Broken Boy

HANNAH GRAY

playlist

Listen to the music that inspired *Broken Boy* on Spotify.

"Get to Gettin' Gone" by Bailey Zimmerman

"Thinkin' Bout Me" by Morgan Wallen

"Flowers" by Miley Cyrus

"10:35" by Tiësto, featuring Tate McRae

"Hate Me" by Ellie Goulding and Juice WRLD

"Just Friends" by Ally Barron

"If the World Was Ending" by JP Saxe, featuring Julia Michaels

"Friends Don't" by Maddie & Tae

"tear myself apart" by Tate McRae

"Hold Me Closer" by Elton John and Britney Spears

"that way" by Tate McRae

"Last Night" by Morgan Wallen

prologue

LINK
AGE EIGHTEEN

Her lips are cracked and dry and her skin pale. Every word she forces herself to speak seems like it hurts her, cutting deep in her throat as she wheezes and coughs. Still, it's the same each time I come home from college to see her. We are getting closer to the end every day, and I know it. We all know it. For the most part, I've avoided coming in here. Not because I don't want to see my mom, but because I can't bear to see her this way. She has always been so happy, so beautiful. Yet I'm watching her wither away to nothing. She's declining rapidly. And there's no hiding the fact that she's in agony.

"You're going to be okay," she says, barely whispering. "I promise."

I suck in a breath. Emotions aren't something I'm good at showing. Not because I don't have them, but because showing them makes me feel weak. And awkward.

"I don't know about that." I feel my throat swell, and I swallow back the feeling of dread creeping up. "None of us will be."

She shakes her head slightly. "I don't mean losing me, baby. I know that'll hurt. I mean, your heart." She reaches up, putting her hand on my chest. "I know it hurts, but I promise … it'll all be okay." Her eyes peer up at me. I can tell she's so exhausted. "She loves you so much. She'll come back to you."

I freeze, holding my breath. I haven't told her that my best friend—the girl I love—left me behind. My mother has enough to deal with, fighting cancer—and losing. She doesn't need me piling on to her with my issues too. So, I have kept it to myself that Tate is gone.

When I don't answer, she clears her throat, attempting to sit up. But when she can't find the strength, I help her. Wrapping my arms around her, I move her upward until she seems semi-comfortable.

"Nothing that's worthwhile is ever going to come easy," she whispers. "But that doesn't mean you give up. It means you fight harder. You have patience. You show unconditional love." Her hand cups my cheek. "You've loved her since the day she arrived here. So, when the anger and spite start to take over everything else, remember that." I know she wants to cry but is too dehydrated to physically do it. "I don't want to leave you, my sweet boy. But I'm going to die, Link. And you're going to need her."

I swallow, my own vision blurry with tears. "She left."

She smiles the smallest smile. "She'll come back. And when she does … let her."

She says the words like it should be so easy to do. But I know two things to be true.

Tate probably isn't coming back.

And if she does … I don't think I'll be able to just forgive her.

THREE WEEKS LATER

Taking a fistful of dirt, I sprinkle it into the rectangular hole in the ground. Small pieces of earth hit the casket, scattering over it every which way, with no rhyme or reason. What's supposed to be symbolic in some way seems meaningless. I don't want to drop a handful of dirt on this cherry-colored piece of wood. I don't want to do anything right now. I just want to wake up and have this nightmare be over. I want to travel back to when life didn't seem so hopeless. No, actually, I'd go back to all those months ago. When it didn't seem like everything was so fucking doomed.

My father sobs without trying to hide it. And my brothers stand beside me, looking down at where we know our mother lies, but not really seeing it. All of us knowing deep down inside that it might be her body, but that it stopped being our mother a week before, when she took her last breath.

Numb. That's what my brothers are. Just like me.

Throughout the service today—hell, the past seven days—that's all I've felt. Numb. Dead. Frozen. Dazed.

I can feel the darkness creeping in, threatening to pull me into its depths, to a place so gloomy that I'll never escape. Yeah, it's trying. And I'm not doing a damn thing to stop it. Honestly, I don't care if it takes me anymore. At least in the pits of hell, nothing can get worse.

There're only two people who could pull me away from it, bringing me back to safety. One of them was my mother. And since she's lying six feet in the ground, about to be covered with earth … I guess I can count her out.

The other, the one who had been my favorite person in the world since I was twelve, disappeared without a trace a month prior, only to send me an email a few days ago.

An email.

A measly three-lined fucking email.

When I saw Tate Tracy's name appear in my inbox, I thought she'd say she was coming home to be with me for the funeral. To stand by my side and help me through this agony. I assumed she'd tell me she was sorry for leaving the way she had. But she said none of that. Instead, she wrote how fond of my mother she was and that she was so sorry for my loss. She even wrote that fucking line that she was thinking of me and my family. Like I was a random fucking person on Facebook who'd just endured a loss and she was commenting on it with some generic message.

Like I meant nothing to her. As if I never had.

So, as far as I'm concerned, Tate Tracy is nobody to me. Not that she has been since she left. But that email was the final nail in the Tate and Link coffin. And now, I hate her. And that hate is growing every single day. Like a disease, deep-rooted inside of me, spreading throughout every single cell in my body with no cure to stop it.

One day, she'll come back. She'll realize she fucked up.

And despite my mother's wishes, that's the day I'll look her in her deep brown eyes, and I'll tell her to fuck off.

Nobody's pulling me away from the darkness now. So, I guess I'd better get used to it.

Because that's where I'll always be.

LINK
AGE TWENTY-ONE

"Yo, little brother," Logan says on the other end of the phone. "The fuck you been up to? I was talking to Carter, and he agrees that your punk ass never calls. You don't text. Nothin'."

"Y'all need to find a life besides worrying about me," I joke, throwing my duffel bag into the backseat before climbing into my truck. "I've been busy training. Something you'd know about if you played for a real team."

"Oh, fuck right off," he tosses back. "We'll see who's the better team when we play you, won't we? We'll mop the ice with your asses."

"Oh, we'll see all right."

"Have you talked to the old man lately?" Logan's voice grows serious. "I keep thinking, one day, he'll get better, but I think he's just getting worse."

"Not since I was home six weeks ago," I say quietly. "Been meaning to call, but, you know … life."

"Yeah, maybe we can take him on a fishing trip for a few days this spring, once hockey season is over," Logan chimes in, sounding hopeful. "I think he'd like that."

"Yeah, that'd be good," I answer, knowing it's likely never going to happen.

He'd never leave our house overnight. Since our mom died, he's done the same thing every single day. Wakes up, drinks one cup of coffee—exactly how Mom made it for him—reads the paper, goes to work, comes home, eats dinner, and watches TV until he goes to sleep. And when we go home to visit, it seems like we throw his entire routine off, and he hates that. So, I've learned that it's best for the both of us if I just stay at Brooks University.

"Well, look, I just wanted to make sure you were still alive and all." He chuckles softly. "Don't be a stranger. You're giving me a dang complex here."

"My bad." I turn the key to my truck's ignition and listen to it rumble to life. "I'm headed to the gym. You behave yourself and keep trying to make that shitty team look better."

"Yeah, yeah. Fuck you," he grunts. "Bye."

"Later," I say before ending the call and pulling out of the driveway.

Out of the four of us brothers, Logan and I were the ones who took to hockey at a young age. Eating, breathing, and living for the game. Only being a year apart also made for some serious competitiveness between him and me. And those few times a year when we get to play against each other, we make sure to bring all the shit-talking, just like the good old days.

For Carter, the oldest of us, football was his life. That was, until an injury took him out his senior year of high school. And Travis, the baby, is in school to be a doctor. He's the brains of the family for sure.

And then there is me. I am the quiet one. The one who takes life way too seriously and lives solely for hockey. Hockey has been good to me, so it deserves my full attention. It was there for me as a kid, when my mother got sick the first time, when my best friend left me, and when my mother died. Proving itself the only true love of my life. That isn't changing anytime soon.

TATE

Taking a long, heavenly sip from my fountain Diet Coke, I sigh. *So. Damn. Good.*

Who really cares that it's filled with aspartame and other bad crap that's probably going to rot my brain and cause bloating or that it has absolutely no nutritional value whatsoever? It's pure perfection. No matter what my friends always say, warning me of how awful it really is. Some people choose tanning beds while they are young even though it'll make them look like a dried-up prune later in life. I choose the goodness that is Diet Coke despite how it's basically poison. The crisp bubbles are something I just can't get enough of.

My phone rings, and on the screen in my car, I see my mom's name. Clicking the Accept button, I wait for her voice to fill my car.

"Hey, Mama," I say, smiling, as I continue to drive toward campus. "Calling to check on me for the thousandth time, are ya?"

"Ha-ha. It hasn't been *that* many times. And I know traffic is crazy at this time of the day. I just wanted to see how you're making it."

"Lady, it's only a two-hour drive, not across the country," I point out. "But I'm about two minutes out. Just stopped and got my second Mickey D's Diet Coke of the day."

"Oh, I'm jealous." She sighs. "Love me a good Diet Coke straight from the fountain. It just tastes different, you know?"

"Oh, I'm aware."

I gaze out the window at the streets I'm vaguely familiar with. I remember when I was in sixth grade, we took a field trip to the Astronomy Center here at Brooks University. I love this place. I always thought I'd end up here for my entire college career, but I guess plans change.

"Are you sure you don't want me to come down and help you settle in?" She pauses. "I should be there. Damn you for being so independent."

"I'm good, I promise. I don't have much unpacking to do, seeing's this apartment is fully furnished." My eyes find Oak Street, and I put my blinker on. "I'm pulling into the place now. So, as long as this dude doesn't kidnap me, I'll call you later."

"You are *so* not funny!" she hisses before she blows out a breath. "It just doesn't feel right, not being with you, babe. Your father or I—or, heck, even both of us—should be there. I hate this. I feel like a shit parent."

"Well, I didn't want to say anything, but …" I say harshly before laughing. "Seriously, Mom, y'all have done enough. Well, *you* have done enough."

While I wait for my mom's answer, I park in front of the adorable apartment that was listed online for rent a few months ago, which was when I decided to come back to Georgia after spending my freshman and sophomore years in Boston. I hated it there. But I was determined to give it a real, honest try before coming back to the only state I'd ever known.

"Your dad loves you," is all she says. "Just be careful, Tate. And if you need anything, call."

"I was in Boston for the past two years. Trust me, Brooks University will be a cakewalk compared to that place. You should see some of the side streets there." I chuckle. "I'll call you later and let you know once I'm settled in. Love you."

"Love you more. Call your daddy too. He worries."

I freeze up at the thought of having to call my father.

"Okay, I will. Bye," I answer quickly before ending the call.

Shifting my car into park, I throw my head back against the leather headrest and exhale, closing my eyes.

For twenty years, my mom put up with my father's shit. His cheating scandals, his eyes that couldn't help but check out every girl who walked by him, and the fact that he was a self-centered asshole for their entire marriage.

Being the wife of a famous hockey player had taken its toll on my mother. And though she wasn't the perfect parent, as she went through times of hitting really low lows, followed by the highest highs, she did her best. And even during the periods she struggled to love herself, she always wanted better for my sister, Meyer, and me. She cared so much that when she knew I was struggling with the hell that came with being the daughter of a professional athlete, she pushed for us to move to Appleton, Georgia. A small town where we could live a more ordinary life. We had gone from living in a mansion to a semi-normal house. Sure, it was still much larger than the average home—no doubt about that. But it was a much homier feel than what I'd had before. And for that, I loved it.

Meyer never minded the attention of reporters following us around at outings. She'd simply smile and wave, being her charismatic self. Me? I hated it. And thanks to having a fainting condition, I was always scared one of my passing-out episodes would be caught on camera.

And then there were the untold number of affairs on my dad's end. And once I became old enough to understand the tabloids, I resented my father for embarrassing our family the way that he had. And for treating my mom the way that he had. And even though we lived in Georgia, he spent the majority of his time in Florida, even during the offseason. God only knows what else he was up to behind my mom's back.

All of this left Meyer and me with daddy issues. Both of us swearing off men who were athletes in the limelight—even if that meant I couldn't be with the person my heart had always longed for.

It didn't help that every time our dad messed up, our mother would mentally check out for a while. She'd lose weight and get depressed. She'd stay locked inside our house. And even though she wanted to be there for us … she couldn't. She'd attempt to smile and pretend to be listening. But we both knew her mind was somewhere else.

But just like a wave crashing on the beach, she'd eventually settle and come back to us. Always. And in my eyes, it's sort of a blessing that he asked for a divorce two years ago. But given he was a retired center for the Tampa Bay Lightning, their marital trouble and divorce were extremely and painfully publicized. Which certainly didn't make it easier on any of us.

So, while it seemed simple enough to swear off athletes, that rule became harder to follow when I was twelve years old, Meyer eleven, and we moved to Appleton. Because right across the street from our house was a mother and father who had not one, not two … but four sons. All unusually good-looking and stupidly athletic. But one in particular, Link, who fell third in the Sterns boy lineup, instantly took me in as a friend from the moment my sneakers hit the pavement of our new driveway. And from then on, we were inseparable.

At first, Link Sterns might have been just the boy who saved me a seat on the bus, invited me frog catching in the pond in his backyard, and bought me a milkshake after school most days, but as he grew up, he became the epitome of what every teenage girl's dreams were made of. Except mine.

At least, that was what I kept telling myself.

Oozing confidence, foolishly attractive, and with a smile that could leave a girl's heart pounding so loud that she couldn't hear anything else, he was hard to avoid. And let's not forget those abs that would leave anyone in a puddle at his feet if they stared too long.

But not me. Because I was his best friend. And best friends weren't supposed to look at each other like *that*. Besides, by the time we were juniors in high school, I'd seen more girls fall in love with him than I could count, and he didn't exactly push them away. But even though I knew I shouldn't stare at him the way I often did when he wasn't looking … I did it anyway. It was like a train wreck, except prettier. And everyone knows you just *can't* look away from a train wreck. Even if you regret it after it's done.

I was the nerd who loved studying outer space and asked for things like telescopes and books about planets for my birthday. And then there was Link. He was my best friend, who would leave the biggest party early just to pull an all-nighter with me on my balcony so I could watch a meteor shower.

I smile at the memory of us taking turns between sleeping and watching the sky. He'd promise to wake me up if it started, and even though he probably didn't care to see what I was waiting up for, he'd make me promise to wake him up too.

Except that one night we both dozed off. And when we woke up, we were tangled up in each other. His arms held me tightly to his chest, almost protectively. Which shouldn't have surprised me because since I had moved there, he had always been protective of me. He might have been obsessed that my father was a professional hockey player, but that didn't stop him from keeping me safe from Dad's infatuated fans. Still, when we woke up that close, something felt different. Something between us shifted that morning even though I tried to fight it. And since he never brought it up, I knew where I stood. In the friend zone. Exactly where I wanted to be.

He was everything I'd sworn off. His dream was to make it to the NHL. And in my eyes, the NHL had not only taken my father's soul, but had also been the demise of my parents' marriage. Link was going to be famous, and I just wanted to be left alone. It could never work—I knew that. But still, I thought about him every night I drifted off to sleep. And when he hugged me every morning before we parted ways to head to class, I'd melt into him like butter, feeling my skin turn cold when he released me. That hug was the best part of every day for me. It was the only time I came to life.

I was in love with my best friend. And that was a problem because if we ever crossed the line, it would ruin me, and I wouldn't even be able to blame him. Because guys like that? It was just what they did. He'd hit me like a freight train and then keep on trucking. And I wasn't about to be that stupid. I wasn't going to let history repeat itself with what my mother had signed herself up for.

So, I drew an invisible line. A bubble to shield myself from ever taking it too far, not wanting to deal with the consequences. Unfortunately for me … even the toughest bubbles can get popped by a man like Link Sterns.

A knock on my window startles me, pulling me back to the present and away from the days when I still had my best friend.

A man who appears to be in his late fifties holds his hand up and waves, and as I roll the window down a little, he leans down.

"Tate Tracy?"

"That's me," I say, nodding. "Are you Harold?"

"Y-yes." He sounds nervous.

As he steps back, I push my door open.

"It's exactly like the picture!" I wave toward the apartment. "I can't tell you how excited I am about this."

He looks down and pinches the bridge of his nose. "Miss Tracy … I'm so sorry. I, uh … the apartment is no longer for rent. Again, I really can't express how sorry I am. I feel like a horse's ass."

I stare at him, narrowing my eyes before I breathe out a laugh. "You're pulling my leg. Good joke, Harold. Awkward but good. But school starts next week, so I'm going to need the keys to get settled in."

He shakes his head. "I wish I were. But my daughter and her husband's house burned down this morning. They have nowhere to go." He pats my shoulder. "She's expecting. Her little girl is due next month. I am so sorry, Tate. I would have called you sooner, but my wife and I just decided this is what needed to be done."

I take one last look at the apartment before sinking against my Jeep. I know I can't be mad. That would make me the world's shittiest human being.

"I understand. I'm sorry about your daughter's house," I whisper.

Pulling a piece of paper out from his back pocket, he hands it to me. "We own a few other apartment buildings around Brooks. All are full, but this one right here, well, I know they have one open bedroom in it. Good tenants, always pay their rent on time."

"So, no chance they're running a crack shack or anything?" I try to joke. "I'm just not all that adventurous."

"No chance in hell. Not these ones at least." He laughs. "The address is written there. It's just a few blocks away."

Looking down at the scribbled writing, I attempt to smile even though I sort of want to cry. I have to keep it together. Besides, it isn't like *my* house burned in a fire. And there's no way I can be mad at this man.

"Thanks. Good luck with everything. Again, I'm really sorry about your daughter's house. She's a lucky girl to have you."

"Oh, I don't know about all that. I do my best. Go see if anyone's home at that address I gave you." He smiles. "I have a feeling they won't say no to you."

"Will do," I say and get back into my Jeep.

I thought I'd have it all figured out after today. Sure, I knew moving to Brooks would be tough. I mean, shit, Link has this campus eating out of the palm of his hand, and I'm coming here after ghosting him years ago.

Even when his mother died, I wasn't sure what to do. I planned to come to his mother's funeral, but my mom told me he was having a hard time with it, and I worried I was the last person he wanted to show up there. Against my better judgment, I didn't attend the funeral. Instead, I wrote him an email.

An email.

Who writes a damn email to the boy who was their best friend for so long?

I type the address in on the screen, and it shows the route with an estimated driving time of three minutes. Shifting into drive, I head to what might be my next home.

LINK

"Are those fucking Crocs?" I scowl down at Cam's feet as we walk out of the gym.

"Damn right they are." He smirks. "You ain't rockin' if you ain't Croc'n."

"Wow. You gonna buy a pair of white New Balances too?" I shake my head. "Never thought I'd see the day when Cam Hardy, legendary puck boy of Brooks University, lost his dignity." I frown, looking him up and down. "Damn shame, I tell ya." I pretend to look around, keeping my face straight. "To be honest, I'm embarrassed to be seen with you. You're killing my game."

"First off, you ain't got game. And second"—he holds his middle finger up, then turns around and moons me—"fuck right off, Linky. One day, the most adorable curly-haired kid might give you a pair of these as a birthday gift. And when they do, you'd best be fucking wearing them with pride."

It all clicks, and I laugh. "Isla?" I say his girlfriend's daughter's name, finally understanding why Cam Hardy has gone to the dark side and is wearing the world's ugliest shoes.

He looks annoyed. "Yeah. Well, at least that's what she and Addison said. Isla said she saw them and knew I'd love them because they're camouflage. But knowing my girl, Addy probably has me decked out in Crocs, hoping the ladies won't check me out. Psst, we both know a little Crocs action ain't gonna stop them from looking." He points to his face. "I mean, come on."

I shake my head, stopping at my truck door. "To be honest, I'm not even sure you'll be able to drive home without the women chasing after you."

"I know, right? Hey, when you get back to the apartment, tell Brody he's a lazy fuck for me, would ya? If he keeps skipping our workouts, we might be more jacked than he is one of these days."

"Somehow, I doubt it," I grumble, knowing I might be extremely fit. But Brody? He's a whole other type of beast. "Trust me, he's still working out. He's just had … other commitments lately."

I know what Brody's new commitments consist of. But the rest of the team doesn't, and it isn't my place to tell. Not yet anyway. But when he does, I can't wait to hear them make fun of him for being a damn underwear model. Cam will have a field day with it.

"Yeah, I bet one of those commitments includes him buck naked with at least one chick, if not multiple."

"Quite possibly." I grin, opening my door. "Catch you later. Don't get into too much trouble, big dawg. Especially with those sweet Crocs."

"I'll try my best," he tosses back. "No guarantees!"

Pulling my phone from my center console, I see a shit ton of texts and missed calls from Brody.

Brody: Dude, answer your phone.

Brody: Some hot chick is here. Harold told her we had an open room. She needs a place to stay.

Brody: You've got one minute to answer, or I'm telling her she can have Cam's old room.

Brody: You'd better not complain. You had your chance to answer.

Brody: Not that you should. You ought to thank me.

Hitting his contact, I put my phone to my ear.

" 'Bout fucking time, asshole. Been calling you for an hour," he answers on the first ring.

"You know I leave my phone in the truck when I'm at the gym, fucker. What are all those messages you sent me? Tell me we don't have another roommate. It's not a damn hotel or some shit."

"Oh, we've got a new roommate. And I personally think you'll be pretty impressed. She's cute."

"She could be a serial killer, you moron. Or a crackhead."

"I don't get crackhead vibes," he says cockily. "And if she's a serial killer, maybe she's into some kinky shit."

I shake my head. "How whipped are you with your mystery girl? Normally, you'd be all over this chick if she was hot."

"Oh, trust me, she's hot. And for the thousandth fucking time, there's no mystery girl," is all he gives me. "Get your ass home to give her a proper greeting. She's unpacking her crap in her room right now. And don't you dare make it awkward and shit."

"Whatever," I groan. "Be there in five."

I head home. Trying to remind myself that having a chick live with us won't affect my life that much. Sure, it'll be annoying if she brings random people over that I don't know, but as long as they aren't complete wack jobs, it should be fine.

I hope.

TATE

Unzipping my last bag, I pull the bottom drawer out and begin putting away my jeans and shorts. I'm tired, and I suppose I could have waited until tomorrow to unpack, but that's just not who I am. It isn't my personality type. I'm thankful as heck that this room happened to have a bed and a dresser in it, but judging by how attractive the dude who let me in was, I'd be scared to take a black light to this mattress. If the guy who used to live here was anywhere near as hot as that Brody guy is … yuck.

When he opened the door, shirtless, revealing his tattoos with a cocky grin on his lips, I almost turned around and went back to my car right then. But given that dorms had been filled up back when I called months ago, I knew this was my only shot at living near campus. Instead, I put on my sweetest, fakest smile and charmed him into letting me have the room. On the bright side, rent will only be a fraction of what it would have been if I had gotten the other place. So, there's that.

He seemed surprised that Harold had given me their address, but he didn't act mad or annoyed. He simply said he needed to call his buddy to clear it with him.

When he came back to the door five minutes later, he motioned for me to come inside with a smirk and said, "Come on in."

Assuming the friend he called is also a man, I can safely say, this isn't how I pictured my living arrangement going for my junior year of college, and I can't push the thought of, *What am I even doing?* from replaying in my brain.

I cringe inwardly as I picture the day when I explain this to my family.

A knock at the door has me quickly closing my suitcase, which still has my bras and panties at the bottom.

"Knock, knock," Brody says against my closed door.

Even through a block of wood, I can tell he's grinning.

Standing swiftly, I smooth my hair down before walking over and pulling the door open. "Hel—" I start to say, but the word dies in my throat just as a set of blue eyes lands on mine.

My body goes numb. My throat feels like I can't breathe. My heart stops beating inside my chest. And I panic that I'm about to faint. And I really, really don't want to do that.

Closing my eyes for a second, I drag in a few breaths before releasing them, lulling my body to calm the hell down before I embarrass myself.

"Sorry to interrupt, but our other roomie got back, and I figured you'd want to meet him," Brody says, jerking his head toward an all-too-familiar face. "This is Link. And, Link, this is Ta—"

"Tate," Link growls, finishing Brody's sentence.

"Well, yeah. How did you know that? I didn't know you were a fucking mind reader of some sort." Brody laughs. "Like I told you on the phone, Harold had some sort of mix-up and sent her in our direction to rent Cam's room."

I take him in. His hair is still the same light-brown color. The sun always made some pieces lighter than others. It's a bit longer than it was the last time I saw him, and he somehow looks even more jacked and toned than he did before too. And I swear, he appears taller.

His ocean-blue eyes cut into mine, looking instantly mad.

God, he's so handsome. Even when he's looking at me like he hates me.

"No," Link mutters. "She ain't staying here. Fuck. No."

"Link …" I start to say something. Anything to smooth over everything between us.

But it's useless. I have no idea what to say. And he sure as hell isn't going to listen.

14

"No!" Link roars. "Why the hell are you here, Tate?! Huh?"

"Okay, now, I'm just confused." Brody's gaze moves from me to Link, and he elbows him softly. "I'm sensing you might know each other, huh?"

"Not anymore." Link's eyes move to my suitcases. "Pack your shit back up. This is my house, not yours."

As he starts to back away, Brody runs his hand over the top of his buzzed hair. "Well, fuck me sideways. Didn't see this coming." Resting his hand on his waist, he sighs. "You know what? There's another hockey house next door. One of the dudes there might be moving out, if he hasn't already." Pulling his phone out of his pocket, he starts to hit a few buttons. "Let me call Hunter and ask him."

"Hell no, she isn't living with Thompson and those clowns." Link suddenly reappears. He looks frustrated, and he paces back and forth, raking a hand down his neck. "Fine, you can have the fucking room. But stay the hell away from me, Tate."

"You know … I'm just going to go now," Brody says, awkwardly shifting on his feet. "This is fucking uncomfortable." He disappears down the hall, and I hear his feet going down the stairs.

As Link starts to turn, my voice finally decides to work. "It doesn't have to be this way, Link. Please," I plead. "I'm sorry."

"Yeah, actually, it does." Taking a few steps toward me, he stops, narrowing his eyes. "*You* made it this way, Tate. You. No one else."

"I know that," I say, looking down. "I was scared."

"I don't know why you're here. To be honest, I don't really care. Just stay the fuck out of my way," he snarls. "Do you understand? Because if not, I'll have you and your shit on the lawn in no time. And forget about the other hockey house because you aren't living there. Those are my teammates. So, if I were you, I'd keep my head down and my mouth shut."

And just as his chilling words hit me, he's gone. And all I can do is sit on my bed and feel my heart breaking in my chest from a guy who looked at me like I was dead to him.

Maybe I am. Maybe I should be.

I chose my fate the day I ran away from him and hightailed it to New England. There's no going back. His eyes are darker now. He's harder. He isn't my best friend from my childhood who watched over me.

He's a bitter man who looks at me like I'm evil. Because I suppose, in his story, I am the monster. But even if that is true, what other choice did I have to make than the one I did?

Because sometimes, you have to be the one to protect yourself. Right?

TATE

The sound of rain pattered off the roof as I lay in my bed. I had graduated high school that day, and in a few months, I was starting a whole new chapter in Boston. I really had no idea why I had chosen a place so hectic and different from what I was used to. It so wasn't me. I supposed, in a way, I wanted to prove something to myself. That without my sister, my parents, or my best friend, Link, I could survive. No, not just survive. Thrive. It also didn't hurt that without any family around, I was certain no one would know who I was. I liked the idea of that. For so much of my life, I had been hockey star Harvey Tracy's daughter. In a city away from everyone I knew, I could just be plain Tate.

A familiar banging noise startled me, making me sit up in my bed, listening to make sure I had heard it right. And when another rock pinged off my window, I climbed out of bed.

In the darkness, as the rain poured down, there was Link. He stood on my lawn, looking up at me on the second story. Lightning struck, lighting his face up for a second before it went dark again.

"What are you doing!" I hush-yelled once I opened my window. "Are you crazy? There's a dang storm outside!"

"You don't say?" He grinned, water pouring down his face. His hair was soaked, and the fabric of his shirt clung to his chest in the most delicious way. "Can I come up or what?"

Staring at him, I eventually nodded my head. "Come through the back door, but be quiet!"

Once he took off toward the backyard, I quickly closed the window and ran to the mirror to look at myself. He was just my best friend. It shouldn't matter how I looked.

But it did. Oh, it did.

My shoulder-length hair was messy, so I pulled it up into a bun and put on a little lip gloss. As I started to walk toward the door, I froze, realizing I was in my sleep shorts and a thin white tank top that left little to the imagination. Brushing it off, I pulled the door open and waited for him to come up the stairs. It was just Link. And even though I loved him, I was sure he didn't see me that way anyway.

Hearing his light footsteps, I thanked the Lord that my parents' bedroom was downstairs in a whole other part of the house and that Meyer wasn't home tonight. It wasn't that uncommon for Link to be over at our house, but sneaking into my room in the middle of the night might not look so good to my mom. Or my dad, who had surprisingly come home for my graduation.

As he reached the top of the stairs, I took his hand and pulled him into my room, closing the door behind him.

Looking up at him, I wiped my hand across his forehead. "You're crazy! Why were you out there in the storm?!" I pause. "I'm surprised you aren't at the party still. Are you drunk?"

"I had a few drinks," he answered honestly. "But I'm not drunk."

Walking to my bed, he took a seat on the edge of it.

"What's going on?" I followed him, standing before him. "Are you okay?"

"Not really," his low voice rasped. "I needed to come see you, Tate."

I stared at him, surprised. "I don't understand. We're going fishing tomorrow, so you'd have seen me then."

"I couldn't wait until tomorrow. I couldn't wait any longer at all." He peered up at me. "I saw you get a ride home from graduation with Jasper." He looked pained. "I've watched him ogle you for weeks, and it makes me fucking sick. Are you into him?"

I couldn't stop the most unattractive snort that came when I laughed. "God, no. My parents were going to the store to get stuff for dinner. Jasper offered to drop me off on his way to the party."

"I wanted to bring you home," he said resentfully. "This was supposed to be our day."

"I'm sorry. I didn't know." I shrugged. "You seemed pretty busy, so I took him up on his offer. I didn't want to bother you."

Once the ceremony had ended, we were all outside, taking pictures with our loved ones, and Link had been surrounded by our classmates. He might have been my best friend, but that never made it easier to approach him when he was in a crowd. Nobody got us. They didn't understand why I was with him so often. Or why we were attached at the hip, but weren't a couple.

"I want you to bother me," he whispered, his gruff voice tortured. "Bother me all the fucking time, Tate."

Suddenly, his hands reached out and touched my waist. Pulling me to him, he positioned me between his legs and dropped his forehead to my stomach. "You can't go to Boston, T. You just can't."

Shocked that he was touching my waist this way, I sucked in a breath before resting my hands on his shoulders. "Why not?"

Gazing up at me again, a broken look on his face, he shook his head once. "Because I can't stand the thought of not seeing you every day. It makes my stomach hurt. I love you, Tate. I've loved you since the day I saw you get out of your daddy's truck behind that moving van. With your overalls and Converse. And those scrawny chicken legs." He rolled his tongue over his lips slowly. "Who is going to protect you when I'm not around?"

"I don't need anyone's protection," I whispered. "I'll be okay, I promise."

"I know that," he snapped. "Dammit, T. I want to protect you. I always will."

"Link—" I started to answer, but he stopped me.

"I know your rule. I know you don't want to be like your mama. But I'm not your dad, and I'm tired of loving you, but not being able to show it, Tate. I want to love you in the open. I can't take another day of having you close and pretending that I'm not dying to fucking touch you."

"You're drunk," was all I could muster up, reminding my heart that alcohol was to blame and that he didn't feel this way.

"I'm not drunk. But even if I were, I'd feel the same way." He pulled me closer, burying his head into my abdomen. "Don't go to Boston, T. Come to Brooks. Or let me go with you. I can make you so fucking happy. You'll see. You just have to let me show you."

I stood there, frozen. Not knowing what to say, but knowing in that moment that all I wanted to do was feel his skin next to mine. And finally … finally know what his kiss tasted like.

I was going to Boston. I had to. And even if this night and finally being close to him made leaving harder—and deep down, I knew it would—it was a risk I had to take.

Without thinking, I pressed my mouth to his and kissed him. "Be my first, Link," I whispered against his lips as he snaked his hands up my legs, gripping my ass.

Even though I knew this was going to complicate things to the point of no repair, I wanted him to take my virginity. And he did.

In those moments, I'd never felt more whole. More loved. More … myself.

But I knew that when the sun rose, it wouldn't seem so simple. And, boy, was I right.

I lie in my bed, looking at the picture of us that was taken on my fifteenth birthday. I open the small box, pulling out the planetarium tickets he gave me, which I saved, along with a book about building rockets. I always knew when I returned one day, he probably wouldn't be thrilled to see me. I never imagined he'd look at me the way that he did last night though. Like he hated my guts. My heart throbs as I imagine his blue eyes that held so much hurt and anger when he spoke to me hours ago. I didn't recognize that person.

He had always been so soft with me compared to how he was with others. Like I was his puppy and he needed to care for me. Heck, even in school, he'd bring me snacks all the time. Because he knew I hated the cafeteria and how overly crowded it was. And because I had a fainting condition that seemed to occur more frequently when I was either hungry or stressed. The passing out wasn't something that happened often, but that didn't stop Link from constantly worrying.

Seeing him now is like being in the presence of a stranger. And truthfully, I'm nervous to see him again. But even though I'm scared to face him, I know I can't hide in my room forever. And I'm in desperate need of a coffee or a Diet Coke, maybe both. The way the past few days have gone, I might just skip both and go straight for tequila.

I haven't told my parents that I'm living across the hall from Link. My mom would tell me to get the hell out of here before I did more harm than good. And although my dad wouldn't care, I haven't talked to him in almost six weeks.

I did, however, text Meyer and tell her. She's always understood my reasons for why I ran from Link after he told me he loved me. She lived through the same childhood, the highs and lows that my mother went through; she gets me more than anyone else in the world ever could.

Throwing my blankets off, I climb out of bed and force myself to leave the comfort of this room, knowing damn well there's a good chance Link is outside that door, ready to declare his hate more than he did last night.

LINK

"You boys have a lot of work to do if we're going to make it to the Frozen Four this year. Goddamn, you're out of shape," Coach LaConte yells, shaking his head in disgrace. "We've been at this for weeks, and we aren't anywhere near where we should be. If you don't get it together, you know what that'll mean? Twofers—that's what." He points to the locker room. "Go shower. You smell as bad as you're playing. Like ass."

We skate off the ice, trudging into the locker room. A few of the freshmen hang their heads, feeling like failures. But we actually aren't all that bad. Or out of shape. Coach is just an extreme hard-ass. And his approach to making us work harder typically entails telling us we're downright terrible.

Those of us who had him as a coach last season don't lead on that we know his tactics. We simply play along.

This is his second season coaching us, and I know he wants us to make it to the Frozen Four as badly as any of us do. I don't even think he wants it so much for himself as he does us. As difficult as Coach can be sometimes, I respect the hell out of him. Our last coach was fired after he got caught getting a blow job from a student under his desk. Coach LaConte is a much more honorable man.

Even if he is a dick.

"We gotta get it together. I can't deal with twofers," Brody says, pouring some water into his mouth. "Hell, I'm barely surviving the one-ers we've been having."

"That ain't even a thing, dude." Cam laughs, pulling his skates off. "I don't want two motherfucking practices a day either though. But we all know that we don't look nearly as bad out there as he's saying. That's just Coach doing his Negative Nancy thing. Y'all know how he is."

"Easy for you to say. He's basically your father-in-law these days," I point out. "If I was gonna be sitting across from him at Thanksgiving, asking him to pass the peas, I'd probably cut him some slack too."

"Either way, I sure as hell won't be asking him to pass the peas, Sterns." Cam makes a sick face. "Peas are fucking gross. Mashed potatoes? Yeah, he can pass them on over all day long. And pie? Hell yes. Peas? Put those foul things in the trash and leave them there."

"I mix peas with my mashed potatoes," Brody chimes in, and we all tell him he's nasty.

Brody, Cam, and I have been best friends since we became teammates, and Cam lived with Brody and me until he went and fell in love and ditched our asses. Now, I get to live with Tate.

Yay for Cam falling in love. Not.

The dude almost left us last year to play for the pros, but a fucked up accident kept him with us. I was bummed for him, but as a winger, it's been awesome, having him as our team captain and the center.

"What's that like anyway, Hardy?" Hunter grins. "Sitting at the same dinner table with Coach and shit? Gotta be weird as fuck, especially since he hated you last season."

"Hate? He couldn't stand the sight of him," I say, pointing to Cam. "Your very presence pissed him off."

"Truth." Brody nods.

"Y'all need a life," Cam says, shaking his head before heading toward the shower. "You've got too much time on your hands. Come to think about it. Maybe twofers are exactly what you need. That way, you won't be worrying about me and Coach sittin' at the same table."

"Whatever you say, big dawg," Hunter tosses back.

Brody struts over to me. "Dude, you were gone before I even woke up. We usually ride to practice together. And last night, you locked yourself in your room. The fuck is going on with you?"

I catch Hunter staring at us, looking highly amused, and when I ask him what the hell is so funny, he laughs.

"You two sound like an old married couple. Poor Brody. Linky left him home to drive to practice all alone." He winks. "You could have ridden with me, O'Brien. I wouldn't ditch you."

"Ignore him. He's just jealous of the bond, my man," Brody says, rolling his eyes dramatically. "If it's the chick, I'll kick her out. I told you, she can probably go stay at the other hockey house."

"And I told you, she's not staying with those motherfuckers," I grumble, avoiding looking at him. "That's not an option."

"So, what is it, brother?" He leans a little closer. "Do you want her or something? Because if it's going to be a problem, I'm not trying to deal with that shit all the time. This isn't the fucking *Big Brother* house, where people are fighting and conspiring against each other. I want Zen and peace, goddammit."

"She's nobody," is all I give him. "Maybe she was at one point in time, but not now."

"So, I can hook up with her then," he drawls slowly, his eyes glimmering with amusement, "and you won't care?"

"Go for it," I say, standing. "But if you do, I'll break your fucking arms off and beat you to death with them."

As I trudge toward the showers, I hear him snickering behind me like a little kid.

"About what I thought, Sterns. About what I thought."

I don't know what I'm going to do about Tate living across the hall from me. I don't know how to not imagine pushing her door open, ripping her blankets off, and making her beg for my cock. But no matter how bad I want to be inside of her again, I can't. Because after that last time, she doesn't deserve to come on my dick again.

She begged me to be her first, and it was the one and only time I got the chance to sink inside of Tate Tracy. I thought that night would bond us together. I thought she'd come to Brooks with me. I mean, everyone knew she didn't really want to live in Boston. She was simply trying to prove something to herself. Or, if you ask me, her dad. He had never given her a lick of respect or attention.

The night I confessed I loved her was the same night our friendship died. I don't know if I would change things if I could go back, but that night ruined me for any other woman. I might have my share of hookups, but it's her face I see when I do.

And now, she's back in Georgia, here at Brooks, and I have no idea why. Maybe it's to fuck with me, or perhaps she's finally admitted to herself that she didn't love the city because it wasn't who she is. She needs to live somewhere she can look up and see the stars without the city smog around. One thing she probably liked in Boston was the fact that, with hundreds of thousands of people, she could blend into the shadows easier. In a way, that was all she'd ever wanted.

Whatever the reason is that brought her here, it doesn't matter. She showed her true colors, and there's no going back now.

TATE

Sitting at the coffee shop on campus, I scroll through the Brooks Connections page on my laptop, desperately looking for a different apartment or room to magically appear. It's no use though. I know better than to think I'll luck out. I thought about asking Brody about the teammates he said might need a roommate, but is a bunch of pompous, conceited athletes really who I want to live with? Not really. I mean, sure, that's my living situation right now, but at least I know Link. He might be angry with me, and he sure as hell isn't being all that nice, but I know he'd never do anything to harm or hurt me. With strangers, who's to say what would happen?

Classes start in four days, and part of me wishes they had already started so that I had something to do. I can't stay cooped up in my bedroom all day, but I also don't feel comfortable hanging around at the apartment when it was Link's place first.

Checking the time, I close my laptop and gather up my things. The Astronomy Center next door opens soon, and I plan to see if I can get a job, helping to run their public shows. It's something I did back in Boston, and I really enjoyed it. This will obviously be a lot smaller of a place and likely with less people, but I'm more than okay with that.

"Don't you have an apartment? With things like a couch and a TV?" I hear a familiar voice drawl slowly. "And, hell, I bet our couch is probably more comfortable than that crappy chair you're sitting on."

My eyes find Brody, and I can't help but smile. He gives off this charismatic energy that you just can't hate. He's charming while also being a complete goof. I'm glad Link has him.

"Yes, well, you see … here at the coffee shop, nobody is glaring at me or telling me to pack up my shit," I attempt to joke. "So, there's that."

"You're safe. We just had practice, and now, he's headed somewhere with Cam." He rests his hand on the back of one of the chairs. "He'll come around, just give him time."

"Easy for you to say. He doesn't hate you." I give him a pointed look. "I really appreciate you letting me live there and all, but I don't know how it will ever work."

He tilts his head to the side. "Oh, something tells me that it'll all work out just fine, babe." Giving me a playful wink, he takes a few steps backward. "Patience, young one. Patience. I gotta run. Catch ya later. At the grump-partment."

I smile, shaking my head at his insanity. "See ya."

I don't have much faith when he says everything will be okay. But I hope he's right.

I want my friend back.

I walk into the Astronomy Center's lobby. With a little cafeteria off to one side and restrooms on the other, the place is much bigger inside than I thought. There's even a gift shop, making it a space-obsessed child's dream. Oh, who am I kidding? This is my dream too.

"Can I help you?" a gorgeous girl with the most beautiful head of curly black hair says, never looking up from her computer.

"Maybe," I say nervously. "My name is Tate Tracy. I'm a junior in the aerospace program. I just transferred here from Boston. I was wondering if you had any available job positions for students."

Finally, her eyes move up, and she studies me for a moment before standing. "Let me go get Oliver He's the manager."

Turning slowly, I look at all the exhibits around the lobby. A scale that can tell you your weight on all the different planets and the moon. A prop to take a picture in front of to make it look like you're in outer space. And a large computer screen with some sort of outer space quiz on it. This building might be smaller than the last place I worked at, but it's got plenty of charm. I allow a sense of comfort to wash over me—something I haven't felt in a while.

I like it here. And I need this job for my own sanity.

Seeing a pair of double doors propped open, I poke my head inside and take in the dome that serves as the actual planetarium. It's on the smaller side, but it's immaculate and in fantastic shape. I look around the walls and ceiling, covered in screens, and smile. I've always loved these places. Even on Earth, you can feel like you made a trip to outer space.

"Tate?" a deep voice says from behind me, and I whirl around.

"Yes, that's me." I try to hide the surprised look on my face when the manager—who I was expecting to be a geeky little guy—turns out to be a complete hunk.

His brown hair is in a tousled mess. It's striking, and it looks like it took hours of styling, though I'm betting he rolled out of bed like that. His lips are slightly full, and his jawline is stupidly sharp. And his eyes? Wow … those things could capture the dang Holy Spirit.

Holding his hand out, he smiles politely, flashing his white teeth. "I'm Oliver. Holly says you're looking for a job." His eyes crinkle at the sides. "Is that true? And if so, what sort of job are you looking for?"

"Y-yes. Yes, it is true." I shake his hand before releasing it. "I worked at the Astronomy Center at the college I just transferred from Boston. Mostly helping to run the public shows and things like that. Also, at the kids summer camps, I'd volunteer to help in any way I could. I'm not sure if that's something you offer here at Brooks, but it was pretty incredible to see the kids of the community come out and learn about something us aspiring astronomers are so passionate about."

"Are you an astronomy major?" He leans against the desk Holly just got up from.

"Aerospace engineer. But my love for astronomy is what put me on the path for aerospace."

"Wow, impressive." He nods. "While I think it's horseshit, I'm sure you're aware that it tends to be a predominantly male-dominated career. So, seeing a woman going through it, ready to trailblaze? I'm fascinated."

I fight the urge to roll my eyes. Barely one minute into our conversation, and he said the words *predominantly male-dominated career*. This dude could be my boss, and while he seems nice enough … well, I find him annoying.

"Uh, yeah." I look down for a second, awkwardly shifting on my feet. "Thanks."

"As far as the summer camps go, we have tried those in the past. Unfortunately, it never took off quite like we'd hoped it would. But I'd love to try it again sometime." He stuffs his hands in his pockets casually. "We do public shows two days a week, sometimes three on school vacation weeks. I'm guessing it's a similar program to what you had back in Boston, though ours is probably much less hectic." He laughs. "We have different movies we play in the planetarium, typically lasting an hour."

"Yep, sounds exactly the same." I nod. "And then I would usually spend about fifteen minutes or so sharing some general facts about outer space, allowing kids to ask whatever questions they had."

"We don't typically do that—"

"Oh, no big deal," I cut him off before he can tell me no.

"Tate, relax. I was going to say, we don't typically do that because we're short-staffed." He sighs. "Sounds like a great thing to add. When can you start?"

"Whenever," I say quickly. "Aside from classes, I'm totally free."

Wow, way to make it known I have no social life at all.

"How's Saturday at nine in the morning work? I'll give you some paperwork to fill out. If you can, bring it back later today."

"Perfect!" I try not to squeal but fail. "That's perfect. Thank you so much."

"Come on," he says, jerking his chin toward the office door. "I'll get you those papers. Welcome to the team. Though I'll admit to you now, it's a damn small one."

"Small but mighty!" Holly calls out, walking from the back room. "Small. But. Mighty!"

"Well, yeah." Oliver grins. "Obviously."

Reaching in his drawer, he hands me a stack of papers. "It'll be great to have you. See you later, Tate."

Taking them from his hand, I blush when my fingers hit his skin, and I pray he doesn't think I did it on purpose. "Thanks again."

I woke up today, feeling discouraged, but that's changed now. I'm going to be working at a really cool place. Life is good.

At least, it is until I walk outside and remember where I live now.

TATE

O nce all our customers leave, I turn off the equipment. Today's show was about Mars. It wasn't my favorite by far, but it was interesting. It's my second day working at the Brooks Astronomy Center, and so far, so good.

Almost two weeks have passed since I moved into Link's apartment. He's gone when I leave in the morning, and somehow, we seem to miss each other most nights. It's clear he's avoiding me just as much as I'm avoiding him. I lie in my bed sometimes, allowing the thoughts to creep in, imagining sneaking into his room and climbing under the covers with him. Running my hands down his abdomen, stopping at his briefs. It's hard not to think about, knowing he's *right* across the hall.

I somehow always end up back to *that* night. Recalling the way he kissed me in the darkness and brushed his fingers along my neck and down my chest. It was beautiful. And even though it was wrong of me to lead him on … I can't regret it. I can't regret it because some part of me came to life when he touched me. When Tate Tracy became a woman and no longer a girl. And even though it was painful, as anybody's first time is, he was gentle, sweet, and patient.

Most people's first-time stories I hear sound awful. Mine … was perfect. Because mine was also with my first love.

Since then, I've ached to be that close to him again. Remembering the small details when my life forever changed. I wish more than anything that things could be different, that we could be together. And in an unflawed world, we would be. But Link's time as a college hockey player is running out, and he'll be headed to the pros. I know myself enough to know that I would be no good for him either. I'd be jealous and insecure. So not what he would need and so not what I'd want to be. It would be a lose-lose situation for both of us.

I just wish he could see that was why I did what I did.

"You did great today." Oliver's voice pulls me from my thoughts as he jingles his keys in his hand. "You're a natural with this whole teaching thing."

My cheeks heat. I've never been great at taking a compliment. "Oh, I don't know about that. I'm just a nerd who loves to talk about space. Hopefully, I didn't bore the children to death." I frown. "One kid literally pretended to be snoring." I cringe. "Next time, I'll cut it back to ten minutes."

"That kid also tried to steal space ice cream from the gift shop and punched the screen of the weight reader. Little jerk." He laughs. "Trust me, don't change a thing." He pauses, looking at me thoughtfully. "Do you want to go get a coffee next door? My treat."

I stare at him in shock. *Is he coming on to me? Did I send the wrong message?*

Oliver might be attractive, but I'm not interested. And he's my boss.

"Um, actually—"

He must see the hesitation on my face because he gives me a small smile. "As friends, Tate. Coffee with a friend. I just figured I could pick your brain about Boston and maybe get some ideas for us to use here."

I chew my lip but finally nod. "Yeah, okay. That sounds good actually. I guess I could use some caffeine."

"Awesome. Ten minutes?" He jerks his chin toward the office door. "I just need to return a few messages from this morning."

"Yep, sounds good."

It's probably strange for me to grab coffee with my boss. But at the end of the day, he is a student too. And we probably have a lot in common that we can talk about. All my friends are back in Boston or all around the country in different colleges. And my sister is in New England. I could use a friend here at Brooks. Even if it is a male friend who signs my paychecks, who really cares?

A friend is a friend when you're desperate, like me.

LINK

"You're staring," Brody says, drinking whatever frozen concoction he's got. "No, wait. You're *glaring*. Hell, I think smoke might be coming from your ears."

"Am not," I grumble, turning my attention away from Tate as she sits next to the window and across from some preppy-looking asshole who's wearing fucking khakis.

She doesn't even know I'm here. We're hidden in this corner booth. She walked in as he held the door open, making it obvious they came together. He even paid for her coffee.

I know her, and even though she drinks coffee, she'd rather have a gross Diet Coke from a fast-food joint. She's a damn addict when it comes to fountain soda.

"You avoid her like she's walking herpes at home. Like if she gets too close, you'll catch the herps, and it'll crawl all over your body, making your dick fall off. But then we come here, and you look like you want to murder Oliver for sitting with her."

"Oliver?" I scowl. "Who the hell is Oliver? And how do you know who that dude is?"

"That astronomy place is pretty sweet. He hooked me up, letting me take a girl there." Brody grins.

"He works there?" I let my eyes go back to their table.

She laughs hard, wiping under her eyes as her nose scrunches up.

I miss that laugh. I miss *making* her laugh like that.

"More like he's the manager. He's studying to be an astronomer or some shit." He shrugs. "He's not a bad guy, Link. If you want him to back off Tater Tot, I'm sure he would."

"Tater Tot? What the fuck? You guys have nicknames now?" I scowl.

"Don't be jealous. She can be your Tater Tot too." His eyebrows wiggle up and down. "You can be her Lincoln Log. Or you can just give her your Lincoln Log."

"What the fuck is wrong with you?" I shake my head, sitting back in the booth as I glare in his direction. "I can't really tell ol' khaki pants to back off when I don't want her, now can I?"

"Whatever helps you sleep at night," he mutters. "I won't point out that when they walked in together, you looked at her like someone had killed your puppy."

"I don't have a puppy."

"Maybe she's your puppy," he says nonchalantly. "Maybe you want to snuggle her."

"Do not. She ain't a good person. You'll see."

29

His face grows serious as he spins his cup with his fingers against the wooden table. "Maybe, deep down, none of us are, Sterns. Maybe we're all bad in our own way. But that doesn't mean there isn't some good in each of us, right?" He nods toward Tate. "She might have done some questionable shit, but haven't we all? But we both know that she isn't bad."

"Y'all best friends now or what?" I scoff. "Whose side are you on anyway?"

"I'll always be on your side, brother. Know that. But take it from a man who lived in denial for too damn long … that isn't a place you want to stay at. It'll leave you bitter and angry. And grumpier than your ass already is."

I'm not buying Brody's bullshit. He's fucked up in the head, just like me. He might not talk about his past, but the fact that he's never had a single family member come to a game or had anyone check in on him in the time I've known him is enough proof that he's in pain. He just puts a front on to hide it. Me? I don't try to hide that I'm a grouchy bastard.

Rolling my eyes, I watch her get up from her seat and head our way.

Fuck, she's going to the restroom. Which means she'll walk right by us.

Her shoulder-length brown hair is curled today, falling perfectly around her angelic face, which disguises that she's actually the devil. And the flower-patterned dress she's wearing is cut just low enough to show off a tease of cleavage, making me curse this Oliver fucker for sitting across from her. Even though I hate her … she still takes my breath away.

Pretending to play on my phone, I look anywhere but at her, hoping she'll somehow miss us and walk by.

"Brody … Link," I hear her say nervously. "Didn't see y'all over here."

"You know, Tater Tot, Cam and Link might also have Southern accents, but yours is so much fucking cuter."

"Gee, thanks," she says, and I don't even have to be looking at her to know she's likely blushing.

Tate's never been good at taking a compliment. Or really even being flirted with. Something in her is wired to tell her she isn't worthy of it or some shit.

"How do you know Oliver?" Brody says curiously.

We glance back at the table where he's sitting, and he quickly looks away when he sees us all gawking at him.

"The job I told you I started? Well, it's at the Brooks University Astronomy Center. He's the mana—"

"Manager," Brody finishes her sentence. "Sweet, Tater Tot. How did I not know you were a hot, nerdy girl who's into outer space?"

Her cheeks only darken as she laughs nervously. "I guess it never came up." She shrugs. "Well, I'll see you at home."

As I peer up from my screen, her eyes cut to mine, slicing me down to my fucking soul.

"Link." She waves softly before turning.

My eyes float to her ass. Even in a loose dress, it's clear how nice of an ass she has. My dick twitches in my jeans, proving itself a traitor.

As soon as she's out of sight, I slide out of the booth. "Let's get the hell out of here before she comes back."

He follows me, and I can hear the smirk in his voice. "Why? So you don't have to witness her kiss Oliver good-bye?"

"She's not going to kiss that douchebag," I grumble. "They're colleagues. That's it."

"Dude, have you looked at him? All girls probably want to kiss that motherfucker. He looks like an Abercrombie & Fitch model."

"Shut up," I say through gritted teeth as we walk past him.

"Later, Oliver," Brody tosses to him.

"See ya, O'Brien," Oliver says. "Try not to do anything weird or inappropriate in public places," he teases.

"You know I can't promise that, man." Brody smirks.

I have to fight the urge not to grab the guy by the shirt and tell him if he puts one finger on Tate, I'll murder him. She might not be my girl, but she sure as hell isn't his either.

But now, she's met this dude, who likes all the same nerdy shit she does, and she clearly doesn't give a fuck about me.

Bad is remembering the way it felt when she discarded me. Shitty is missing her every day and craving her like a drug. But having her share a campus, a fucking house with me? All while I put an act on that she's dead to me? Well, it's unbearable. And truthfully, I don't know how much longer I can do it before I lose my mind.

TATE

I walk next to Oliver as we make our way back to the Astronomy Center, where our cars are parked. Once I saw Link, something shifted. The coffee not-date was no longer fun, and my mind was suddenly a thousand miles away. Well, not a thousand miles away … just out the door, leaving alongside Brody.

The way Link looked at me—or I should say, looked through me—it was like I was no one now.

He's over me. I should be happy. I should be breathing easier. So, why the hell does it feel like I can't breathe at all?

"You're awfully quiet over there. Everything all right?" Oliver says, nudging my side lightly.

Giving him a fake smile, I nod. "Oh, yeah, I'm fine. Just tired—that's all. The first week of classes always wears on me." We reach the parking lot, and I walk toward my Jeep. "Thanks for the coffee. It was fun."

"You're welcome," he says, eyeing me over. "You sure you're good, Tate? Did I do something wrong?"

"No, no. Definitely not," I assure him. "See you Thursday. The show is at three, but I figure I should get here by one to make sure everything is set up?"

He doesn't look convinced, but takes a few steps back toward his sporty-looking little black car. "Perfect. Thanks. And great work so far. We're happy to have you on board."

"Happy to be here," I say honestly. "Have a great rest of your night."

And then I get in my car and head home. Because even though it's the last place I want to be, I'm almost out of clean laundry. So, I need to be an adult and face my past.

And by past ... I mean, Link Sterns.

When I get home, Link's truck is here, but Brody's isn't.

Great. I don't even have good ol' Brody as a buffer.

I don't know him all that well yet, but he's so lovable. I can see why the buzz around campus is that the ladies love him, and from the sound of it, he's pretty fond of them too.

Because the football and hockey teams are both basically royalty, I have to hear about a lot of things around campus. Including Link and some of his former hookups. The girls gush as they talk about how hot the sex was with Link Sterns. They act like he's some brooding dude, which seems to fit the bill on how he is now.

I've been that girl before ... I *know* what that man can do in bed.

It might pain me to think of him with other women, but I'm not exactly an angel. Sure, I haven't physically *been* with anyone but Link, but I've dated. Or tried to anyway. Back in Boston, I was determined to find the one who would sweep me off my feet, making me realize I could get over Link once and for all. I was smarter about who I spent time with. No athletes, just ordinary men who weren't going to be in the limelight one day. I'd learned all too well to be careful with who I let into my heart. Because they might just dig themselves in there, refusing to leave. I'd learned that even though it was said life was short, the days could feel like eternity when you were missing someone.

So, even though I'd tried to get over him, the truth was, I couldn't stand another man's hands on my skin. Their lips were too soft or too slobbery. Their scent wasn't *his*. So, before we could take it too far, I'd push them away. To be honest … they all made my stomach turn. It wasn't them, and it wasn't me either.

It was Link.

Link was to blame for the simple fact that I couldn't move on. How could I when I was so stupidly in love with him?

Grabbing my bag, I force myself out of the Jeep and head inside. I know the second he sees me, he'll likely bolt out the door like his ass is on fire.

When I push the front door open, my chest feels tight, and my stomach feels like it's about to fall out of my ass.

Goddamn this man for making me feel this way.

When I hear the TV in the living room on and see the back of Link's head as he sits on the couch, I press my back to the door and squeeze my eyes shut.

Blowing out my breath, I give myself a silent pep talk to stop being a little bitch and act like this is my house too. Because it is.

Hearing the couch creak, followed by footsteps, I know he's coming toward me. And there's nowhere to hide from him and his dark, angry energy.

"Did you kiss him?" Link's deep, gritty voice rasps.

"What?" I say, my eyes flying open as I take in the man at the other end of the hallway.

"That Oliver clown, with his khaki pants, like Jake from fucking State Farm." He takes a few steps forward. "Did you kiss him?"

"I guess I don't see how that's your business, Link." I drop my tote bag on the floor and toe my shoes off. "I think you've said, like, five words to me since I've been here. And none of those words were nice. This is the first shit you've got to say?" Walking toward him, I put my hands on my hips and stand tall. "Word around campus is, you bang girls. Lots of girls. *Loads* of girls. Hell, your penis probably fell off a long time ago from whatever STD you'd gotten. So, tell me, what the hell does it matter what I do or who I —"

His lips are on mine, and his strength pushes me against the wall before I get the words out. He kisses me roughly, growling against my mouth, "Shut up, Tate." His mouth hovers over mine as his chest heaves against my own. I feel his heart beating with mine. "Shut your mouth, or I'll shut it for you by showing you just how much my dick is very much still intact."

My back arches against the wall, pressing my chest against him as I glare. "What? Don't want to hear what I have to say?" I drive my hand into his chest. "Quit being a dick to me, Link."

"You're lucky I haven't been worse to you," he says, his eyes darkening as he glowers down at me. The smell of mint making me dizzy. "I hate your fucking guts."

"If you hated me, you wouldn't care whose lips I was kissing, would you?"

"So, you *did* kiss him?" He backs away slowly, leaving my body cold again. "Wow."

As he makes his way toward the front door, I feel the tears gather in my eyes. "Link … you can't keep running from me. Eventually, we're going to need to face the elephant in the room."

Not turning around, he stops with his hand on the doorknob. "I might care whose lips you're kissing, Tate. But I promise you, I still hate you just the same."

And he's gone. And I touch my fingers to my lips, still feeling the electricity pulsing through them from his kiss, wishing I could feel it again. Yet knowing I shouldn't.

LINK

How fucking dumb am I?

I kissed her. On her lying, conniving mouth.

I've always known Tate's rule. *Don't fall for a professional athlete. Or someone who is going to be one someday.*

I can't blame her for being skeptical. Hell, look at her mother's situation and how shitty that turned out to be. But I'm not her piece-of-shit father. That dude barely showed up for his wife and daughters. Even during most of Tate's and Meyer's biggest moments, he wasn't there. He was off, banging some young chick, flying her all around the world behind his wife, Meg's, back. When the guy showed up at Tate's graduation, it was like a fucking unicorn sighting.

But even if she couldn't be with me, she also ran from the friendship we'd had since we had been twelve, for Christ's sake. I trusted her more than anyone. Even my own brothers. And then she threw it away after one fucking night.

When I had gone over there, drunk, and confessed my love to her, I had known I was changing our dynamic. Sure, we'd both felt that pull the universe refused to let us dodge. I'd held her in my arms at night and probably hugged her too long sometimes. Looked at her in her bikini more than I should have.

Kept most guys away from her simply because they knew she was mine even if she technically wasn't. But when she told me to be her first, a voice in my head was screaming she wasn't ready for that. It told me that if I did this, we'd never come back from it.

Selfishly, I did it anyway. How the fuck was I supposed to tell her no? It was all I'd thought about for years. And I guess a part of me knew that even if she ran from me … I'd always be her first. In some weird, fucked up way, I'd felt like that would make her mine. For life.

The only way I'm going to keep her from hurting me again is if I avoid her and ice her out, the way she did me. And whenever I start to feel that same weakness, like I just did inside a few minutes ago … I need to think back to that email she sent when my mother died. That's the only way living with her will ever work.

Putting my truck in reverse, I back out of the driveway and get the hell away from her.

Tomorrow, I'll be stronger. Even if that means I have to be an even bigger dick. She's kissing her coworker. It's obvious she's moving on with her life. I guess I should too.

Driving around for a while, I turn the music on and try to drown out my complicated reality. That is, until my phone rings, and I see Cam's name on the screen.

"What's up?" I answer, mustering up any energy I have for this conversation.

"Not much. Hey, look, I can't find my knee brace anywhere. I don't need it often, but right now, I do. I'm thinking it's in my old closet. Can you check?"

I groan. "Fine. But only when Tate isn't there."

"Well, I hope she ain't there right now. I need it for practice tonight."

"I'm not even home. I have my shit for practice in my truck and was just going for a ride to kill time." I sigh. "How bad do you need it, Hardy?"

"I mean, I suppose I can skip wearing it. Maybe injure myself and be out for the season. Your call, big fella."

Turning my truck around, I smack the steering wheel. "Fuuuck," I hiss. "You owe me, motherfucker."

"Yeah, yeah. I'll pay you back by leading us to the Frozen Four. See you in a bit. Thanks." And then that asshole hangs up.

And now, I'm stuck going into Tate's room after storming out not even half an hour ago.

It only takes me ten minutes to pull back in front of the apartment. And just like I dreaded, her car's still here.

Pushing the truck door open, I head inside to get this shit over with. Maybe I'll luck out. Maybe she'll be in the bathroom. Or on a walk.

I go into the apartment and head to her door, and I sigh in relief that it's halfway open.

That is, until I push it the rest of the way, and she's completely naked, reaching in her dresser for clothes, fresh out of the shower.

"Link! What the fuck?!" she screeches, attempting to cover her breasts. "Get out!"

I try to play it cool, but Christ almighty, every ounce of blood flows straight to my dick at the sight of her. I look down, but it's no use; the image is stuck in my damn brain.

All of it takes up every molecule inside my mind. The small of her back that leads to her full ass. Her wet hair combed back. Or when she swung around, cupping her tits in an attempt to cover herself. It's all I can see.

Looking at her again, I try to ignore the fact that my cock is growing by the second. "I just need something out of your closet. Don't flatter yourself, Princess. I'm not trying to look at you, Tate. Those days are long fucking gone," I say and watch her shoulders slump the smallest bit, yet it isn't enough. I need to hurt her more. At some point, hurting her will make me feel better. It's got to. "The last thing I want to do is fucking look at you."

Pushing past her, I open the closet and reach up to the top, patting around until, eventually, I find Cam's brace.

When I turn around, she is holding her towel around her, crying.

"Fuck you, Link. Get out."

I stand there, frozen, waiting for some sort of feeling of satisfaction as I watch her cry.

She marches toward me, shoving me. "Get out!" she screams. "Get out! Get out!"

Grabbing her wrists, I hold them against my chest, stilling her. Her towel falls, leaving her completely bare.

"No, you're in my house."

Her eyes narrow, and her mouth forms a pout, her lips quivering the smallest bit. "Guess what. This is my house too, asshole!" She attempts to wrestle against me but fails. "You're stuck with me, so get used to it! I'm not going anywhere!"

I always loved that, even as quiet as she was with everyone else, she was anything but that when she was around me. But right now, it's plain pissing me off.

"Bullshit!" I growl, gritting my teeth and throwing the brace onto her bed. "You'll always be going somewhere. You'll never fucking stick around!"

"What do you want me to say?" she says, her lips trembling more. "You really didn't leave me a choice, Link. Things changed that night. They won't ever be the same."

Even in my rage, red hot as it is, I crave to reach out and hold her when she cries. On one hand, it's hell to not be able to comfort the one person I want to, but on the other, I'm so angry that I want to be the one to cause her pain. I'm going insane. An absolute, utter fucking mess.

Fighting through the need to brush her trembling lips, I root myself to the fury, not letting myself soften from her sadness.

"An email, Tate," my voice barks. "A fucking email is all I got from you during the worst time of my life. My best. Fucking. Friend sent an email when my mother died," I snarl. "You never gave a fuck about me or my family."

She sucks in a breath, her chest swelling. "You don't know what you're talking about, asshole. I *did* come back for you when I found out your mom was sick. And you know what? It seemed like you no longer needed me."

Her words numb me. I wonder what the fuck she means.

Tears stream down her beautiful face, and my fingers spasm, wanting to reach up to brush them away.

"You can be angry with me for leaving in the first place. And you can hate me for not showing up for the funeral because I should have been there. But I did come back as soon as I knew." She bites down on her bottom lip, raking her teeth along it so bad that I'm surprised I don't see blood. "The only reason why I didn't come home for the funeral was because I didn't want to make the day harder for you than I already knew it was going to be. Trust me, I wanted to be there. I did."

I don't want to ask her when she came back. I don't want to know. Because if it's true, if she really did come back … I'll forgive her and fall right back into needing her.

"Friends are supposed to have each other's back forever, Tate." I release one of her hands, pointing in her face. "Not just when it's convenient for them. I looked after you. I fucking protected your ass and treated you like a queen even though we weren't dating."

"Don't you get it?" she whimpers. "It was hard enough, being your friend before you told me you loved me. Before we … did that." Her voice turns to barely a whisper. "After that night, there was no way I could stand to be around you." Tear-filled eyes gaze up at me. "You were my best friend for so long, Link. But being your best friend was torture."

"How the fuck was it torture?" I scowl. "I did everything for you!"

"Because I had to see you with God knows how many girls, knowing I could never be one of them. And watch you be Appleton's most beloved jock. I got to be in the friend zone with the man I thought about every damn night I went to bed. I got to be known as the nerdy girl who you felt responsible to look after even though you probably didn't want to." Her nostrils flare. "And my entire time in high school, you made sure no one else could have me, driving every single guy away who showed interest. While you stuck your dick in whatever hole you could."

"And then I told you I loved you, Tate! Goddammit!" I hiss. "I told you I wanted you. That I wanted us. And you fucking ran away like a coward."

"I know!" She pulls her hand away and covers her face. "You knew what my rule was. You knew I would never marry someone like my dad. I'm sorry." She sniffles. "Running away was to keep myself safe. I couldn't bear to be around you any longer. It was killing me." She sucks in a breath. "*You* were killing me."

"So, you wanted me, but were tortured because I fucked other girls. But then, when I admitted I wanted you, it scared you because you couldn't be with me because I played hockey." I throw my arms up. "That makes zero fucking sense."

"I know. I know that!" she shouts, her beautiful face soaked with tears. "I just had to put distance between us. It was the only way."

"Yet here you are. Back in fucking Georgia." Gripping her chin, I tip her face up. "Hate to be the bearer of bad news, but, even if you *did* come back for me at some point, when you sent that email instead of coming home to the funeral, you made me fucking hate you," I roar. "I should have never fucked you that night, Tate. I should have never buried my cock between your thighs. But you asked me, and even though I fucking knew better, I did it anyway. But make no mistake. It's my biggest fucking regret."

Backing away, I grab Cam's brace from the bed and walk out.

The worst thing I ever did was hook up with my best friend. Because now, we can't even be around each other.

LINK

"Sterns, nice play," Coach LaConte calls out. "Hardy, I suppose you were all right too." He looks around to the entire team. "You're looking better, but we've still got a long-ass way to go. And guess what. Time isn't on our side here. We've got our first season game in two weeks." He points to the exit. "Get on out of here. I'll see your cheerful faces bright and early tomorrow morning."

We all sigh in relief. We've had two practices on most days lately, and we're all starting to feel it. It's been a week since I saw Tate naked, and because of Coach's insane expectations from us, running into her really hasn't been a problem. I've seen her for a few seconds in passing and caught glimpses of her going from the bathroom to her room, but we've managed to awkwardly skate around each other.

Keeping busy has also kept me from asking her when she came back to me. Even though it's killing me not to know.

"Yo, Sterns," Cam says from behind me. "What do you say we go grab a beer? Or some food? O'Brien, Thompson, you in too?"

"I can't. Sorry, Cap," Hunter calls back. "Have a cold one for me."

"I'm in. I'm fucking starving," Brody mutters before yawning. "I'm so exhausted that my nutsack is even tired."

"If that's the case, I suppose you won't be sneaking out for any secret hookups tonight, huh?" I call out to him. "Tired nuts seem like a good reason to lie low."

Turning around, he winks. "I'm never too tired for that."

"When do we get to meet her anyway?" Cam asks as we all walk into the locker room. "I thought we were family, and now, you're keeping secrets and shit."

Brody gives him a pointed look. "Oh, gee, I wonder who else did this same fucking thing not long ago." He shakes his head. "Pot, meet kettle. You hypocritical dick."

"I guess that's fair," Cam says. "But in my defense, if I hadn't kept it a secret, Coach would have cut my balls off and probably let you guys use them as a puck. And then I would have had to join the women's hockey team instead." He grimaces. "That shit had to stay under wraps."

"So does this," Brody mumbles. "For now. And, no, it isn't because I'm embarrassed. It just isn't the right time to be dropping bombs—that's all. Besides, it's easy. Fun. Nothing else."

"So, you wouldn't care if she hooked up with someone else?" I taunt him.

"It ain't like that." He shrugs.

I walk to the shower and step in, letting the hot water wash away the sweat and ease my aching muscles. With Cam in a serious relationship, Hunter chasing his ex, and Brody sneaking around with God knows who, I can't help but think the guys are losing focus on what matters this year.

Making it to the Frozen Four. That's the goal.

And up until this point, I never had anything distracting me. Now, I'm living with my distraction. How the hell is that supposed to work?

We sit at the bar at Club 83, and I finish off my second beer. It feels good to let off some steam tonight, but we all know we have to wake up early tomorrow morning. So, unfortunately, this night can't last forever.

"So, this chick who's living with you," Cam says, peeling the label off his beer mindlessly, "you gonna tell me the story about that? Did y'all date?"

"Nah, nothing like that," I mumble. "Remember that friend of yours, Bama Bishop?"

"Beau Bishop," he corrects me. "I'm from Alabama, too, and do you see me, walking around, calling myself Bama? Fuck no."

Cam is one of the only people I know who calls Bama by his real name. Probably because they've been friends since before Beau was Bama. And like he said, Cam's from the same exact town in Alabama that Beau is.

"All right, calm your pickle and stay on track. Jesus." I scowl. "As I was saying, you know how you and *Beau* had a falling-out after years of friendship, but you forgave him, and now, you're good?"

"Yeah, I guess."

"It's like that. Except I'm not about to forgive her," I say bluntly. "Ever."

"You're missing a key difference here, my friend." Cam looks thoughtful. "She has a vagina. And not that I've seen it personally, but I'm pretty sure Beau has a pecker."

"What the fuck does that matter? She was my best friend, just like he was yours. Same fucking thing."

"So, you've never put your D in her V?" Brody says skeptically.

"Nope," I lie.

"Not even the tip?"

"No. How fucking dumb are you, dude? On a scale of one to ten."

"Eleven," he deadpans. "Also, are guys and girls really ever just best friends though?" Cam asks, strumming his fingertips on the table. "I think not. I've seen enough chick flicks and Hallmark shit with Addy to know that they always, always, fucking always fall in love with each other and shit. Or worse, one falls, and then the other is like, *Nah, I'm good.* And that shit is awful to watch, really."

"Not to change the subject here, but who doesn't love a good Hallmark movie from time to time?" Brody chimes in, taking a sip from his Sprite. "Hell, I sometimes enjoy a Lifetime one too. They are kinky as fuck."

"Lifetime is where it's at. Straight-up filthy," Cam agrees. "The acting is shit, but I'm not mad at it."

I stare at them. "What has happened to the two of you? Christ almighty. Coach must have cut your dick off, and you just don't remember it. You have a vagina now."

He smirks, raising his eyebrows. "Ahh … Addison would beg to differ," Cam says slyly. "Either way, my man, I'm picking up your vibe. You want this chick. I say, go for it. I'm all about that romantic shit these days."

"When did I ever say that?" I groan. "I don't want her."

"I gotta take a piss," Brody says, standing.

Just as he leaves, a pretty blonde thing takes his seat. Smiling at me, she leans a little closer. "Link Sterns, right?"

"Maybe." I look at her.

She is no Tate Tracy, but maybe that's not a bad thing. Seeing as Tate is probably off, kissing dudes who tuck in their shirts and wear fucking khakis and talk about planets.

She smiles, trying to appear super confident, but I can sense she's nervous.

"I know you're Link Sterns. I'm Kaylee. You're one hell of a player."

I hear Cam snort behind me, but I ignore him.

"Hockey fan, I take it?"

"Something like that," she says playfully. "Can you keep a secret?"

"I'll try my best."

Dipping her lips to my ear, she looks nervous. "My friends dared me to come talk to you. It was this or something way, way worse."

"Worse than me?" I narrow my eyes. "I doubt that."

She swallows. "The other was, well, to have a one-night stand … with a stranger." She looks up at me uncertainly, biting her lip. "Don't worry … I won't hold you to that one."

The thought of Tate sitting across from Oliver assaults my mind, and the fact that she wouldn't tell me he didn't kiss her must mean that he did. His lips were on hers. Lips that are supposed to be mine. They could be off together right now; his hands could be all over her body. She might even fucking like it.

"Why not?" I drawl slowly. "I'm free. And you did say you're a big fan."

Her eyes widen before she glances over at her friends. "O-okay. I mean … yeah. Yes."

Suddenly, Cam nudges me. "If you're catching a ride with me, let's go. Addy is waiting for me, and I can't keep my honey waiting." Standing up, he slaps me on the back. "Choppity chop."

"Told you … no balls anymore," I mutter just as Brody stands next to him. "Big ol' vagina."

"Nah, Cam Hardy just *loves* the one vagina he's getting." He winks. "Let's go, motherfuckers."

"Is there room for one more?" I mumble to Cam.

His eyes float to the chick next to me. Keeping his voice low, he gives me a hard look. "Really, dude? Wouldn't it be easier to just go tell your new roommate you want her and fuck her brains out and live happily ever after? I feel like that'd be better."

"It ain't that easy, Hardy. Not everything in life is like that. Some shit can't be fixed."

Patting me on the shoulder, he shakes his head. "If you say so. But take it from me, this won't help. Maybe for a second, when your balls are tingling, it'll take the edge off. But then, once it's over? That pain will be right back."

Pushing what he just said out of my brain, I nod toward Kaylee. "Ready to complete that dare, sweetheart?"

Staring at me, she eventually nods. "Hell yes."

As we walk toward the exit together, even I don't know what the fuck I'm doing. Or why.

I just hope it'll stop me from imagining Tate with another man for at least a few minutes.

TATE

"Goddamn it," I groan, seeing the lights on in the apartment and knowing the boys are back from wherever the heck they were. Looking down at my pizza, six-pack of beer, and ice cream, I sigh. "At least you'll make this night better."

My plan was to run to the store and get back in my room before they got home. I have some homework to finish up, and I was going to stuff my face with pizza and ice cream after treating myself to a beer or two to take the edge off the past few weeks.

Gathering my things, I get out of the car and walk inside the house.

"Pizza, beer, and ice cream? Just marry me already, would ya?" Brody says when he spots me. "A girl who isn't afraid to eat … now that's what I'm talkin' about."

"You only live life once, right?" I shrug, closing the door behind me with my butt. "I'm not spending my days eating salad."

"You and me both." He nods. "Shit's for the birds."

"Help yourself. I won't eat this all." I shrug. "Actually, that's not true. I probably could. But I shouldn't."

"I'm good, Tater Tot. We just went to Club 83."

I hear a girl giggle from upstairs, and my heart sinks. Brody must see it because he walks toward me.

"Don't let it get to you. That's what he wants."

"How the hell are we supposed to live together?" I drop my stuff onto the counter. "It was one thing to be across the country, thinking he was with other women. It's another to have to witness it firsthand." I try to hide the way my voice cracks by clearing my throat. "I know I walked away, but that doesn't make it easier."

He looks sympathetic before a devilish grin spreads across his face. "Link is my boy, and I'd kill for that motherfucker. But right now, he's hurting, and what he's about to do won't make it better." He grabs my hand, pulling me toward his room. "Want to fuck with him?"

Quickly, I shake my head. "No … I've done enough of that for one lifetime, thanks." My shoulders sag. "He should be able to do as he pleases.

Like he said, this was his place first. And I'm the one who left. I chose this as my reality."

I hear her make a squealing noise, and I have to mentally tell myself not to puke. And before I know what's happening, Brody is pulling me into his bedroom. Closing the door and locking it behind him.

"Brody, wh—" I start to say, but he covers my mouth.

"Play along, would you? I need some entertainment in my life."

Sitting on the edge of the bed, he moves up and down, causing a creaking noise before growling a few not-so-appropriate words out. "Tate," he moans. "Oh ... fuck ... Tate."

My cheeks must heat to the deepest shade of red. And as hot as they feel, I'm guessing I could cook a damn egg on them. One thing is for certain ... Brody has experience. *Lots and lots* of dirty experience.

Brody gives me a nod, raising his eyebrows, and I know what he wants me to do.

"I can't do that!" I whisper, appalled. "I'm not even sexy when I'm trying to be sexy! Besides, this is dumb! And soooo wrong."

"Come on, girl. Show me your game," he murmurs. "I know you've got some. Nobody has an ass like *that* and doesn't." He cocks his head toward my butt and winks.

"Trust me, I have no game."

Standing abruptly, he slaps my ass so hard that it makes a loud smack, and I cry out in pain.

"Fuck yes. You like it when I spank you, dirty girl?" He moans so loud that I'm sure the neighbors can hear him. "You want more, Tate? You're going to have to earn it. Get on your knees like a good girl."

Holding up his hand, he puts three fingers up, dropping one at a time until there's only one left. And when the last one goes down, someone begins pulling on the doorknob, desperate to get the door open. Only it's locked, and so whoever is trying to get in starts pounding on the door.

"What the fuck is going on?" Link roars. "Open this motherfucking door before I break it down."

My eyes must be the size of dinner plates as I turn toward Brody, begging to know what the hell we're going to do now.

"Little busy, Sterns," Brody calls out, trying to keep a straight face. "Come back in ten. No, five should do."

"Fuck that," Link snarls.

I know what he's about to do. So, before he can, I pull the door open.

There he stands, tousled brown hair that looks like someone's fingers have been running through it, and that thought alone makes me sick. His shirt is off, but thank God his jeans are on even though I suppose he could have slid them on before coming in here.

Looking me up and down, he notices I'm fully clothed before his eyes shift to Brody, and he charges in.

"What the fuck are you doing, O'Brien?"

"Same thing as you, it seems," Brody replies with a shrug. "Must be a good night for it."

Pulling me by my arm, Link drags me into my room and slams the door. Crowding me against the wall. "Do you really have to whore around with my best fucking friend, Tate?"

My hand connects with his face, landing a slap so hard that my palm stings. "Don't you dare call me a whore, asshole! You have a random girl in your bed right now. Just because I'm a girl doesn't make it any different." I glare up at him, standing on my tiptoes to get in his face. "What I do, or *who* I do, is none of your business. But for the record, I wasn't doing anything wrong with Brody. It was a joke."

"You're right, Tate. I do have a girl in my room. And she's fucking hot too," he coos back. "Maybe I'll go back in my room and let her ride my cock so hard that she'll cry out, and you'll have to listen to her screaming my name." He puts a hand on my chin and tightens his grip. "Is that what you want? You want me to fuck someone else? You want to listen to me plow into her so you can imagine it's you? I bet you'd even slide a finger or two inside those panties, knowing that's the closest you'll get to me fucking you again."

"I. Don't. Care," I mutter, gritting my teeth. "I'll go ride Brody. I'll fuck him, and you can listen to that," I spew. "Prick."

I attempt to duck from his hold, but he grabs me, pinning me to the wall harder. "Shut your filthy fucking mouth before I have you on your knees, driving my cock so far down your throat that you won't be able to even think about fucking another man. You'll be too busy gagging on every inch of me."

His eyes are like that of a rabid animal. His pupils damn near filling his entire irises. Even through his jeans, I feel his hardness push against me, making me whimper.

Damn my nipples for betraying me. And my stupid vagina for tingling the way it is right now. My heart pounds in my ears, silencing any rational thoughts I might have.

"Fuck you," I breathe out.

"Keep pushing me, Tate. See what fucking happens."

We stare at each other for God knows how long. Both frozen in time. His anger radiates off him like an overheated engine. Even so, all I want is to climb him like a tree and never leave this room.

"I don't want Brody," I rasp, calling a truce. "You and I both know that. We were just trying to get to you."

Leaning closer, he continues to grip my chin as his lips barely hover over mine. "You don't know what you fucking want, Tate. That's the problem. It's *always* been the problem."

He's right. I don't. I'm all over the place. I know what I need, and that's to protect myself. But when it comes to what I want, it's always been him.

"Poor, sad, broken Tate. With her daddy issues and her stupid fucking rules," he says, cruel words continuing to flow from his lips like nothing. "You make no sense."

"I know," I whisper, peeking up at him. "I know it's none of my business who you bring home. But that doesn't make it any easier." My head hangs. "Everything is complicated, Link."

"Yeah, well, you chose to come back, didn't you?" he says, emotionless. "You could have stayed away from Georgia. So, if it's hard for you … that's your own doing. And if you can't take it, go on back to Boston. You know, where you can *blend* into the crowd."

I've never said out loud that I wanted to go to Boston so that I wouldn't be noticed. So I could stay under the radar. My mom never figured it out. But Link? Of course he did.

He sees everything that I am. He sees the dark and the ugly. The parts of myself I hate.

There was never any hiding it from Link.

When he leaves, I don't try to hold myself together. I fall into a pile on the ground, thinking about the girl in his bed … and how she'll get Link tonight and I'll be alone.

LINK

"I'm sorry," I say, driving Kaylee back to her place. "I didn't mean to put you in an awkward situation."

"It's fine, really," she assures me, but I can tell her feelings are hurt.

When I brought her home, we started making out even though I wasn't really into it. I had her shirt off within two minutes, kissing her neck and making her moan. But I was struggling with taking it further than that. Mostly because I didn't want to use this girl, who seemed nice enough. And just when her hand slid to my dick, rubbing me through my jeans, I heard Brody moaning Tate's name. At first, I thought maybe I'd heard it wrong, but when I heard her squeal, followed by him yelling her name again … I lost my fucking mind.

I know it was just a setup to get to me, but when I get home from dropping Kaylee off, Brody had better be ready to fucking talk to me.

When Tate is indifferent, it's easy for me to hate her. But when she shows herself to me, even just the slightest bit, and I see the Tate I knew is still in there, I feel myself weaken.

And when she muttered the words, "I don't want Brody. You and I both know that," I was so close to taking her clothes off and reminding her of graduation night.

No matter the consequences, I wanted it. But I willed myself out of whatever trance that girl had put me in, and I got the hell out of there before I did something even dumber than I already had.

When I got back to my room, I apologized to Kaylee and explained it was a fucked up night and I couldn't have sex with her. I felt like a dick, but it wouldn't have been right. Not because Tate was next door, but because this woman deserved more than sex from a dude who was cringing while kissing her.

"Is she your ex? Or … what?" Her voice is quiet. "The girl back at your place."

"It's hard to explain. We have history. And sometimes, history comes back to bite us in the ass."

"I see," she says curtly before pointing to a house. "Right here. You can just pull up front."

When I pull along the curb, her hand immediately goes to the door.

"Kaylee, I really am sorry. And I want you to know, it wasn't you. You're gorgeous. And if I wasn't so screwed in the head, I would have given you a night you'd never forget. Forgive me?"

She offers me the smallest smile before pressing a kiss to my cheek. "Consider yourself forgiven. You're a good guy, Link Sterns. I hope you figure out your … history. And decide if it's also your future." Climbing out, she waves before closing the door.

TATE

"Your pizza is cold, your beer is warm, and your ice cream would have melted, but I just put that shit in the freezer," Brody says after pushing my door open. "You're welcome."

I hug my pillow against me, wiping under my eyes. "Thanks. I'm not that hungry anymore."

I've never been one to cry much. I've always figured, what's the point? But when it comes to Link, consider me a damn water fountain.

I feel the bed shift as he takes the spot next to me. Flipping over, I watch him open two beers before handing me one.

Sitting up, I press my back to my headboard. "Thanks." I sniffle. "Sorry. Before I moved in, your life was probably much simpler. Now, I'm here, messing it all up. Even your friendship with Link."

Gripping my shoulder, he chuckles. "Sweetheart, Link and I might not be blood, but we're brothers. There's no one coming between us. I love that dude. What I did tonight was meant to help him, not hurt him."

"I never wanted to hurt him," I say, as if trying to explain myself. "He's the last person I ever wanted to cause pain. I just … got scared. I'm still scared."

"Deep down, everyone is scared. And if they aren't, they are one dumb motherfucker." He scoots back, sitting next to me. "You're gonna be fine, Tater Tot. I promise."

"Yeah," I whisper, not believing it.

"Yeah," he says back. "He took that bitch home, by the way. He didn't fuck her. I know that for a fact."

When I look over at him, a tear rolls down my cheek. "Really? What, did you have a glass on his door, listening?" I try to joke, but my voice cracks.

"Something like that, but far less creepy." He shrugs. "Now, find something on TV. I'm going to get that half-melted ice cream. But you'd best share with me." Getting up, he winks. "Besides, I faked my best sex sounds for you."

"I microwave my ice cream for fifteen seconds before I eat it anyway. It'll be perfect."

"Are you a serial killer?" he whispers.

"Har-har, not funny." I chuckle, remembering earlier. "Also, about the whole fake sex noises. First off, I heard you and Link talking the other day. You're an underwear model, but what else? Are you a damn porn star too?" I fan myself with my hand. "Because you only set my cheeks on fire, no biggie."

Laughing, he shrugs. "I like sex. What can I say? Most would say I'm pretty good at it too." Backing toward the door, he points toward me. "Now, I'm going to get the ice cream while you find us something to watch on TV. Nothing sad though. I'm not in the mood to cry and shit."

"Deal," I say and point the remote at the TV.

Somehow, I've found an unlikely friend in Brody. But I'm not dumb. I know that will only hurt Link more. And for that, I feel like a complete ass.

Link

I walk into the apartment after riding around for an hour to clear my head, and immediately, I hear Brody and Tate tee-heeing and chatting like they are long-lost best friends or some shit. Only proving more that she's here to ruin my entire life.

Heading toward her room, I sigh in relief when I see the door is open.

Stepping in the doorframe, I take in the image of the two of them on her bed, eating ice cream and hanging out like they've known each other for years. Irking me to my core. Not because I'm jealous they want each other, but because he's acting like her new best friend. And that was always my place in her life.

"What the fuck are you doing? We have early practice tomorrow, O'Brien," I scold him. "And we already ate dinner at Club 83."

Patting his stomach, he smirks. "Link, you really should know by now that I can always eat." Leaning back, he yawns. "But you're right. It's time to hit the hay." He pats Tate's head. "You'd better not watch the next episode of *Outer Banks* without me. I got a bad feeling about Sarah's old man. I'm telling you, he's bad news bears."

"Don't be so sure. I feel like he's just a loving father." She smiles until her eyes connect with mine, and then she looks nervous.

"Good night, Tater Tot," Brody says before throwing his arm around me. "Night-night, Linky. I love ya even though you're a dick. And before you ask, no, I didn't put my dick inside of Tate's vagina. Or her mouth. Or her ass. Nor am I going to."

Even though I knew it was a setup, I still sigh in relief, hearing it from his lips, even if he does put a visual in my head that makes me see red.

Once he's in his own room, I look at her. "I don't know what you're doing, but cut the shit. He's my best friend. Find your own." I glare at her. "I shouldn't have kissed you earlier. That was a mistake, and it won't happen again. I don't care whose dick you let inside of you as long as it isn't my best friend's."

Her face looks slightly pained. "So, you're saying you don't care who I have relations with as long as it isn't your best friend."

"Or my teammates," I answer curtly. "The *only* thing that matters in my life right now is hockey. It's all I have. Don't fuck it up for me."

"Okay," she says softly. "I won't. But for the record, I don't see Brody like that. He's been kind to me. I think of him as a friend. But if that upsets you, I guess I can avoid him."

I look away. "I don't give a fuck. Just don't fuck my friends, Tate. You've done enough, haven't you?"

My eyes find hers again, and I hold her gaze to make myself clear. I guess, in some way, I think if I convince her of what I'm about to say, maybe I'll convince myself too.

"I don't care who you kiss, fuck, or date anymore. I lost my head when you first showed up and again earlier tonight. But I can see clearly now." I nod once. "And what I see is … you're just a traitorous, lying bitch who never cared about me or my family. You can live here, but I'm going to pretend like you don't." I take a step back. "I'm going to pretend like you don't exist at all actually."

And then I go the hell to bed. Because I've had enough of this shit for one night. And I'm sure we both know every word from my mouth was a lie.

5

TATE

After two weeks of hanging out at the coffee shop for at least an hour or two a day, I decide to change my scenery up and head to the library. It isn't always that easy, studying in my room, knowing Link is across the hall. Or never knowing who is coming in and out of the damn place either. Weeks ago, he told me to sleep with or date whoever I wanted as long as it wasn't any of his friends. Which I never had any intent to do anyway. And truthfully, in the short time I've been around him, Brody has become sort of a big brother.

I gaze around the library, listening to the half-dozen conversations going on, and it takes me by surprise how noisy this place is. When I spot a beautiful girl sitting behind the librarian's desk, I immediately recognize her. She attended my high school's rival school a few towns over.

"Sloane Silvine?" I say, my mouth hanging open when she glances up at me. "Wow! It is you. You probably don't remember me. I'm—"

"Tate," she says with the same sweet smile I remember from the few times I've met her. "Tate Tracy."

"Wow! I had no idea that you were at Brooks. I just got here a few weeks ago." I wave toward the desk. "Do you work here?"

"I do. Always been a book nerd, so it seemed only fitting." She smiles. "So, where were you before?" She pauses. "If you don't mind me asking."

"Boston." I sigh. "Just wanted to be back closer to home, you know?"

Though I only saw her a few times during our high school careers, she always came off as such a genuine, kind person. Though word around town was that her father was a crooked man who was doing some illegal dealings from their car dealership.

"I know exactly what you mean."

"So, listen, is there anywhere else in the library that's … well …"

"Less noisy?" she says, raising an eyebrow. "More—oh, I don't know—library-ish?"

I laugh. "Well, yes." I shrug my shoulders. "I hate to sound like a grouchy, old bitch, but my apartment isn't quiet, so I was looking for somewhere that is." I grimace. "The coffee shop was working till one of the guys who works there thought I was hanging out there in hopes of a date. With him." I roll my eyes. "Men."

She giggles before her gaze flicks to the culprits of the noise. "I am so sorry. Today is the only day it's like this because they have some study groups even though it's clear they aren't doing much studying. I've spoken to them a few times, but honestly, it's useless." Standing, she points to a secluded back room. "Tutoring sessions often take place in there, but it's free right now." She jerks her chin upward. "It's all yours."

Before I can answer, the entire library erupts in whistles as an excruciatingly attractive man struts in, making his way toward Sloane.

"Peach, there you are," he says, walking around the back of her desk and pulling her against his side, kissing her forehead. "I see it's the loudest day of the week in here. Sounds like a fucking frat party."

"Knox." She blushes, shoving him gently. "Sort of working here."

His eyes float to mine, and he grins. "Sorry. See how gorgeous my girl is? I do an awful job of keeping my hands off of her."

Sloane shakes her head, but can't stop the smile that continues to spread across her face. She was always a quiet girl. It seems like she's really happy, not that I can blame her.

"Knox, this is Tate. Our high schools were rivals. She was in Boston, but just transferred to Brooks."

She pats Knox's abdomen, which I'm betting is rock hard.

Just like Link's.

"Tate, this is Knox. My boyfriend."

"Oh, you're claiming me today, huh?" He looks down at her before holding his hand out to me. "Nice to meet you, Tate. How'd you like the cold winters? Heard they're brutal in New England."

"It was hell frozen over," I say firmly. "Zero out of ten would recommend."

Sloane covers her mouth as she laughs. "Knox is from Maine."

"Oh shit." My eyes widen. "Sorry."

He shrugs. "It's all good. If I hadn't grown up there, freezing my nutsack off for five months out of the year, I'd say the same thing."

"On the bright side, Maine is beautiful." I smile, shrugging my shoulders. "My sister goes to college there. I've gone to visit a few times. I just prefer the seasons when there isn't three feet of snow on the ground."

"Your sister lives in Maine? No shit? That's cool." He grins before pressing a kiss to Sloane's lips, then releasing her. "I've gotta run, baby. I'll be home after practice."

"Bye. Love you." She waves as he backs away.

Pointing to the dozen loudmouth college kids, he narrows his eyes. "Y'all better do as she says. It's a fucking library, not a damn kegger. Act like it and shut your mouths." And then he looks at her, giving her a grin.

"Oh. My. Gawd," Sloane groans. "He means well. But, Lord, that's embarrassing."

And once he's gone, there are no more loud conversations going on—that's for sure. Just a lot of quiet whispering and nervousness as they all glance around.

"Y'all seem really happy. That's awesome." I jerk my thumb toward the back room even though I don't really need it now that it's quiet. "Guess I'd better get to it. It was really nice to see you. Let's get together sometime and catch up."

"For sure." She nods. "Let me know if you need anything."

"Will do."

LINK

Studying the game tape, we know that for this opening game, we'll have our work cut out for us.

The first game of the season sets the tone. Not just for our opposing teams and how they'll view us, but also for how we'll see ourselves. How strong of a team we really think we are. If we have what it takes to take it to the end. If we lose this first game right out of the gate, forget about an undefeated season. And while being undefeated isn't the most important thing, it sure would be nice.

"All right, boys. Head home. Don't fuck off. Get rested," Coach says, turning the TV off. "Got it?"

"Yes, sir," we all mutter before standing up.

Class, practice, and game tape. That's all this day has consisted of. And tomorrow night, on that ice, we'll show how well our team works together. Personally, I think we're a well-oiled machine.

We have a kick-ass coach. Our unstoppable center, Cam, who was handpicked from the hockey gods. Brody O'Brien, who is basically what you'd get if you thought of the most protective dog you'd ever seen and combined it with a giant. Only instead of a bone, he protects his puck and his teammates at all costs. Cade Huff is another defenseman, who also takes no shit and is feared the moment he steps onto the ice. Hunter Thompson is the team's right winger, and he's a complete animal. And our main goalie, Watson Gentry, is hands down one of the best in the nation. Tons of other talented dudes make up our team, making it one of the strongest in college hockey this season. If we all keep our eye on the prize, we'll be unstoppable.

"Y'all best be eatin' your Wheaties tomorrow," Cam drawls slowly as we head out to the parking lot. "Or in Brody's case, protein shakes."

"Hey, I didn't get this damn sexy, eating carrot sticks and celery, Cam-Cam," Brody tosses back proudly.

"What about you, Linky Winky? You gonna be ready?" Cam punches my arm. "No distractions, right?"

"Dude, do you hear the shit that comes out of your mouth? You've been hanging around Isla too long now. You're starting to rhyme shit."

Cam's eyes widen. "You ain't even joking, dude. Last week, I called steak steaky. And this morning? I called eggs … eggys." He looks down. "Kid is killing my mojo."

"I didn't realize you had any to begin with," I joke, earning me another punch. "And, yeah, I'll be ready. You know that. Catch you later."

When I hop in the passenger side of Brody's truck, he wastes no time climbing in and peeling out of the arena's parking lot. "I'm starving. So, I say we get Chinese takeout on our way home."

"Fine with me."

He glances over at me. "Text Tate and see what she wants picked up, would you?"

"You fucking kidding me?" I deadpan.

"No. She's probably hungry. Be the nice guy that I know you are and ask her."

"You don't feed the enemy. That isn't how it works." I grind my back teeth together. "Why the fuck are you always so concerned about Tate? Do you want her or something?"

"I mean, I thought it was pretty clear that our love runs deep. Like … deeper than the ocean," Brody says, keeping his voice serious as can be. "You can be a groomsman, if you want."

When I stare at him, he bursts out laughing. "I'm just fuckin' with you, man. It's not like that." He relaxes in his seat. "She's more like the little sister I never had. Besides, broken people gravitate to other broken people for friendship." He punches me. "That's why we're best friends, my man."

"What the hell does that mean? I'm not broken."

"Dude, you're a straight-up tortured soul," he fires back unapologetically. "We don't have to talk about our deep, dark shit. But we know it's there. We're damaged goods, and we're both fucked."

"Whatever. How the fuck do you figure Tate is damaged?" I ask him, knowing myself that she is, but not understanding how he would. "Her dad was a professional hockey player. She grew up in a mansion. Doesn't scream broken girl to me."

"Her eyes," he says thoughtfully. "It's always the eyes."

"Whatever," I mumble, staring straight ahead, knowing exactly what he means.

Tate's eyes have always been empty. Her old man was a poor excuse for a father to her and Meyer both. And when they were growing up, their parents' relationship was what they got an up-close look at. To them, being a professional athlete automatically meant that you were a lying, cheating dirtbag. When it came to Tate Tracy, I never stood a chance, and I knew it.

And even though I knew she'd never be mine, I protected her with everything I was. Until she went against me.

"Anyway, text your old lady before I do," he teases.

"She isn't my lady. In case I haven't made it clear, I can't stand her presence."

Grabbing his phone, he shrugs. "Guess I'll call her then."

"I'll do it. You're driving, moron." I hit his hand down from his phone. "You're annoying as fuck tonight."

"Yeah, yeah. Sure I am." He smirks.

I don't need to text or call her to see what she wants from a Chinese restaurant. I've known her order since we first met. But I'm not going to admit that, so instead, I pull my phone out and pretend to text her before getting Brody's order and calling it in.

TATE

I type the last word on my essay and hit Save.

"Thank God that's over," I mutter, shutting my laptop and yawning.

I feel the smallest bit of weight lift from my shoulders—for a moment anyway. Until my phone rings and it's my father.

Even though my mom pushes for him to stay connected to Meyer and me, the truth is, being a parent has never really been his strong suit. He provides us with everything money can buy, but emotionally, physically, and mentally, he isn't around. And when he is around, it's worse. He somehow always makes us feel inferior. Or not enough. He wanted a son to carry on his hockey legacy. When he ended up with two daughters, well, he was less than thrilled. That still hasn't changed.

Only now, he's dating a model who's the same age as me. Actually, I'm a month older.

Clearing my throat, I slide my thumb across the screen. "Hey, Dad."

"Just calling because I miss you. The only way I hear from you is if I call first," he says with an arrogant laugh. "I know; I know. You're busy."

I roll my eyes at his audacity. Up until a year ago, I called him weekly. Sometimes, he'd answer, and sometimes, he wouldn't, but he's never ever called to check on me first. Him calling right now could only mean he wants to tell me something important. Or important to *him* anyway.

"I, uh, miss you too," I say awkwardly. "How's everything been going?"

"Good. Real good," he answers quickly. "That's why I called actually. Had to share my terrific news with my oldest kid first."

I instantly feel my heart begin to race, knowing he's going to tell me something that might not be the best news for me to hear.

Still, I force myself to be polite. "Oh, yeah? What's that?"

"You're going to have a little brother, Tate!" he blurts out. "Margo is pregnant. Isn't that damn good news? Had some fancy blood work done to confirm that I'm finally gettin' my boy."

"Uh—"

"I knew you'd be excited. I told Margo that you would want to babysit and spoil him rotten. Isn't that right, Margo?"

I realize I'm on speakerphone when Margo, one of my father's mistresses he cheated on my mother with, starts to chime in too. But then they start a conversation between just the two of them on baby names, and it quickly becomes hard for me to get a word in or keep up. At one point, I even pull the phone away from my ear and hope they'll stop talking.

"We've decided we're going to get married right away," my dad says. "I got Margo a big ol' ring on her finger. Course, she picked it out."

"In Hawaii!" Margo chirps. "You and Meyer can be in the bridal party."

"Wait, what?" I gasp. "Um … I don't—"

"Oh, come on. It would mean a lot to me." She pauses. "And your *father*."

"That's right, sweetie. Don't you want to do this for me? You know, I am your father and all, and I can't celebrate this big day without you and your sister."

Squeezing my eyes shut to stop the tears, I lie back on my bed. "Sure. Yeah. Of course," I barely squeak.

"There's my girl. I knew you'd say yes. Besides, what else have you got to do? Build a rocket?" He laughs. "I knew you wouldn't miss my big day, Tate."

"Right. Yeah." I pause. "Oh no … I need to get going. I'm actually at work, and my boss needs me," I lie. "Congratulations. This is, um … it's great."

And before either of them can respond, I hang up the phone.

I don't know what was harder to hear. My dad's excitement about a baby he hasn't met when he has two kids he doesn't care about. Or the very fact that they expect me to be in the wedding, knowing my mom was deeply hurt by this woman. To me, Margo is just another affair. And in the end, I don't blame her. I blame my dad. She didn't owe my mother anything. Or us. He's the shithead who couldn't keep it in his pants.

The truth is, my dad has never even told me or my sister he is proud. In fact, he has mocked my love for aerospace and astronomy since I was a kid.

On one hand, I pray he will be different with this baby. On the other, I know it will hurt to see it if he is. And all because, what? The kid was born with a penis. I know a lot of people with penises. I've yet to be impressed by the majority of them.

This night sucks.

Pulling my pillow over my face, I cry into it pathetically. Even though I feel like, deep down, I know I'm being a baby. There are people all around the world with far worse problems than this. And usually, I remember that. Normally, I don't get hung up on things that don't really matter.

I grew up in a nice house. I have a mom who loves and adores me and my sister. And a dad who … does his best. Well, maybe not his best. But … he's okay. He isn't a serial killer or running a drug ring at least.

I enjoy my job, and most of all, I'm healthy. So, while I'll be stronger tomorrow … tonight, I'm going to let myself actually feel the pain.

No, for once, I'm going to relish in it. Letting it spread through my entire body. After all, my mom has always said, sometimes, you have to cry out all the bad feelings to make room for more happiness.

The hot water feels good against my body as I stand under the spray for God knows how long. After crying for a solid half an hour, I dragged myself to the shower to wash away whatever funk my father had put me into. I hate being like this. I loathe acting like I'm some sort of victim.

My eyes feel raw and scratchy. And every time I swallow, my throat closes up on me.

It isn't just that my dad is getting married and having a baby boy. Or that I am invisible to everyone besides my mom and sister. Honestly, I don't know what it is.

I just feel lost. And sad.

And if I'm being honest … broken.

When someone pounds on the door, my eyes fly open.

"Tate, what the fuck are you doing in there?" Link yells. "Trying to dry up our well?"

I don't have the energy for him right now. I can't deal with it. So, instead of answering, I just continue to stand in the spray, hoping he'll give up and walk away. Leaving me to my own despair. Aware that it's completely selfish to waste this much hot water, but not caring.

After a few more yells, the door opens with a thud, and Link yanks the curtain across, exposing my bare body.

"I thought you were fucking dead in here!" he roars. "What the fuck, Tate?"

"I just needed a minute."

Taking me in, he steps back and closes the door.

"What the hell is going on?"

"Nothing," I answer quietly, continuing to let the water wash my body, not giving a shit that he can see everything.

Reaching forward, he cranks the water on cold, making me scream.

Leaping out of the shower, I land right against him. "Goddamn you, Link!" I pound my fist against his chest. "Can't you just leave me alone?" I cry, continuing my assault. "I know you hate me," I sob. "But, just for today, can you pl-please just cut me some slack?"

Burying my face into his chest, I breathe him in. He smells so good. He smells like home.

"You can hate me tomorrow. But tonight, please … just take me back to before."

"Before when?" His voice vibrates in my ear.

"Before I was the enemy," I mutter as I continue burying my icy-cold nose against the cloth of his hoodie. Desperate to just fill this empty, homesick feeling that resides in my gut. "Before I had no one."

"Tate—"

"My dad's finally getting his baby boy," I say, trying to sound happy. "Oh, and he's marrying Margo. Margo, who is our age." I sniffle. "My mom's going to go off the deep end. She's already there, but this … this will ruin her. She was finally doing better."

His body is rigid against mine, and I know he doesn't care. I don't know why I'm venting to him. I guess because I have no one else. My sister would have called me if my dad had reached out to her. That means, he hasn't yet. My mom will say it's okay and that I should go to the wedding, but deep down, she'll be gutted inside. She'll stay home alone, drinking wine and falling into yet another deep depression. And if I go, I'll sit there, being a resentful brat, worried about my mother the entire time.

"Tate … I can't help you," Link's deep voice says, softer than usual. "Your problems aren't my problems anymore."

Slowly stepping back, I wipe my eyes and start to turn around. "I understand," I croak out. "It's no big deal. I'm just being a baby." Grabbing a towel, I wrap it around myself. My eyes are filled with so many tears that everything is hazy.

He's quiet for a moment. "I told you to fuck other people because I need something to remind me of how much I hate you, Tate," his voice rasps. "Having you here, having you close … I'm forgetting that hate. It's fading, and I can't let it. Because we both know, once I'm drafted … you aren't sticking around."

His hand touches my waist, and I suck in a breath.

"Remind me, Tate. Fucking remind me why I hate you." He crowds me against the wall. "I'm begging you. Make me hate you so much that I don't care. That it doesn't faze me to see you cry." He swallows. "Because right now, seeing you cry, all I want to do is fucking fix it. But that isn't my responsibility. Not anymore."

Dropping my towel, I step closer to him. "Neither one of us is capable of hating the other," I whisper. "Even if it would be easier if we did."

I stand before him, unsure of what the hell I'm doing. Every line. Every reason. Every boundary is blurred, and I don't know what's right or wrong.

"I've missed you every single day since I left." Sliding my hand under his sweatshirt, I press my palm on his abdomen. "I swear to you, leaving was the hardest thing I've ever had to do. That's why I came back."

"I don't want to hear this. It doesn't matter now."

"No, I guess it doesn't," I say softly. "You can hate me—or pretend to—Link. And I can keep saying how much I can't be with you till I'm blue in the face. But we might as well feel good while we're at it."

Moving my hand to his sweatpants, I swipe my hand over his hardness. "If you hate me so much, why are you so hard right now?"

I don't know what I'm doing. All I know is, I can't stop.

When he doesn't answer, I press my hand against him harder. "Tell me, why?"

He glares down at me. "Because I want to show you how mad I am at you, Tate. I want to fuck you so hard that you're ruined for anyone else." His filthy words only leave me wanting more as he grabs a fistful of my hair, tilting my face to gaze up at him. "That's why I'm hard. Not because I love you, but because I want to fill you so full of my cock that no man will ever want you again."

"Then, do it," I say as the tears spring into my eyes again. "I'm ruined anyway."

I lurch forward, my lips attacking his as I grind my body against him like a crazed animal.

Lifting me up by my ass, he pushes me against the sink. His hardness pressing to my belly, starting an ache between my legs that turns to a throbbing need.

He kisses me—hard—fisting my hair.

"Please, Link," I moan against his lips. "I need you right now."

When I go to kiss him again, his hands leave my body.

"Right now," he mutters, shaking his head. "Yeah. You need me right now, but that's it."

Blinking a few times, he shakes his head and steps back, heading toward the door.

"Brody brought you dinner. It's in the kitchen. You need to eat."

And then, with a turn of the knob, he leaves me.

Naked and confused. And still wanting him.

Eventually, I gather myself up and put my pajamas on before heading downstairs. And just as Link said, food sits on the counter, still in its to-go box.

As I get a plate out and open the small paper boxes, revealing Chinese food … I sigh. Brody didn't order this for me. Link did. Brody would have had no idea what I would order. This is everything I've loved since I was a little kid.

Orange chicken, a spring roll, and pork fried rice. Even extra duck sauce, which has always been a necessity for me.

"Oh good, you didn't drown in the shower." A shirtless Brody appears from around the corner. "You found your food, Tater Tot."

"The food *you* ordered for me, you mean?" I raise an eyebrow. "Thanks, by the way."

"Right, right … yeah." He laughs. "Even when he's nice, that grouchy bastard doesn't want the credit for it." He shakes his head. "He cares, Tate. He cares so fucking much."

I breathe out a sad laugh. "He's got a strange way of showing it." I sigh. "He shouldn't care. I did him wrong. And the thing is, Brody? He's never done anything wrong. I'm just …"

"Damaged?" he mutters. "Broken?"

I scowl before elbowing him in the side. "Hey, I wasn't going to say that! Jerk! I was going to say, confused. Scared. A coward."

He pulls me against him before heading to the fridge and grabbing a water. "Damaged people know damaged people." He winks, heading toward the stairs. "Night, Tater Tot."

I look at him, puzzled. Wondering what has happened in Brody's life to make him consider himself damaged. While also feeling shook that he figured me out so quickly.

"Night, O'Brien."

I glance down at my plate of food, and my stomach turns. Because even though I know I need to eat … I don't think I can.

6

LINK

The energy in the locker room is on ten as Coach finishes his pep talk, handing it over to Cam, who stands up, looking around at each of us.

"This is our house, fellas. This is our school. Those voices we can hear in that arena," he says, pointing to the door, "they are those of our fans. It's our arena. Our ice. This team is tough—we know this. They aren't going to go down without a fight, but they're going down nonetheless. Because we're ready for this. For some of us, this could be our last season. I don't know about y'all, but I want to start the season by proving that we aren't a team to be fucked with." He continues to look around, making eye contact with each and every one of us. "So, what do you say? Who's ready?"

The room erupts into cheers as we all jump up, forming a huddle.

"One, two, three … *Wolves*!" we all scream.

The game might not have started yet, but our heads are in it. We have a hunger to win. Because each win will bring us closer to the goal. Closer to the Frozen Four. This is our season—I can feel it. I meant what I said when I told Tate hockey was all that mattered. It's all that matters because it's all I have. My mother is gone. My dad checked out when she took her last breath. And the only girl I've ever loved, besides my mother, doesn't want me. This really is it. And I'm not failing at it.

Though Tate has drifted into my mind a few times, I push it away.

We've lived together for a month now. And last night, I saw her break down. I wanted to be there for her, but I knew I couldn't be. And even though she wanted me to fuck her, that wasn't what she really wanted even if she was confused for a moment, thinking it was. She was hurting.

Her dad always said God gave him girls for all the bad shit he did wrong. All he ever wanted was a boy. A boy that—I have no doubt—he'll push so hard to play hockey, pressuring him to live up to his own name. I don't envy that boy. And while I can understand why Tate's feelings are hurt, she shouldn't envy her baby brother either.

Just as I'm starting to wonder if she is coming to the game, I feel her eyes on me. Burning into my helmet like a laser. I don't look around to see where she's sitting, but I know she's not far. Maybe she didn't come to watch me particularly, but she still came here, knowing I was going to be on the ice. And to me, that means I'm still somehow inside her head too.

I hope I'm in her head, haunting her every single day. The thought alone brings me peace.

TATE

"Thanks for asking me to come to the game." I smile at Sloane. "I probably would have just sat at home and eaten ice cream, watching Netflix."

Ally, Sloane's friend, pokes her head in front of Sloane and looks at me. "Girl, that sounds *much* better than this shit." She looks at Sloane. "Tell me you don't agree?"

Sloane elbows her and rolls her eyes. "Oh, hush. The boys are gone at their away game. This will be good for us to take in another sport besides football."

"Wait … there's another sport besides football?" Ally widens her eyes. "Who knew?"

"You're so dang bitchy sometimes," Sloane says to her just as Ally holds her phone up for us to see.

"Henley had the right idea—staying home, ordering a huge-ass pizza by herself, and watching *One Tree Hill* reruns." She sighs. "It's cold in here."

Ally, Sloane, and Henley all date football players.

I went into the library this morning to use the printer, and Sloane was working. She invited me to the hockey game, and even though I wasn't originally planning to come, it sounded sort of nice.

I hadn't met Henley until tonight, but she likes large pizzas to herself and *One Tree Hill*, so I'm pretty sure we might be soul mates.

"So, are you living in the dorms? Or do you have an apartment?" Ally asks, shifting her eyes from me to the ice.

"An apartment. Well, I rent a room at an apartment."

"She lives with hockey players," Sloane gushes. "Link Sterns and Brody O'Brien. Since, you know, Cam Hardy is practically married now, he moved out, and—bam!—Tate got his old room. Homegirl moves fast, apparently."

"Sounds kinky," Ally says, unfazed, nodding her head. "I mean, I love my man, but, damn, those puck boys are easy on the eyes."

"Ally!" Sloane giggles. "Cole would probably cry and then beat them up if he heard you."

"Sure would," Ally agrees. "Anyway, how's that going? Are they nice? Are they gross? Like, does it smell like garbage and stale underwear in there from their parties?"

"Not at all actually. Both are weirdly neat." I knew Link was, but Brody surprised me. "They have been too busy with hockey to party much, luckily."

Suddenly, Sloane turns. "Wait. I totally forgot that Link went to high school with you, right?" Her eyes widen. "Are you long-lost lovers? The few times I did see you when our schools were playing each other, you were with him. It's all clicking now. I get it."

"It's complicated," I huff. "Really, really complicated."

"So, you aren't friends?" Sloane asks, looking at me suspiciously.

"We were best friends. And … maybe more for one night. But I ran. I ran because I had to." I watch as number twenty-two, Link, skates across the ice with ease. Even in hockey gear, he moves in a way that melts me. "And fate, being as messed up as it is, landed us in the same damn apartment. Woo-hoo."

Ally's mouth hangs open. "Girl, we have *so* much in common. I take back everything bad I said about you."

Sloane nudges her, but I can tell she's joking. I don't know Ally well, but it's obvious she's tough. Sort of a little intimidating, but I like her.

"Do you have any advice for me?" I ask Ally softly. "To make it better."

She's quiet for a moment, and I wonder what she's going to say.

"Blow jobs. They fix everything in the small brain of a man," she answers seriously before shaking her head. "I'm playing, though a good blowie doesn't hurt. But in all honesty … to get over the past, you sort of have to face it first." She pats my hand. "If Cole and I can get over me ghosting him, so can the two of you. All you can do is try."

"Yeah," I whisper.

Jerking her thumb toward Sloane, she cringes. "And this chick? Well, her man used her to get info on her dad's highly illegal secret business. Now, they are the epitome of a fairy tale. So, I feel like if they weren't doomed, none of us are."

"Ally!" Sloane elbows her. "Rude!"

I stare at Sloane, completely shocked that that's how her and Knox Carter's relationship started.

If she could forgive him, maybe Ally's right. Maybe I'm not doomed after all.

LINK

"That's right, baby! That's right!" Brody yells, hitting my helmet before gripping Cam's shield. "One down, a shit ton to go!"

Even through his helmet, I can see Cam grin. But I know that just because he's excited we won, he still can't let himself relax. He and I are the same that way. Intense when it comes to the game, and even though he has Addy and Isla, we both live for the game.

The whole team does. But we all just have different ways of handling the pressure. Cam has the constant need to do better. He never believes he's done enough, and he's always trying to improve his game. Brody plays it off that everything's fine, pretending it's all fistfights and good times, but I've seen him freak out before, and it's scary.

We all carry the weight differently, but it's still there.

As much as the boys want to party, we have to face this team again tomorrow. Same place, same time, proving again that we are the better team and didn't get lucky tonight. So, we all know better than to celebrate this win too hard, if at all tonight.

"Dude, nice bottle rocket on that last goal." Cam laughs, referring to the goalie's water bottle breaking the last time I scored. He nudges me. "I love when that shit happens."

"Nice fancy footwork, Cap." I squirt some of my Gatorade in my mouth. My head is soaked with sweat, and I can't wait to shower. "Showing off for your girls up there?" I nod to Addison and Isla in the stands, both waving like crazy at Cam.

"Fucking right I was." He grins, blowing them a kiss. "Go get rested, so we can do this shit all over again tomorrow."

When he turns back toward me, my eyes are on Tate. And before I can look anywhere else, he spots her too.

Lifting his helmet up, he narrows his eyes. "Is that her? Your new roommate, who you have some deep, dark history with?"

I exhale, annoyed. "That'd be her."

He glances from her to me and back to her. "Dude ... I've seen her before. At our old dorm."

"What?" I glare. "No, you haven't. She lived in Boston before this."

His eyebrows lift, and his lips pull to the side. "I hate to break it to you, my man. But she showed up at the dorm freshman year. She knocked on the door, and when I answered, she asked for you." He cringes. "I was hammered—I know that. I don't remember much, but I remember telling her something along the lines of ... you were probably balls deep in your date, but I'd see what I could do."

I suddenly feel sick, my knees growing weak. "Are you fucking kidding me, Hardy? How far into freshman year?"

He thinks about it for a moment. "Probably a few weeks in."

Tate said when she found out my mother was sick, she came back. I wasn't sure if I should believe her, but the math is there. My mom told us right after I graduated that she was sick again, but she was hoping to get into a clinical trial, so she opted to not make it public knowledge until she had to. Which was right after I left for Brooks. That means Meg heard and told Tate, and Tate came back. She came back to be there for me and instead was met by my best friend, who informed her I was fucking someone else.

"Jesus Christ, Cam," I mutter, looking up at Tate for a split second before turning away.

He holds his arms out. "How the fuck was I supposed to know this was the chick who had turned you into the grumpy fuck you are?" His eyes light up, and he punches my shoulder. "But now that you know the truth, you can forgive her."

And as he skates off, I turn my head to look around, and my eyes land on hers. And for a second, it's like I'm transported back to high school. When she cheered my name, proudly wedged between her mother and my parents. Even if we were supposedly only friends ... she was always there.

And I miss that so fucking much.

This might change some things. But it doesn't change that she left in the first place or that she wasn't there for the funeral. She's no good for me, and I need to keep reminding myself of that.

TATE

I sit there, entranced by Link's stare as his teammate skates away from him. The second Cam Hardy looked up at me, I knew he recognized who I was.

I think back to that night and how he answered the door. Shirtless and smelling like booze with a grin that could light up any room. Even though he was delivering me the worst news, Cam Hardy was a hard person to hate.

In a way, I'm embarrassed that Link probably knows now that I was on his doorstep while he was shoving his penis into some random chick. Despite feeling nauseous, I waited on those steps for twenty-five minutes in case Cam actually went and got Link for me. But it was clear he was intoxicated, and I knew him actually going to find Link would be unlikely.

His eyes stay on mine, and for the first time in God knows how long, he isn't glaring. His eyes are far from warm and accepting, but it's an improvement from how he's looked at me since I arrived at Brooks.

In a perfect world, if Cam confirmed that I had indeed come back, maybe Link would be more apt to forgive me. But if I'm being honest, would it even matter if he did? And what the hell am I hoping from Link? Even I don't have a clue.

Slowly, he blinks and turns his head, breaking the moment before skating away.

And yet I watch that jersey with *Sterns* on the back and the number twenty-two until he leaves the arena.

TATE

After finishing the show, Holly and I lock up the Astronomy Center and head to our cars. Oliver had to leave early today, but I didn't mind feeling like I was in charge of getting everything done.

"See you this weekend!" Holly says before getting in her car. "Hey, there's a party at Oliver's place Saturday night. You should totally come."

"I'll think about it." I smile, heading to my own car and climbing in.

This past weekend, the hockey team won both their games. They were as close to flawless on the ice as a team could get. Even Brody—rough, wild Brody. It was like watching art or something. And Link? If I thought he could play in high school, I think he's a damn star on the ice now.

All of his dreams are going to come true. And I'm happy for him. He was never destined to blend in. He was meant to have his name known. He was meant to have crowds cheering him on and people wearing his jersey around the world.

As I drive toward the house, I'm about three minutes away when my Jeep sounds louder than normal. And when I go a little farther, I know my tire is flat.

Pulling onto the side of the road, I throw my head back. "Dammit. I'm tired. And I'm hungry."

Today was one of the busiest I've had since being at Brooks. And it left very little time for food and water. Which is really dumb of me, considering I'll probably pass out now. Alone and on the damn side of the road.

I'm not a complete moron when it comes to cars, but I can't change my own tire.

I decide to bite the bullet and call Brody or Link—whoever will answer first. That is, until I remember I left my phone on my nightstand this morning, like an asshole. It's not like I ever need it much. Well, until times like this.

It's dark outside, but Brooks is a safe campus. I'll be fine. In Boston, I didn't even have my car. Walking was how I got everywhere. This should be a cakewalk.

Grabbing my tote bag, I take the keys from my Jeep and start toward home. When I get there, I'll call to have the tire changed.

I'm not one who's all that scared of the dark. Yet, when I look around the quiet side road I'm on, I'm creeped out as hell. And when I hear a car coming from behind me, I realize how stupid I am for not remembering my phone. This could be a serial killer, and I could end up in someone's basement.

The vehicle gets closer and closer until it slows.

"Tater Tot, what in the hell are you doing?" Brody calls out. "We saw your Jeep back there and thought you'd been kidnapped."

"Get in the fucking truck, Tate." Link's voice comes next, not nearly as playful as Brody's. "Now."

Turning toward them, I hold my arms out at my sides. "I'll get in the truck, but only because I don't want to walk. Not because you're telling me to, asshole."

I glare at Link before walking toward the truck. Link opens the door, letting me in. Grabbing the handle, I pull myself in and slide into the middle seat.

"Why the hell didn't you call?" Link snaps. "Why would you walk at nine o'clock at night in the dark?"

"Sterns, I think she—" Brody starts to say, but Link cuts him off.

"Answer the question, Tate."

"I forgot my phone at home this morning." I blow out a breath. "I couldn't call."

Turning the truck around, we head back toward where my Jeep is parked.

"Can I use your phone?" I glance between them. "Either of you. I'll call a tow truck."

"We don't need a tow truck. I'll change it," Link mutters quickly.

Once we get to my Jeep, he jumps out without saying another word, and Brody gives me a sympathetic smile before patting my arm.

"Sit tight, Tater Tot. We'll get her up and running before you can say *Link is an asshole*."

"Link is an asshole," I deadpan just as Brody pushes his door open.

LINK

I don't want to worry about her, but I do. I worry all the damn time. And then on nights like tonight, I remember why. She doesn't realize that even in the safest places, danger lurks. And that walking at night alone, on a college campus, isn't safe. She doesn't get it. I won't always be around to save her.

I want to be, but she'd never let it happen.

It was so much easier to hate her when she lived halfway across the country.

We finish changing the tire, and I see her climbing out of Brody's truck, heading for the Jeep. An older Jeep. She could have any vehicle she wants. Her daddy is that rich. And even though he isn't present much in her life, he throws money around like it's nothing. She could have bought a nice car. Instead, in high school, she got a job and bought herself this. It's not flashy or overkill. Which suits her. Because I think her entire life, she's wanted to stay hidden. Being my best friend didn't help that either. But somehow, our dynamic always worked.

I open the door to the driver's side and nod toward her. "I'll drive. Just to make sure it's fine." Looking at Brody, I ignore his grin. "See you at home."

Once we're in the Jeep and Brody pulls out, I stare straight ahead. "Someone could have hurt you. You could have been hit by a drunk driver. What were you thinking, walking alone?"

She doesn't say much. She just sits quietly in her seat, looking out the window. "Can you just take me home, please?" Her voice sounds weak. "I'm really, really hungry. I don't feel that well."

"Jesus Christ," I mutter before quickly peeling off the dirt and onto the pavement. "When was the last time you ate?"

"Around nine this morning." I hear the cringe in her voice. "It's been a day."

"That's twelve hours, Tate. And then you were going to walk home?" I can't help the anger in my voice. "That's about the dumbest thing I've ever heard. Did you forget that you, gee, I don't know … have a fucking condition that makes you faint?"

71

"I know; I know. Don't call me dumb," she hisses. "I can call you worse."

"Don't do dumb shit then," I throw back. "And call me whatever the hell you want. I don't care."

"What do you want me to say? I had class. And work." She rests her head against the window. "I got busy, and time just got away from me."

"Too busy to eat a pack of crackers or a granola bar? Something? Anything?" I swing my head toward her.

She doesn't answer. And a few minutes later, we pull into the apartment, but Brody isn't here. Quickly pushing the door open, she steps out, slowly walking toward the apartment.

I fight the urge to scoop her up and carry her inside because I know that would be stupid. I should just get in my own truck and go for a ride, but I want to make sure she eats something. I want to make sure she's okay. I don't want to, but I need to.

I follow her into the kitchen, and she fumbles, trying to find something to eat—fast. She's as pale as a ghost, and I know she doesn't feel good.

"Go sit down on the couch," I tell her before washing my hands. When she gives me a questioning look, I scowl. "You look like Casper the Friendly Ghost. Except you don't seem as friendly." I point to the couch. "Go."

Sluggishly, she makes her way to the couch and sits down. I feel her eyes on me as I get everything out to make her a grilled cheese. I can't do shit in the kitchen. But a grilled cheese? I don't ever fuck those up. One might even call me a master, but I'm not bragging or anything.

After a few minutes, I take the plate to her, passing her a Diet Coke with it.

She tries not to smile but fails. And that look—that one tiny look where I see her as nothing other than an angel—has my breath hitching. I'd do anything to not react the way that I do. But she's Tate Tracy. She'll always be mine, even when she isn't.

"Thank you," she says as she takes both from me, setting the drink on the coffee table. "And for changing my tire."

Slowly, I back up. And after washing the pan and cleaning up my mess, I head toward the stairs. The elephant in the room is what Cam told me, confirming that she really did come back to me. But it's not the right time to address that. I'm not sure when is.

"How'd you get it to be this good?" she asks me, taking another bite. "I don't want to make your head any bigger, but this is the best grilled cheese I've ever eaten."

I look at her for a moment. The truth is, my mom always says the key to grilled cheese is buttering both sides of the bread and then sprinkling it with garlic powder. But I'm not going to tell her that. So, instead, I turn away. "I'm headed to bed. Night."

Her answer is delayed and laced with disappointment. "Night."

Stopping midway, I glance over my shoulder. "Don't go all day without eating. You know it messes with your blood pressure."

Nodding once, she smiles sadly. "I know. I won't."

TATE

As tired as I am, sleep should come easy tonight. Keyword: *should*. But it doesn't. Glimpses of the old Link—that's what's keeping me awake. He's in there. And he's showing himself to me again. He has every right to be guarded, but dammit if knowing he's still in there doesn't make me consider throwing all caution to the wind and just saying to hell with being afraid. If he'd have me, that is. I'm not so sure he would.

My phone vibrates on my nightstand, and when I see Meyer's name, I smile.

> *Meyer: Are you awake?*
>
> *Me: I am now.*
>
> *Me: No, I'm kidding. I already was. Long night.*

Seconds later, she calls me.

"Oh, heyyyy." I grin into the phone.

"Dude … do we really have to go to Hawaii?" She groans. "Like, no. Just no. Also, when were you planning on telling me this? Dad said he already told you this shit *days* ago."

I sigh. "So, he told you. And for the record, I wanted to, but I figured I'd let you continue living in your Dad-free bubble for as long as humanly possible."

"Yep, well, he popped that shit. And then in true, narcissistic Dad form, he basically guilted me into being in the bridal party."

"Same," I say, frowning. "I'd rather put, like, twenty crabs in my pants and let them bite my vagina to the point of no return than smile while they exchange meaningless vows."

"I'll do you one better. I'd rather pass, like, ten kidney stones. I've heard they hurt like a bitch." Meyer laughs. "Still, I'd take that over standing on a beach, watching the two phoniest, most self-centered human beings exchange vows."

"Jeez, tell me how you really feel." I chuckle. "Really, don't hold back."

"Sorry. He just knows how to kill my whole vibe." Her voice turns to a whisper. "And by the way, the vibe was good—really good. I was just about to get laid!"

"Do tell." I sit up in my bed. "I'm getting no action, so tell me about yours."

"There's nothing to tell," she whines. "Dad's phone call killed the engine, if you know what I mean. Anyway, this is going to suck."

"At least we can go together." I lie back, looking at the old popcorn ceiling. "We can get really drunk."

"Duh." She yawns. "Hey, did Mom tell you about the benefit dinner for Mrs. Fenton? I feel so bad that she had a stroke. Poor Mr. Fenton must be lost while she's in the hospital."

I nod silently in my empty room. I got a message from my mom a few days prior, explaining what had happened to Caroline Fenton. Our neighborhood's sweetest lady.

"I did," I mutter. "I'm going to go home for it."

"I feel bad that I'm not." She exhales. "Actually, I feel like a complete dick for not coming home for it."

"You live halfway across the country. I live a few hours away. Big difference," I assure her. "I'll give everyone your best."

"And to make the situation worse … guess who's showing up at it. *With* their new young woman. Just to flaunt that he's making a big, fat donation in front of Mom," Meyer grouches.

"Are you serious?" I growl. "Dad doesn't even know Mr. and Mrs. Fenton. God, he's such a douchebag."

"Everything he does is selfish," she says quietly. "The only reason why he's going to go to Georgia and roll into that benefit dinner is, one, to be all like, *Hey, Meg, look at my hot fiancée. She's as dumb as a pounded nail, but her tits are huge, and she's my daughter's age.* And, two, because he loves flaunting around that he has money. So, obviously, a donation—a tax deductible donation—is right up his alley."

"Ugh. He's annoying. Also, her tits are huge because they are fake. Mine would be ginormous, too, if I dumped as much money into my boobies as she has." I groan. "I creeped her Instagram. She really *is* my age and already getting so much Botox. By the time she's thirty, she'll be like the guy in the movie *Just Go with It*, who spits out water when he tries to take a drink."

"She's just so mean and condescending. She basically calls me an airhead every time I talk to her. Is it mean if I hope she gets hemorrhoids during pregnancy and shits all over the table?"

"Yes, that's terrible," I deadpan. "And … same."

"We're going straight to hell." She laughs. "How's your roommate situation going? Have you accidentally woken up in Link's bed yet?"

"What? No! Of course not. We have a pact. No athletes."

"Yeah, but … you two have always loved each other. I wouldn't blame you for breaking the pact." She pauses. "And besides, if you aren't busy in Link's bed, how come you haven't made me that hat you promised me you would?"

"I actually just picked out yarn yesterday." I smile. "So, I'll be working on it this week."

"Did you get a pom for the top?"

"Does a bear shit in the woods?" I deadpan. "Obviously, I got the cutest, biggest pom I could find."

"My badass sister, just knitting hats and taking names." She laughs before another yawn rips through the phone, making me yawn too. "Okay, I'm going to bed. Love you," she mumbles.

"Love you." I smile before ending the call.

Talking to my sister always puts my mind at ease. Maybe some siblings annoy each other, but she's my best friend. And I can't wait to make her the cutest beanie hat. It's going to be her favorite color—light pink. I got some baby-blue yarn for my own hat, but I know I probably won't get a chance to wear it unless I go and visit Meyer in Maine. Knitting might not be the coolest thing for a college kid to do, but I learned from Mrs. Fenton last year when I was home for Christmas break, and I really enjoy it. Truthfully, it's sort of therapeutic. And who knows? Maybe I'll go to another hockey game with Sloane, and I'll need a hat. It's cold as hell in those arenas.

Even if Link probably didn't want me at the games last weekend, I loved watching him again. And besides, I can always cheer on Brody.

I continue to lie in bed, awake, debating on if I should start working on Meyer's hat tonight since I'm already up. But even though I'm restless, I'm too exhausted. And eventually, I drift off.

The sun peeks through the window as my alarm rings on my nightstand. Turning it off, I stretch my arms over my head. I wish I could stay in bed just a bit longer. But that's not an option. I might not have to work today, but I have a full day of classes.

So, forcing myself to sit up, I slide out of bed and saunter to the bathroom.

Brushing my teeth and scrubbing my face quickly, I go back to my room and throw on some clothes. I plan to take a kickboxing class tonight, so I'll shower after that.

Slipping my shoes on, I head down the stairs.

"Hey, Tater Tot. Before you go, I got these for you. You know, to throw in your bag." Brody approaches me, passing me a huge Ziplock bag, filled with granola bars, crackers, a water, and a bag of chips.

Link, I think instantly but toss it into my tote bag and raise an eyebrow at Brody.

"You must be a mind reader, knowing all my favorite brands and flavors."

"Oh, yeah, basically a psychic really. Probably should start reading palms and shit," he says, playing dumb, knowing that it was Link who got this stuff for me and made him say he did.

"Mmhmm," I say playfully. "I guess so."

Even when Link wants to pretend he doesn't care, he can't help himself. And he doesn't even want the credit. For him, it's easier to make me think he hates me.

The thing I'm starting to realize is, Link Sterns isn't like my dad. But is that really enough to break my rule on athletes?

I just don't know the answer to that yet.

LINK

The past week has flown by. Between classes, practice, and training, I'm on autopilot. Just going through the motions. And whenever I'm around the apartment, I have the urge to do nice shit for Tate. It's like I can't stop myself. And since I don't want to do that, I've been trying to stay busy and away from home as much as possible.

Last week, I got up early and ran to the store and bought a shit ton of her favorite snacks to make sure she always had something in her bag. Of course, I had to make Brody play it off like it was him; otherwise, she'd get the wrong idea.

"Where are you headed to?" Brody says from the table, eating cereal, even though it's after noon now. Brody basically eats around the clock though. It's probably the reason why we can't keep this place stocked with groceries.

"I told you the other day. I have to go home for a benefit thing." I guzzle water and wipe my mouth. "An older lady who lived on the same street I grew up on had a stroke. Due to her age and other health issues, she had to be transported to a fancy hospital in Atlanta, and that shit isn't cheap."

"Is it a dinner or something?" He frowns.

"I guess." I nod. "It's only two hours away, but I'm going to head out soon. You know what that means? You'll have the place to yourself since I'm sure Tate will be going to this benefit thing too. She was close with Mrs. Fenton. So, you won't have to sneak around tonight, you dirty dawg."

"Why don't you be an honorable man and ask Tate to ride with you?" he suggests. "That'd be nice."

"No," I say quickly. "Tate will plan to stay the weekend, I'm sure. I'll stay the night, but I'm getting the hell out of there at the ass crack of dawn tomorrow. So, you'd best have your dick tucked in bright and early before I get back."

"Fine, you grumpy fuck. And for the thousandth time, I'm not sneaking because I'm hiding anything." Getting up, he walks to the sink and rinses his bowl. "You have a good night, my man. Be nice to my Tater Tot."

"She's not *your* anything," I mutter. "Remember that."

"Yeah, okay. If you say so." He smirks and walks upstairs.

Heading to my truck, I start my trip toward home.

TATE

I sit at Delilah's, my favorite café in Appleton, across from my mother.

I woke up first thing this morning and drove to her house. The benefit dinner isn't until tonight, but I wanted to see my mom and go to all my favorite places at home. Starting with this place. She's seemed so good the past few times that I've talked to her. And seeing her smile again means the world to me. And thanks to social media and the fact that my mom can't help but snoop, she already knew my father's news about the baby and the wedding, so I didn't have to rip off *that* Band-Aid.

I look around the café, loving that it hasn't changed at all.

Link and I would spend so much time here after school. Getting milkshakes. I'd get cheese fries, and he'd get mozzarella sticks, and we'd share. It was located conveniently a mile from the school, so we could walk or take the bus. Even in high school, we'd make time to come here. Sometimes, Meyer or his brothers would join. It was sort of our spot.

My eyes stare at the corner booth we always sat in. I couldn't bear to sit there today, to risk seeing the small carved letters—*L* + *T*—there. We did it when we were thirteen. It seemed so funny and innocent. Now, I cringe that we did that to the owner's property. Though she never seemed to care much.

Even being here makes me slightly sad as I think back to a much easier time. Still, I wanted to come. I had to.

"I hope there's a big turnout tonight. She deserves it, you know." I pick at my fries. "They both do, Mr. and Mrs. Fenton." I drag in a breath nervously. "You know Dad is coming tonight, right? Or that's what Meyer said."

Her mouth forms a flat line. "Yeah. I heard he was."

"Yeah, and it's probably just because he'll have someone there to document him dropping a huge-ass donation." I roll my eyes. "That's the only way he'd do jack shit for Caroline and Clyde—is if it benefits him in some way." My nostrils drag in an annoyed breath. "I bet he won't even show up. He'll probably be busy recording a podcast or filming another awesome hair color commercial."

I wait for her to scold me. To say something along the lines of, *Tate, that's your father. He loves you.* But she doesn't. Instead, she laughs.

"Yeah, or he could be too busy showing people his old hockey stats, pretending he's still relevant and not getting old and saggy."

I stare at her for a moment before I start laughing. "That is so not what I thought you were going to say."

Shrugging, she holds her coffee cup and brings it closer to her lips. "He sucks. I know he's always been a slacker when it comes to his duties as a dad. And I'm aware he has never been you girls' biggest cheerleader. But the past six months or so? It's completely inexcusable." Her eyes grow sad. "I know you see me as weak for putting up with everything I did. I'm supposed to be your role model … and I failed." Her shoulders slump. "I can't take it back, but I am really sorry for that. If I could go back, I'd do things differently. I'd prove that I'm stronger than that."

"I don't view you as weak, Mom," I assure her. "But I have to ask you … why did you put up with it all? Why did you turn a blind eye?"

"For you and Meyer. I thought, if I just stuck it out, if I just ignored it, I could spare you both the embarrassment of everything being blown up in the press." She sighs. "I guess it was all for nothing because, eventually, it *all* came out at once."

"I think it's better it was all at once," I say softly. "Better to be that way than little by little but constantly." I reach across and pat her hand. I'm not one who is usually affectionate, but I know she needs it right now. "You did your best. And your best was great."

Her eyes look lost. "If I could do anything differently, I'd go back and protect you more from the media." She sets her cup down and wipes her eyes. "I know how rough that was on you, growing up in the public eye, and I'm sorry." She smiles sadly. "But despite my mess-ups, I need you to know I'm so proud of you. You moved to Boston, thrived in school, came home to Georgia despite me telling you not to," she jokes. "And I know you're still thriving here." She squeezes my hand. "My daughter is going to be a freaking engineer."

I don't correct her on the fact that I might have been thriving academically in Boston, but that was it. I wasn't flourishing emotionally, mentally, and certainly not socially.

"An aerospace engineer," I say, correcting her playfully. "I'm over halfway there. Thank God. Though I'll admit, I love working in the Astronomy Center too. But I'm ready to get into the engineering part of it all."

"One day, I'll be able to say you worked on a rocket that's headed for outer space."

I laugh. "I hope so. But I have a long way to go before that."

Since I was a kid, I was interested in putting things into space. I'd come up with crazy ideas, oftentimes rattling them off to Link. He never laughed or called me crazy. Neither did my mother. Even though, in hindsight, my ideas *were* crazy. But now, I'm getting closer and closer to this dream coming true. Sure, I'll need another year or so after earning my bachelor's to complete the requirements to earn my master's degree, but I'll get there.

My dad didn't feel the same way. He'd scoff at my ideas. And laugh when I told him my plans for college. He told me it was time to get off whatever cloud I was on. But I refused to do that. One thing that has never let me down is the sheer, bewildering galaxy. I'm going to follow this dream through—even if it kills me.

Just another reason why Link and I wouldn't work. He'll be heading for the pros soon. Whatever lucky lady ends up with him will need to basically follow his dreams and give up her own. Riding his coattails, cheering him on. I have my own dreams. Except mine allow me to stay in the shadows, where I like to be.

"So, where to next?" my mother asks, interrupting my thoughts—fortunately. "We still have hours until the dinner."

"Pedicures?" I suggest, smiling. I know how much my mom loves having her feet massaged.

"Um, yes, please." She claps. "I haven't had one since Meyer and I went a few months ago! My feet are scary."

"Do you think Krystal would have time to do my hair today?" I say, thinking about how much I need a change. "I'm thinking it's time for a new me."

"We can stop in and check." She smiles. "But I like you the way you are."

I take a sip of my soda and tilt my head to the side. "Sometimes, change is good. It's nice to be home, Mom."

"Happy to have you. Are you staying the whole weekend?" Her eyes look hopeful. "Please say yes."

I frown. "Sorry, I have to work at the Astronomy Center tomorrow night for a show. But I'll be here till lunchtime tomorrow." I smile. "So, we can come back here for breakfast."

She pretends to give me a dirty look, sticking her tongue out. "Fine. If that's all I get, I'll take it. You ready to go? These feet aren't going to rub themselves."

Sliding out of the booth, I nod. "Lead the way."

I'm still debating whether or not I want to go to the party at Oliver's after work tomorrow night. On one hand, it sounds sort of fun. On another … it sounds like work. And I'm lame enough to admit, I typically like staying in, alone, watching Netflix. Besides, I could always get some knitting done

And then I wonder, *How lame am I these days?*

Lame enough to choose sitting in my room, knitting, risking listening to the man I'm in love with having sex with some random girl, just to avoid being social at a party—that's how lame.

LINK

My brothers and I walk behind our dad toward the high school gymnasium, where the benefit dinner is being held. Appleton is a small, tight-knit community, and the entire town pulled together to make this happen for Mrs. Fenton.

She and Clyde have been married for over sixty years. They never had any kids, but if I had to guess, it wasn't for a lack of trying. They love kids, so I have a hard time believing they didn't want a family of their own. Still, they've made do by basically adopting the entire neighborhood's kids. At Halloween, their house is the most decorated on the block. It also has the most candy. My brothers and I grew up mowing their lawn and trimming everything around the property. In return, Mrs. Fenton, or Caroline, would make us the best doughnuts I've ever had. Among lots of other desserts.

Now, Caroline is sick, and truthfully, it doesn't sound promising that she'll get better. And if she doesn't, I really don't know how Clyde, her husband, will survive.

"Clyde is so depressed. I wish there were something we could do," Travis says, frowning. "Just isn't fair. She's, like, the sweetest person in the world."

"Yeah, but she's old," Logan says, completely unfazed. "And that happens when you're old."

I land a punch right on his arm, and he throws his hands up.

"What the fuck was that? You asshole. We're all thinkin' it. Y'all just don't want to say it."

"Logan …" Dad warns. "Can you just try to be normal for one day?"

"I'm not saying it ain't sad. I'm saying she's old. And when people are old, their bodies start fucking up on them. It's sad. But it's life."

"Are you sure no one dropped you on your head when you were born?" I say, dragging my hand down my face.

"For real. Your brain isn't right," Carter says, shaking his head as he pulls the door open. "You're young, and your brain is already fucked up. So, what's that say about you?"

This shit is constant and always has been, growing up with three brothers. It doesn't help that my mom's gone, so nobody is around to smarten us up. Well, to smarten Logan up. The rest of us aren't *that* idiotic.

We make our walk in, and instantly, I'm taken back to my high school days. Nothing here has changed. Even in the years I've been gone. The place is filled to the rafters. Dinner is set up in a self-serve type of deal with tables scattered everywhere.

I don't feel her here. Which means she's not in the gym. Not yet anyway. But I know she will be. And the second she is, I'll know it.

"Well, fuck me sideways. Tell me that isn't Brooks University's infamous Link Sterns I see."

I hear a familiar voice and turn to find Jessob Gilson grinning at me.

Smirking, I tip my chin up. "JB, the baller from Tennessee." I bump my fist against his. "How's it going, ol' boy?"

JB and I were in school together since kindergarten. But where football became his life, hockey became mine. And once sports overtook our lives, it was harder to hang out. And since I went to Brooks and he went to Tennessee, we haven't seen each other at all. But he's a good guy. And from what I've heard, he's killing it on the field.

"It's going. Had to come home for this though." He looks around. "What a turnout."

"Yeah, I knew it would be. It's Caroline." I suddenly feel Tate's presence, and I know she just walked into the building. "I'll catch up with you in a bit. Good to see you, JB."

"You'd better," he says before his eyes dart behind me. "Holy hell, you lucky bastard."

I don't need to ask him what he means because I know when I turn, Tate will be there. She might not be mine technically, but JB knows there will always be something connecting her and me. He was one of my few friends who knew how I truly felt about her. I kind of had to tell him because if I hadn't, I knew his ass would've been trying to bag her.

Slowly turning, I see her. Only she looks different than the last time I saw her at the apartment. The same empty, lost eyes. And her petite figure is unchanged. Her lips are still full, and her face is still angelic. But the brown hair I became accustomed to … is lighter. And even though I watch every head turn to stare, I liked her the way she was before.

The way she always was.

Things are constantly changing in life. People have strokes or get sick. People die. They disappear. Players get injured and are done with the game, or they get the phone call we all dream of and head to the pros. Nothing is ever meant to stay the same. I know that. But Tate Tracy was perfect the way she was. I didn't want her to change. I didn't want her to be like every other woman I came across.

Her eyes dart around the room as she smiles to those she passes by, her mother close by her side. Her dress hugs her toned stomach and stretches across her waist and thighs, which are thicker than you'd think they'd be if you were only looking at her upper body. And when she turns around to wave to someone, I get a view of the dark blue fabric that hugs the curve of her ass so perfectly, making me curse silently.

Whatever god made her must have taken his damn time. There's no way on earth that an angel like that was made in a day.

When her eyes find mine, I look away. Eyes that have always seemed to be searching for something, anything, when she looks at me. I had to look away because when she looks at me like that, I'd give her anything, except she doesn't want that. She doesn't want me.

"Tate looks good." Logan whistles low. "I'm digging the blonde hair. Well, it's sort of blonde. Sort of brown. The fuck would that be called? Bronde?" Eventually, he shrugs. "Either way, it's hot."

I don't even entertain whatever the hell he's going on about. I just grab a Coke from a server carrying a tray and talk to a few people as they come up to me.

TATE

For the past hour, I've caught up with person after person. People I went to school with, teachers from kindergarten all the way to my junior year of high school. I even saw the bakery lady from town. All in the midst of trying my best to avoid looking anywhere near where I know Link stands. People gather around him, no doubt wanting to congratulate him on having such a successful college hockey career thus far. Girls from high school flock to him, not that I can blame them.

Once everyone has eaten and the music starts, Caroline's niece, Priscilla, steps in front of the crowd.

"I just want to take a moment to thank everyone who came out tonight. And for those who couldn't make it but sent a donation or some kind words, it means so much. As you all know, the past week has been a tough one for our family. But even in this hard time, it truly means the world to us that our community has gathered to make something this wonderful—and on such short notice." Her eyes gloss over. "So, eat, drink—well, drink soda and juice because that's all we can offer here."

The crowd laughs.

"And dance!"

Once she sits back down, I look at my mom to find her eyes the size of the dinner plates here tonight.

"Holy shit," she utters. "Oh God, I'm not ready for this."

"What?" I follow her gaze to find my father walking in. Alongside him is Margo. "Fuck me sideways. I was just starting to think maybe I'd luck out and he wasn't going to come," I murmur, making my mom snap out of her trance.

"Watch your mouth, little lady," she whispers as she turns her gaze to *anyone* but the pair of them. "Shit, she's pretty. She's, like … really pretty. I'm old. I'm old and wrinkly. My skin is loose in places. Places *her* skin certainly isn't."

"Oh, yeah, you're straight-up decrepit." I roll my eyes. "Get it together, Mom. Don't give him what he wants. What *they* want is to see you squirm, to see you hurt." I grip her hand in mine. "Excuse my language, but … fuck them."

She swallows, nodding nervously. "Yeah, fuck them."

"That's the spirit!" I chime in just as my eyes catch sight of Link laughing.

His eyes squeeze shut, and his head tips back slightly as his youngest brother continues to talk.

Logan has always been the funny one. They all like being jokesters, but Logan? He could have you in stitches in a matter of seconds.

"I'm being silly," my mom mutters from next to me. "You don't need me putting you in awkward situations. I'm sorry. Maybe I should go say hello."

"Trust me, you aren't. And maybe you should. But not yet. Play it cool," I assure her, continuing to watch Link, unable to pull my eyes from him.

I haven't seen him look so happy in the short time I've been at Brooks. Even with his friends, even on the ice, he constantly carries something with him. Something that weighs him down.

Once Logan struts off slowly, Link's expression turns somber. And as he looks around, his eyes landing on the pictures of Caroline and her husband that are spread out on the tables, his shoulders slump.

And when he leaves the auditorium, headed into the hallway, I know I need to follow him. I need to make sure he's all right.

LINK

I've always been an avoider. I avoid feelings. I run from despair. And I sweep my shit under a hypothetical rug that is probably so thick that it could touch the clouds.

I've always done this because, well, it's worked for me my entire life. I take my issues, and instead of drowning in them, I just use them to better myself at hockey. All the pain I don't allow myself to feel has become a super force to help me stay ultra-focused on the game I love.

The game is my life. And the ice, my safe haven. When I'm on it … nothing else matters.

Not that my mother is dead. Not that my dad is depressed. And not that I can't have the one thing I want more than anything else.

Tate.

Maybe that's why I hate to leave it—the arena. Because I know when I do, everything I've tried to run from will chase me down.

Everything like … my mother getting sick. Watching her fade before my very own eyes. Her inescapable death—something my father will never come back from.

The day she took her last breath is the same day my dad stopped actually existing. He spends most of his days since then keeping the house exactly how she left it. Taking care of her gardens. Keeping everything of hers right as it was. If any of us accidentally moves something when we're home … it's hell.

Which is why none of us go home much since we all graduated high school. When we're at our house, we stress him out. He is always constantly behind us, cleaning up our messes. Even if it is a simple cup or a pair of shoes. It puts him over the edge because it makes the house different than it was the day she left it before she died. A day that is etched in my brain forever.

The lights weren't on in the ambulance. Neither were the sirens. They didn't need to be. She was dead.

Hospice had done their job. They had kept her comfortable. Or as comfortable as she could be.

I knew she was finally free of the pain. But that didn't make it easier. Not really anyway.

I sat on the doorstep, watching the ambulance drive away until it was out of sight. And then I closed my eyes and tried to go back in time. I wanted to remember my mother baking cookies with us at Christmas. Or dyeing eggs at Easter. And the times she'd drive us all to the sports we played, keeping her so busy that I didn't know how she did it all.

But she did. She did everything. And even when she was dying, she would call and check in. Something our dad doesn't do. He's angry, and I understand. I'm angry too. I'm angry because every day, people do bad things but are healthy. Or given second chances. She was a saint and had to die a painful death, leaving us all behind.

I walk into Mr. Levi's room, my old homeroom class, and look around. It looks different yet the same. The windows face outside to the senior parking lot. If anyone ever tried to skip out early, Mr. Levi would pretend he didn't see them.

Selfishly, I need a minute to clear my head. Seeing all of the pictures on the tables took me back to the benefit dinner the town had put on for my mother years before. My parents didn't really need the money. My father did good for himself, owning his own construction company, and my mother had been a registered nurse until she got sick. But the town insisted on rallying around her. Which meant getting together.

"You all right?" Tate's soft voice says from the doorway.

Not turning around, I stuff my hands in my pockets. "Yep. Fine."

She takes a few steps, and I feel her getting closer behind me. Closer until she stops right next to me, our arms almost touching.

"Why did you do that to your hair?"

Out of the corner of my eye, I see her stiffen before her hand runs over her head.

"I wanted a change. It was time for one."

"Now, you look like every other chick here," I retort coldly, wanting to hurt her feelings.

It's true though. Before, her hair was natural. Something not many girls can say. I loved it because it was one hundred percent her.

She's quiet for a bit before, eventually, she brushes it off. "Clyde was just walking in when I came. Took them a while to convince him to come out to this, I guess. But it will be good for him to be around everyone."

I blow out a snide breath, glancing over at her for a second. "Nobody knows what is good for him. The man said he didn't want to come; they shouldn't have made him."

I was the same way when my mom got sick. I didn't want to come out and pretend everything was great. Or receive hugs from people, like it would change a damn thing. I just wanted to be left the fuck alone. Same with Clyde.

He's scared his wife isn't going to be okay. And from what I'm hearing … he has a right to be scared.

"Maybe so. But he has no children to be home with him. We're the closest thing he has to family. So, like I said, he shouldn't be alone right now."

"And since when has that mattered to you?" I swing toward her. "Since when have you given a flying fuck if someone shouldn't be alone?"

"Link … that's not fair—"

"You know what's not fair? You walking around like everything is fine. Like you aren't the fucking devil underneath that pretty face."

"I am not the devil," she answers sharply. "You don't believe that either."

"I bet the devil's eyes are empty too." I step closer, glaring down at her. "Just. Like. Yours."

She stares up at me, looking so small against my height.

"Like I told you … I came back as soon as I found out that she was ill." I hear the unmistakable sound of pain in her voice. "It was clear that you no longer cared if I was around."

"I had to get over you somehow, didn't I?" I mutter.

"Yep," she says coldly. "I guess so."

"Why'd you let me fuck you, Tate?" I ball my hand into a fist. "What was the point if you were just going to leave?"

She closes her eyes for a moment, dropping her head down. "If I'd stayed, I could never have pushed you away, and … I couldn't stand the thought of just being friends with you for another second." Lost brown eyes look into mine. "The truth is, being away from you sounded easier than being tortured with seeing you every day, but knowing you could never truly be mine."

"And was it?" I growl lowly. "Was it easier? You know the day you left is the same day she told us she was dying. I needed my fucking friend."

Her eyebrows pull together as tears gather in her eyes.

"No. Because the truth is … there's eighty-six thousand four hundred seconds in a day … and since we were kids, there has never been one of them when you weren't the only thing that mattered," she whispers. "And even though I needed to put space between us, if I had known your mom was going to tell you she was sick, I would never have packed my car and left that morning." Her hand slides down my abdomen the smallest bit. "I hope you know that."

"I don't know anything anymore when it comes to us," I snap. "You were my fucking person, Tate. I'd take that night back just to go back to when we had each other's back. But I was being selfish. I knew you couldn't handle it, but I did it anyway."

"You regret that night?" she utters. "You wish it hadn't happened?"

"Yes," I say instantly. "That night ruined everything."

The tears fill her eyes so full that they drip down her cheeks as she looks away from me, moving her hand down from my shirt. "I'm sorry you feel that way." She sniffles. "I regret a lot of things. More than I can say. But being with you? Having you as my first?" Her voice drops so low that I barely hear her. "That will never be one of them."

As she starts to back away, I step toward her, pushing her against a desk. "I've been with a lot of women since that night, Tate. And when I squeeze my eyes shut as I bury myself inside of them … all I see is you." I glide my hands to her ass, lifting her up onto the desk. "I *always* close my eyes."

Stepping between her parted legs, I nudge the bulge of my jeans against her dress. "You ruined me for anyone else. And all I dream about is ruining you back. Fucking you so hard that nobody would ever want you again and making you come so good that all you'll ever think about is me fucking you."

My cock grows, pushing against her dress as her lips part.

"You're all I think about already," she whimpers. "You already ruined me."

As badly as I want to slide inside of her, pounding her against this desk while her nails claw my back with my name under her breath, I can't. It's been too long, and she doesn't deserve that. So, instead, I slide my hand under her dress and up her thigh. My fingers stop at the fabric of her lace panties, but I push them to the side, dipping inside.

"Why are you so wet, Tate?" I growl, keeping my voice low, knowing that we stupidly left the door open. "Is it because I live inside of your brain? Is it because you dip your own fingers inside sometimes, imagining it's me?"

"Yes," she whimpers.

"Have you done that since you've lived across the hall from me?" I push deeper.

"Yes." She licks her lips, sucking in a breath. "So many times."

With my thumb, I rub circles against her in a spot she must love because through her dress, her nipples harden. Sliding two fingers deeper, I move in and out. I never kiss her even if I wish I could.

"Link," she moans, looking down at herself as I continue to fuck her with my fingers.

I know I should stop. I should make this traitorous bitch pay the ultimate price, not letting her come the way I know she needs to.

"When I think about another man doing this, I lose my mind," I groan. "And when I think about someone else fucking you, I see red." I dip my forehead to hers, moving my fingers in and out. "I'll never forgive you, Tate. I was ready to give you the world, and you ran off to Boston. Doing God knows what."

I'm telling the truth, though I have no idea why I'm saying any of this. It doesn't matter now. In fact, she doesn't deserve to know. Still, I can't stop.

"There has never been anyone else," she sighs just before her lips catch mine and she kisses me. "Only you."

I stop, pulling my lips and fingers from hers. "What?"

"I might have run away from you, but you followed me. At least, your memory did." She presses her lips to mine again, but I don't respond. "If you think it's been easy for me, you're wrong."

A single tear falls down her cheek. "Leaving you behind was the hardest thing I have ever done. And I picked up the phone and tried to call you … it must have been hundreds of times."

I stand there, frozen, for another moment before I slide my fingers back inside of her. She's soaked, needing me, wanting me, just like I knew she would.

And when I drop my head down, pushing her dress over enough to drag my tongue along her nipple, she squeezes around me. Coming so hard that I think she might bruise my fingers.

When she's finished, I pull away.

"That's right, Tate. I'm in your mind again. You'll go to bed, thinking of my fingers fucking you the way I just did. And when you wake up, you'll be thinking about the same thing all over again."

I grip her chin. "No man will ever satisfy you. Not the way I have." Bringing her lips to mine, I kiss her hard, leaving her breathless. "It'll be a long, lonely life. But you chose this. Remember that."

And when I leave her there, wide eyes and messy hair … I know that even though I gave her an orgasm, I took more than I gave. Because as long as we're living together, I'll make sure from this point on to remind her that I'll always be there, in her brain.

Making it impossible for her to ever move on. Or to feel normal.

Because if I can't, why should she?

TATE

Looking in the mirror one last time, I give my hair one more run through with my hands and make sure I don't look like I just did what I really did do in my old homeroom classroom.

I hadn't expected it to happen. Any of it. His hands on my body. His lips on my lips. His mouth on my breast. His fingers … inside of me. I'd thought he'd yell at me and tell me to go to hell, at best.

One thing is for sure: we just made things a whole lot more complicated than they already had been.

Heading out of the bathroom, I walk back toward the gymnasium to find my mom. I left her not long after my dad walked in. I know it was shitty timing, but the need to be there for Link was instinctual. Even though I assumed he'd be pissed that I followed him, I just wanted to make sure he was okay.

The thing is, I don't know if he is. He holds himself together like he's fine. Unaffected. But at the end of the day, Link lost his mother. And from what my mom has told me, his dad isn't doing well. So, how could he be all right?

I pull the door open and walk into the gym, immediately looking for my mother. Instead, Margo and my father beeline it for me, hand in hand.

"Guess I have to find you, huh?" he taunts, releasing her hand and pulling me against him.

"Sorry. I was using the restroom." I hug him awkwardly, and next, it's Margo's turn.

Her hug is cold, but she attempts to smile. "Your dad is just so excited for this baby."

"Finally getting my boy!" my dad cheers. "I know you're gonna love him, T. I just know it."

"Yeah … it really is something," I say, stepping back. "How, uh, have you been feeling lately? Everything good?" I ask Margo.

"I'm just so tired. But thank the Lord, your daddy has been waiting on me hand and foot." She tucks herself against him, beaming. "This baby and I are sure lucky to have such an incredible man."

I swallow back the vomit that so badly wants to come up my throat and land on her dress and his shoes. Instead, I do what I always do. I smile and nod. "Yeah. For sure. The luckiest."

They stare at each other as his hand snakes down and rubs her stomach. And like so many times before, he forgets I'm here.

"Well, I guess I should go see Clyde," I mutter. "Nice seeing you."

As I start to turn, Margo stops me. "Wait, we didn't even get to talk wedding details. So, we've decided that Hawaii just isn't feasible right now. With your father's appearances and podcasts, it would be tough to travel that far."

I sigh in relief. *Yes, I get out of this wedding! Thank you, Jesus—*

"So, we've made the decision that we will get married on the beach at the resort where we met in Florida." Her eyes widen, and she squeals, "In two weeks!"

"Wait, what?" I frown. "Two weeks? That's, like … really soon."

Fuckity fuck. Something could come up to save me from this. Something. Anything. Brain surgery. A kidnapping perhaps. Maybe a meteorite will fall from the sky and knock me out cold for the entire day.

"Baby girl, Margo's fixin' to start getting real big. She wants to fit in the wedding dress she's having custom-designed." My dad leans down, kissing her. "So, you'll be there? Gonna be on a Sunday."

"I don't—I'll have to see." I stand there in shock. "I have classes. And work. And—"

"Work at the Astronomy Center, doing public shows, you mean?" Margo says, completely unimpressed. "I'm sure they can survive without you for the weekend."

An obnoxious laugh sounds like a bark from my father's chest. "That's right. I'd say so. What do y'all talk about to a bunch of snot-nosed kids anyhow? Aliens? I think you can skip out for the weekend. What are you getting paid, twelve dollars an hour?"

"Eleven actually," I say with a snide smile.

I open my mouth to come up with something to shut them up, but before I can, Link's voice stops me.

"There you are, babe." Suddenly, an arm wraps around me. "I've been lookin' all over for you."

Craning my neck, I see him just before he pulls me against his side. "Um …"

"Link?" my dad says, sounding confused. "What's all this?"

Releasing me, he holds his hand out to Margo while glancing at my dad. "Well, where are my manners? I guess I haven't formally met your fiancée, Harvey. I'm Link Sterns." He pauses. "Tate's boyfriend."

"I didn't even know Tate had a boyfriend," Margo says rudely. "And certainly not one like"—she swallows—"well, like you."

I know her words are a direct blow. I'm plain and ordinary. Link is stupidly attractive, and she's in the sports world enough to know how talented he is. In her eyes, he could have anyone he wanted. And I guess she's right.

"I know," he says, grinning down at me. "She's way out of my league. She's always the smartest person in every room and definitely the most beautiful. But for some strange reason, she slums it with me."

I swear I see smoke coming from Margo's ears at the mention of me being the most beautiful, and she thrusts her plastic boobs up further.

"So, you'll be at the wedding then? Right?" Margo looks at us suspiciously. "Two weeks from this Sunday in Florida?"

"Well, yeah," he answers, never breaking eye contact with me. "I wouldn't let my baby go alone."

"That's great," my dad says coolly. "You know, if my daughter ever called to check on me, I might know things like—oh, I don't know—who she's dating." He winks at me. "I'm teasing. I know you're busy with all your *rocket* studies."

"Damn right she is," Link chimes in protectively. "Hell, one day, she'll be making more than all of our asses, combined."

"Huh. Well, I guess we'll have to see," my dad scoffs.

"Yes, well, I never want to call and interrupt an intense game of golf these days. Or a super-important podcast about a game fifteen years ago. And I never know when you're filming your hair color commercials. Which, by the way, is working great. Your hair *almost* looks natural," I throw back sweetly, watching my dad's smile die. "It was so great to see you guys. I wish we could talk longer, but we really should go visit Clyde now."

Before they can respond, I step from Link's hold and turn.

"So nice to see y'all. Congratulations," Link drawls from behind me.

I have no idea why he did what he did. Or if he even really plans to attend the wedding with me. But one thing was clearer than ever.

And that thing is … Link still has my back. Despite everything I've done wrong.

"What was that?" I mutter as we walk toward where Clyde sits.

"If anyone is going to be a dick to you, it's me, not your pompous asshole father and his bitch fiancée," Link coos in my ear. "Glad to see he hasn't changed."

Turning before we reach Mr. Fenton, I grab Link's hand. "Did you mean it?"

He doesn't look directly at me, instead looking around. "I don't know."

When I sink into myself, frowning, Link's thumb slides over my bottom lip. "For now, just be happy I saved you from that conversation. Deal?"

Nodding slowly, I look up at him. "Deal."

TATE

"Are you sure you have to go?" My mom pulls me against her. "One night wasn't enough."

She's right; it wasn't enough. I'd love to visit more. She's been in such a great mood, even despite my dad rolling in last night and trying to make himself look like a hero in front of the crowd. Luckily, most of the people there know that he's a dick. Despite the check for five thousand dollars—which, let's face it, is like chump change to him.

"I'll be back in a few weeks, promise," I assure her. "Besides, when Caroline comes home, I want to visit her." I say the words, hopeful, though nobody sounds very optimistic that she's improving.

My mother stiffens but nods. "Yes. Yes, you will."

As she releases me, I turn toward her and put my hands on her shoulders. "I am proud of you for being strong when Dad and Margo walked in. I know that wasn't easy, but maybe it will get easier every time."

She gives me a sad smile. "I sure hope so. I know I didn't end up saying hi, but maybe one day, I will be strong enough to." Kissing my cheek, she steps back. "I didn't mention it at breakfast, worried maybe you weren't bringing it up for a reason. But I have to ask you … what was the whole ordeal with you and Link when he walked up while you were talking to your dad?" She looks worried, but I don't know why. "Y'all looked *really* cozy."

I chew my lip nervously. "So, here's the thing … you know how my apartment fell through?"

"Yes." Her eyes widen. "Why?"

"I sort of somehow ended up renting a room at one of the hockey houses." I cringe, feeling bad I didn't tell her sooner. "Anyway, Link heard Margo being, well, sort of rotten to me. And long story short, Link stepped in and pretended we were dating." I gulp. "And now, they expect us to attend the wedding … together."

There we stand, in her driveway, as she stares at me with nothing but shock.

"I'm so confused. So, you and Link are, what, friends again?"

"Not really," I say, leaning against my car. "He's done a few nice things for me, sure. But it's evident he hasn't forgiven me for leaving. Or for missing the funeral." Shame washes over me. "Not that I can blame him. I should have just come home for it. I just figured he wouldn't want me there."

"Don't feel guilty for doing what you thought was best. It's hard to know what the heck is right in those situations." Her hands rest on my upper arms as her eyes look into mine. "Just be careful, okay? Don't forget why you left to begin with. Why you needed that space. Okay?"

Surprised that she doesn't seem happy for me, I tense the slightest bit. "I will." Jerking my thumb toward the car, I give her an apologetic smile. "I really should get going. Love you."

Giving me one more squeeze, she kisses the top of my head and steps back. "Drive safe. I love you."

Once I'm in my car, I look across the road at the Sterns' perfectly kept house. Nothing ever looks amiss there; it never has. Just like I wish my mom would move on, I wish Link's father, Reed, would too.

As I am turning out of my driveway, I notice Link's truck is gone already. When I went outside to get my charger earlier this morning, it wasn't there either. Perhaps he had early practice and needed to get back to Brooks. Either way, it doesn't seem like he travels home much since he left for college years ago. When I was in Boston, I didn't travel home much either. For holidays, Mom would fly to us most of the time. And Dad, well, he usually claimed to have a work commitment.

I have no idea what Link I'll get when I arrive back at Brooks. It could be grouchy, tortured Link. Who seems to be annoyed at the very sight of me. Or I could get the dude who jumps in when I get in trouble, wanting to help. *Or*, if I'm really lucky … I'll get the guy from my old classroom last night. The one who gave me pleasure with his hands, never wanting anything in return. Honestly, as hot and cold as he's been lately … it's hard to say.

And even if he doesn't plan to actually take me to the wedding or follow through on pretending to date me, he did me a solid. One I didn't deserve.

I've never been one who can stand having the music too loud. It hurts my brain. So, turning the music on just loud enough, I attempt to drown out the thoughts that haven't left my mind since yesterday.

Just like *he* said they wouldn't. Link had already been taking up most of the space inside my brain. After last night, when he brought me to heaven with his fingers … it's only gotten worse.

LINK

I walk into the apartment to the smell of pancakes, and when I hear a girl's voice, I'm pretty positive I'm about to see Brody and his chick, bare-assed, probably eating pancakes off of each other. Brody's *that* adventurous.

Before I can back out the door, Brody appears.

"Thank fuck your pecker isn't out." I sigh, dropping my bag down.

He's shirtless, but that's nothing new. In fact, I wonder if he's like the dude from *Guardians of the Galaxy* who can't wear shirts because his nipples are sensitive. Then, I remember it's Brody, and he just likes to show off his body.

He looks nervous for a moment before he grins. "Bria, guess we're busted."

I only know one Bria. And that's Kye Collins's sister, Bria. I've only met her a few times. Last I knew, she lived in Florida—if it's the same girl, that is.

Walking around the corner with a sports bra and sweatpants is none other than Bria Collins. Surfer chick who is insanely hot and could probably be a fitness model.

"You're just in time for my pancakes. Which happens to be the only thing I can cook." She walks back into the kitchen, and I don't miss Brody checking her ass out.

"So, you're the mystery girl, huh?" I follow them into the kitchen and lean against the counter. "The one keeping him up all night and making him sneak out for some lovin'?" I shrug. "I'd say nice to meet you, but I already know you."

Picking up a pancake from the insanely tall stack, she throws it at Brody, hitting him in the chest. "Ew. With this guy? What in the world have you been telling your friends, O'Brien?"

95

He gives her a sly grin. "I had to have some fun with them. I didn't even tell them we were friends because they'd have automatically thought I was bagging you and would have annoyed the fuck out of me over it. And if I'd told them we weren't banging, they wouldn't have believed me."

"I don't really buy that you aren't," I say, walking over to the pancakes and piling a few onto a plate. "But, okay, I'll play along."

"Dude, I don't want my vagina to rot out of my body. I like it too much for that." She pushes herself onto the countertop and sits, swinging her feet. "He's nasty. He probably has a dirty dick. He's like Magic Mike, but an underwear model instead of a stripper."

"Do not," he snaps. "No glove, no love." Pointing to her, he raises his eyebrows. "And this fuckstick finally started to leave me alone about the model shit. So, hush your face."

"What's wrong with modeling?" Bria raises an eyebrow at me.

"There's nothing *wrong* with it." I shovel some food into my mouth. "But do I still like to give him shit for it ? Hell yeah. I really do." I change the subject, knowing Brody gets mad when I tease him. "How'd you two become friends anyway? I thought you lived in Florida."

"I'm an underwear model," she deadpans, and I almost choke on the pancake in my mouth. "And I moved here this year to get my master's degree. Brooks has one of the best programs in the country for studying fine art."

"You're an artist?" I ask. "That's cool."

"Photographer," she corrects me. "But, yeah … it's all the same."

"She's badass." Brody winks.

Rolling her eyes, she ignores him. "Anyway, why did you drive back home so early?"

I look away from her, clearing my throat. "Just had some shit to get done today. Didn't want to be tied up there all day."

Nodding slowly, like she somehow gets that I don't want to talk about it, she hops down from the counter and begins cleaning her mess up. "Gotcha. Well, I guess now that the cat's out of the bag, I'll be seeing ya."

"Guess so, but I still don't buy that y'all ain't knocking boots." I smirk and move quickly to my room because she seems like the type of chick you wouldn't want to piss off.

Once I get into my room, I flop onto my bed and put my hands behind my head, staring at the ceiling.

I couldn't get out of my house quick enough today. And even though my brothers were staying the entire weekend, they understood why I wasn't. We all get it. The tension and pain inside of our house, it's crippling.

And then there's the fact that I swooped in to save Tate even though I had no business doing it. I was in a group of people behind her. I'd watched Tate's dad degrade her for years, and now, this devil woman was doing the same. I tried to tell myself to walk away, but I couldn't. So, now, it looks like I'm supposed to be going to a dang wedding.

Truthfully, I don't know if I will or not. I wasn't thinking two weeks away when I said yes. I just knew that at that moment, she needed someone in her corner. And like always, I wanted to be that guy for her.

I yawn, my eyes feeling heavy. And slowly, I feel myself drift off to sleep.

"What do you mean, she's gone?" I say, looking up at Tate's house. "I just saw her this morning."

Her mother's face looks pained. "I'm sorry, Link. She decided to head out to Boston early. She called the landlord, and the apartment was available and waiting for her. She thought it would be for the best to go get acquainted with the city early. Before classes start in the fall."

She's lying. I know she is. Nobody goes to college that early. And I already talked to Tate about it. She wasn't going to leave until a month after I was going to head to Brooks to begin training.

"That doesn't make sense, Meg."

Her eyebrows pull together, and she pats my arm. "My daughters have both suffered from all of the allegations about their dad. Trusting anyone will never be easy. I'm just so sorry she hurt you in the process," she answers softly. "Please understand, she didn't come to this decision lightly."

My face must show my disgust about the said allegations. Everyone knew Tate's dad was a dirty fucking dawg. I knew Tate and Meyer had sworn off athletes, but I thought I would be an exception. After last night, everything seemed to fall into place. I don't understand how she could just leave.

"I love her," I say boldly. "I'm not her dad. I'll never be her dad." Taking a step back, I take another look at the house. "I'll get her back. She loves me too."

"I'm sorry, Link," she whispers. "I really am."

Storming across the road, I try to call Tate for what could be the tenth time in the past hour. Of course, it goes to voice mail.

Yanking the front door open, I start toward the stairs, but the sight of my mother and father and all of my brothers at the dining room table stops me. Mom and Dad look depressed, just like they did six years ago when they sat in those same two chairs. That was her first round with cancer. Something tells me it's back.

"What's going on?" I say, stopping in my tracks.

"Mom needs to tell us something," Logan mutters, looking scared.

My father looks as pale as a ghost, and I see my mother breaking even though she's trying to stay strong.

"Come sit, baby," she whispers. "I need to talk to my boys. All of you."

Staring at her, I wait for her to tell me what I already know. Only this time, I have a bad feeling it is worse.

I sit down, and then she tells us the worst news any of us have ever heard—that her cancer isn't just back, but that it is returning with a vengeance. She is dying. But to me, it seems like she is just giving up.

I guess some days really do last forever. Even when you wish they wouldn't.

I drag in a breath, sitting up in bed. My head soaked with sweat.

That was the worst day of my life. The day my mother died could be too, I guess. But the day she told us her cancer had returned was somehow worse. Because from that point forward, we knew the clock was ticking.

And there was no stopping it.

I had woken up that morning, on top of the world. Next to Tate in her bed as she slept soundly, her hair a mess on her face and pillow. I kissed her cheek and snuck out before anyone else was awake in the house. I left there, feeling like we'd turned a corner. Like … she was finally, rightfully mine. And within hours, I learned she'd left me and that my mother was going to leave soon as well.

The day my mother had found out she had cancer the first time, the universe had delivered Tate to me like some sort of healing gift. Only the second time, Tate left. And the cancer wasn't going to leave until it took my mother with it.

Whoever says karma doesn't exist has never had a day from hell like that one. I knew one thing for sure: whatever I had done in a past life must have been really fucking bad for me to be handed a day like that one.

Gazing at the time, I realize I've been asleep for hours. I can't remember the last time I took a nap, but I know I didn't sleep for shit last night, so it's no wonder why I dozed off.

I can't fathom why I did what I did yesterday. From that moment when I knew that I needed Tate to remember how much she had fucked up, all by making her come on my fingers. Or when I lied to her daddy, pretending we were together.

In that classroom, even though I knew she was trying to keep quiet, with every time I pumped harder or rubbed those circles with my thumb, she'd moan. And like a drug, I needed more. I ate her moans up like fucking crack.

The blood rushes to my cock as I squeeze my eyes shut, remembering how flicking my tongue on her nipple made her squirm at my touch. She was desperate for more. I owned her.

What I wanted to do was climb over her, demand her to open those plump lips, and slide my dick into her mouth. Or pull her off the desk, flipping her over and fucking her from behind, feeding her every inch as she begged for more, whimpering in pain, but not wanting me to stop.

I want to be etched into every crevice of her brain. But I know that with every touch, kiss, and moan … she's imprinted right there in mine too. There's no outrunning her. She's always there.

Stepping out of bed, I push the door open and make sure no one is in the hallway before heading to the bathroom and turning the shower on.

I'll never admit out loud that my fantasies of her are much more satisfying than any other chick I've physically been with. But it's true.

So, palming myself, I close my eyes and imagine her dropping to her knees and taking me into her mouth like a good girl. Even if she probably isn't.

I imagine hitting the back of her throat and feeling her gag against me. Yet still not wanting me to stop.

And like so many times before, I fuck my hand to the thought of Tate. Because I know I shouldn't let her suck my cock in real life.

TATE

I get back from Appleton with plenty of time to spare for work. Tonight's show is more geared toward toddlers and young children, and I'm actually stoked. It's the tween and teen showings that are my least favorite. To be honest, that age group scares the crap out of me. So judgmental and … mean.

Heading up the stairs, I hear the washing machine on and make a mental note that I need to do laundry myself tomorrow. I'll take any chore out there, but I despise doing laundry.

Slowly pushing the bathroom door open, I somehow miss the shower running until it's too late, and through the clear shower curtain, I see a naked Link. His body is slightly blurred, but I know it's him. He doesn't turn his head toward me, though I have no idea how he didn't hear the door creak open.

And that's when I see the stroking motion coming from his hand. And I gasp when I realize he's pleasuring himself. His head tips back, his eyes squeezed shut.

I should back out of this bathroom and shut the door. I shouldn't disrespect his privacy by standing here and watching like a pervert. Only I can't look away.

His motions slow before getting faster again, causing a deep ache between my legs. I grip the sink counter as my breathing picks up, completely spellbound by him.

My phone rings, and even though I try to silence it, he hears it before I do.

Pulling the curtain back, he glares. "What the fuck are you doing in here, Tate? The door was shut."

"I'm—I'm sorry," I stammer, my eyes floating to his length again as his hand still grips it even though the movements have stopped.

Quietly closing the door, I lick my lips and start toward the shower.

Not thinking, I step inside, still dressed in my pale blue dress.

"What are you doing?" he growls. "I don't want you in here."

I look up at him, the shower spraying over us. "Really?" my voice croaks, hoarse from need.

His expression only hardens, but so does his dick. "Really."

Reaching out, I slide my hand under his. "What were you thinking about, Link?"

He doesn't answer, so I push further by sliding my hand.

"When you were stroking yourself like that, what were you imagining?" I whisper. "Who were you imagining?"

He doesn't respond right away until, finally, his eyes move down my body, taking in the now see-through fabric as it clings to me from the wetness. "I was thinking about shoving my dick down your throat, making you gag on me."

"And then what?" I quiver, needing him to tell me more.

"And then you swallowing me like a good girl even though we know you aren't one."

I can't help but wonder what he means by that. But I'm also too turned on to find out right now.

Putting my hands on his sides, slowly, I drop my body lower, dragging my tongue down his abdomen until I'm on my knees.

Pushing my hair back, I gaze up at him. "Show me."

"Tate," he growls, his eyes burning into mine with anger, "why do you deserve to suck my cock when we both know it's exactly what you want? In fact, I bet you're dripping, just thinking about having me in your mouth."

"Because I've done some things wrong and I need to show you how sorry I am." I tilt my head slightly. "And you want this. If you didn't … you wouldn't be in here, pleasuring yourself to the thought of me." I don't know what comes over me, but I smirk. "And besides, my mouth will feel better than your hand … I promise."

After a beat longer of glaring, he fists my hair with his hand, dragging my mouth to his hardness.

"Open up wide then, baby. You asked for it." He glowers. "Now, suck."

Doing as I was told, I open my mouth and inch forward until I taste him. Even though his body blocks most of the water from me, the overspray trickles over my body, keeping my lips wet. His grip tightens on my hair, pulling my head upward just as I take as much of him as I can into my mouth before letting him slide back out, repeating it all over again. And when I get too cocky, he hits the back of my throat, and just like he wanted, I gag.

A moan escapes his lips as his hips jerk toward me.

Without hesitation, I go right back in, never breaking eye contact as I watch the man made of stone wither at my touch. He might think he's punishing me, but he's not.

I want him inside of me. I want him to take me every way known to mankind. But I know he won't. Everything has to be on his terms. Or at least, he has to think it is. He isn't ready to give me that. Probably because he thinks I don't plan to stick around.

"Good girl, sucking my cock like it's your fucking job," he hisses. "Remember how turned on you are right now, Tate. Remember being this excited to have my dick down your throat because I promise, you won't be for another man." He pulls my hair back further. "Those lips were made for sucking my cock and my cock only."

I take him as deep as I can, humming as my tongue runs down his length. His eyes stay on me as he pushes himself just that much deeper into my throat. And he doesn't give me an option to finish him off or not. Because seconds later, he's pouring himself into my mouth. And I take it. Without so much as trying to pull away.

"Fuck," he mutters, throwing his head back.

Putting a hand on the wall behind me, he attempts to steady himself, sucking in a breath.

Pushing myself up, I stand, looking right at him. I could pretend to play his game, but instead, I smirk.

"Every girl who strokes you or gets on her knees, begging to take you into her mouth … you'll think of me. This vision isn't going anywhere … so I guess we're both in the same boat. Huh?"

His eyes stare into mine, and the corner of his lips turns up the smallest bit. "Think what you want, Princess."

He knows I hate the nickname Princess. Since my parents were clearly well off because my father was a professional athlete, I was called that, growing up, more times than I can count. And no matter how many times I heard it, I hated it all the same. Reaching down, I pull my dress over my head, leaving me bare besides the pink thong I'm wearing.

"I don't need to think it, Link. We both know it's true." Stepping around him, I stand in the spray as he turns to face me. "After all, it was *you* in here, thinking about me."

I need him so badly right now. And maybe if I toy with him enough, he'll give me more. I'll take anything because pleasuring him the way that I just did, as deliciously hot as it was … was torture.

Reaching down, he cups between my legs. "I'd fuck you right now, but you'd like that too much. And guess what, Tate. You don't deserve it. Not yet anyway."

When he drags his fingers along the fabric of my soaked thong, my knees weaken, just before he drops his hand and steps out. Making me realize, I not only didn't win that battle …

But I probably won't win the war either.

"Link!" I call out. "We need to talk about yesterday. We need to talk about what you said to my dad."

I peek out and see him drying himself off before reaching for the doorknob.

"No, Tate, we don't."

And when he leaves without another word, going from hot to cold once again, I decide right then that I'm going to that damn party tonight. I need it.

LINK

I continue to lift, making my arms scream. Hell, my entire body is pissed off right now, probably wondering what the fuck I'm doing to it.

After the whole shower ordeal, I rushed to the gym. Just like she always does, Tate had me all sorts of fucked up, and I needed to blow off some steam.

I just blew my load right down her throat.

Even though that happened only an hour ago, blood rushes to my cock, just from my imagining doing it again. She puts me under a spell, making it impossible for me not to continue to do stupid shit.

She knows she's just as in control as I am. Hell, maybe more. I can try to play that game like I'm calling the shots, but it's all bullshit. The truth is, I'm not sure who's driving the car and who's the passenger right now.

I was so close to spinning her around, pressing her face against the shower wall, and diving in so deep that she'd yelp. I wanted to, but I knew I shouldn't.

I had imagined her going down on me for as long as I could remember. That vision was nothing new, and yet … it still got me just as worked up every time I imagined it. Now, it's been done in real life. And the reality was even hotter.

I have no idea what I'm doing. I don't have any sort of game plan. Because when it comes to Tate, I might as well throw every rule book out the window. I'm clearly not capable of following it anyway.

She said if she had known my mother was ill, she wouldn't have left the way she did. But I'm not ignorant. I know that even if she hadn't left that day, she would have left eventually. She'd made up her mind that we couldn't be together long before then. Come hell or high water, she was going to leave someday.

And then there was the kicker that I was the only man who'd touched her, which put me right over the edge … in the best way. I feel a possession over her that I know isn't healthy or right. But she's mine. She's always been mine.

Pushing the bar up, I sit and grab my Gatorade. If I go home, I'll have to face her. And seeing as I made her come undone on my fingers and I came in her mouth, all in twenty-four hours … I'm not sure how well that would go over. But I can't avoid home forever. Just for right now will have to do, I guess.

TATE

Closing the tube of mascara, I pull out my lip gloss, applying a layer. Smacking my lips together, I give myself one last look in the mirror. I look decent. What more could I ask for than that?

I'm not a supermodel, but for a frat party, it'll do.

I curled my shoulder-length hair and then combed through it. Turning it into soft, big waves. Despite Link hating the color of it now, I love it. It's somewhere between brown and blonde, giving me the change I needed. For once, I took my time doing my makeup. And by taking my time, I mean, I put on mascara, eyeliner, and lip gloss. And for my outfit, I dusted off my black crop top, pairing it with straight jeans and Nikes. Because this is a frat party, and my ass might need to run home if there're any creeps there. Or mean girls. I could run from them too.

"What am I even doing?" I whisper to myself. "Why am I pretending I want to go be social?"

I don't know what I think I'm gaining by going out tonight. But both Holly and Oliver texted me this morning, asking if I was coming. So, I guess I feel like I should. And this is college. I should be out, making friends. Not holed up at home. Besides, it's the weekend. I'm sure Brody and Link will both be off with God knows who.

As I head down the stairs, a shirtless Brody pulls his attention from the TV and turns to look at me.

"Damn, Tater Tot. You showin' some skin tonight?" He gives me a cheesy wink. "I approve. Oh, and by the way, I am digging the new hair. You're giving me Sarah Cameron vibes. And you know how I feel about her."

Brody and I binge-watched *Outer Banks* in a matter of days. It was hard to stop once we started. And he wasn't lying. He is obsessed with Sarah.

I giggle, feeling my cheeks burn. "Thanks. I'm trying something new."

"I like it," he says with a grin. "Where are you headed?"

"My friend Holly is picking me up. We're headed to a party."

His smile dies a little. "Where at?"

"It's at Oliver's fraternity house. You remember Oliver from the Astronomy Center?"

"Yeah, I do. But maybe I should go. I like Oliver, but some of those dudes he lives with … well, I've heard things. I don't really like the thought of you being there alone."

"Good thing I won't be alone," I remind him. "Oliver and Holly will both be there. And I'm sure dozens of other college kids. I'll be safe."

He doesn't look convinced, but he nods. "Call if you need me. I'm serious, Tate."

"Yes, *Dad*," I say and start toward the door. "I'm kidding. I will, I promise. I'll probably stay an hour, tops, and need a lift anyway."

"Tate," Link's voice says from behind me, coming out of nowhere, like *always*, "where are you going?"

"To a party at Oliver's frat house," I snap. "Because, you know … I'm in college."

"Fuck that. Those guys are creeps," he throws back bluntly. "I don't like this, Tate."

"Agree. I like it when you stay home and knit," Brody chimes in, pissing me off further. "Can't you just do that tonight?"

"Nope, because I already finished my sister's hat the other day," I answer playfully, seeing Holly's headlights pull in. "I swear, if I need you … I'll call! This is just something I feel like I should do."

My hand reaches for the door, opening it a crack just as Link slams it shut.

"It's not safe, Tate," he hisses through gritted teeth. "Use your fucking head."

I poke his chest. "If I stay home, we can talk about what happened at the benefit dinner." I glance back to make sure Brody isn't looking. "Or the shower."

He grows more frustrated. "There's nothing to talk about, Tate. I was helping you out."

"Both times?" I raise an eyebrow.

"Yep." He shrugs. "You don't need to go to this party. Go outside and tell that chick you're staying home."

"Are you staying home, Link?" I cross my arms.

When he doesn't answer, I blow out a breath. "That's what I thought. So, why should I? Besides, I lived in Boston. You know, that big *city* in Massachusetts? I did just fine, protecting myself there." I smile sadly. "I appreciate your concern, but I promise … it's okay."

When he looks unconvinced, I try a different approach. Standing tall, I press a kiss to his cheek. "I am so thankful that you worry about me. But I like Holly. And Oliver. They have become my friends, and I want to go." Stepping around him, I pull the door open. "Have a good night."

I beeline it for Holly's car before Link can throw me over his shoulder and tell me I'm not going.

Holly seemed so sweet and innocent at work. I totally had her pegged wrong. And truthfully, that scares the shit out of me.

Thirty seconds into us being here, she was already on her second shot. And not long after, she found some weed, and now … approximately thirty-two minutes upon arrival, here she is, dry-humping the shit out of some random dude on the couch for everyone to see.

"There you are," a familiar voice says behind me, touching my shoulder. When I turn, my eyes find Oliver, and I sigh in relief. "Hey!"

Pulling me in for a hug, he puts his lips closer to my ear. "I'm so glad you made it!" He speaks loudly over the blaring music. "Where's Holly?" He smells like a mix of Abercrombie & Fitch cologne, liquor, and mint gum. So unfamiliar and so different from Link's fresh, woodsy scent that I wish I could drown myself in.

Jerking my head toward the couch, I scrunch my nose up. "She ditched me pretty fast for that fella. To be fair, he looks much more fun."

The guy's hand grips her ass as she grinds herself against him greedily. Their tongues attack each other's mouth in a way that makes me think of a couple of slugs doing the tango, making my stomach lurch.

After he sees her, his hand grabs mine. "Need a drink?"

"Um, that's okay." I shrug. "I'm not drinking tonight."

If I were home, I'd probably have a few beers or maybe a White Claw or two. Maybe three. But not here with all of these dudes looking at me like they're the lions and I'm an antelope. I've never been someone who puts herself in risky situations. In fact, being here, at a frat party, is about as adventurous as I get.

Moving his free hand to my shoulder, he gives it a squeeze. "Come on. Loosen up, beautiful. You deserve it after working so hard. Besides, you aren't on the clock."

"You're right. I probably do. My boss is a wicked hard-ass," I joke. "I'm kidding. You're a good boss. And Holly is great. Y'all have made my transition to Brooks easier."

The way he suddenly rubs my shoulder, massaging it lightly, makes me feel uneasy. He's never given me creeper vibes, nor have I ever thought he was into me like this. But right now, looking at his eyes twinkling and the energy in his hands as he touches my body, I think I've read the entire situation wrong.

"You look gorgeous tonight," he says before his hand leaves my shoulder, brushing a curl away from my face and dragging his fingers through to the end. "I like your hair this way. It's much more you."

I frown. *How does the color of my hair have anything to do with who I am?*

My eyes must widen as I step back awkwardly, tearing myself from his touch. "Thanks," I answer flatly before waving around. "This is some party, huh?"

He shrugs his shoulders lazily. "I suppose so. That's how they all are. We throw a party, and people come."

Jerking his head toward the sliding glass door, he smiles. Suddenly not looking like a creep. Suddenly back to the guy I know from work. The one I've come to know and respect. "A ton of people are out back by the fire. Wanna check it out?" He nods toward Holly, who looks like she is about to bite the dude's tongue off. "Your wingwoman is kinda busy, it seems."

I chew my lip nervously. But when I'm about to say no, he makes it seem much less harmless.

"Some more of the astronomy majors are out there too. You know I have a telescope back there, right?"

"Um," I mutter, knowing I would be much happier at home, in my bed, with snacks, "okay."

Throwing his arm around me, he leads us to the door and pushes it open. But as we walk outside, I gaze around ... and there isn't a soul to be found.

"Um ... where is everyone?" I pull away from his hold. "There isn't even a fire out here, Oliver."

As I start around him, I see he's shut the door. And all I hear are Link's and Brody's voices in my head, telling me to be careful.

What a moron I am.

Putting his arm out, he stops me. "Tate, we don't have to pretend. *You* don't have to pretend."

"Pretend?" I frown, feeling my heart begin to race. "I don't know what you mean."

When he drops a hand to my waist, I feel my skin crawl.

"I know you want me. I know you're scared it will look bad because I'm your boss." He licks his lips, dipping his head lower. "It won't, I promise. We can keep it a secret."

Shaking my head, I stumble backward. "I don't—I don't know what you're talking about. I don't … I'm sorry, but I don't feel that way."

He continues toward me, crowding me against the house. "I saw the way Link looked at you. He wants you too. But he can't have you. At least not until I do." He runs his hand over my hair. "Fuck, you're so hot."

This time, when he tries to grab my waist, I punch him right in the nose. But before I can turn and run to the door, he grabs my wrist, his fingernails digging into my flesh, pulling me against him, and his lips attack mine so hard that I taste blood from my own lip. His tongue snakes inside my mouth, making me want to puke. And even more so when his hand stretches over my breast.

"Come on, baby. Don't fight it," he whispers.

And when he tries to kiss me again, that's when I knee him right in the balls before turning and bringing my elbow up, assaulting him in the nose again. He might have tricked me, but that's the only thing he'll do tonight.

"Bitch!" he groans, grabbing his junk. "I know you want me! You little fucking tease!"

Somehow, by the grace of God, I get the door open, and I bolt inside as quickly as I can. Swallowing back the puke threatening to come out.

Keeping my head down, I run through the crowd of people blindly and run right into a massive, hard body.

And when I peek up, I see him. The person who is always saving me.

Link.

Whoever claims angels are females doesn't have a guy like him in their life.

LINK

Tate's brown eyes stare up at me, only this time, they aren't filled with nothingness. They are filled with paralyzing, bloodcurdling fear.

Her lip is smeared with blood, and I see fingernail marks on her wrist.

Wrapping my arms around her, I look down at her. "Tate, what the fuck is going on?"

"Oliver, he—"

As she starts to say the words, I watch her eyes roll back, and I know what's going to happen next. Fastening my hold on her, I wait for her to go limp.

When I first met Tate, I had no idea that she had a condition that made her faint. But within a year, she fainted at school—in the cafeteria, in front of everyone. And scared the shit out of me. It seemed to only happen a few times a year, more so when she was stressed or hadn't eaten.

And judging by the way her body was shaking when I caught her … something fucking horrible had just happened.

"What the fuck, Sterns?" Brody yells, looking at Tate's lifeless body. "Is she okay? Was she drugged? We need to call an ambulance!"

"She faints sometimes," I say back, looking around. "But she's not okay. I know something happened. I'll kill that Oliver motherfucker—I promise you that."

Within seconds, she's waking up, and I carry her outside.

"Talk to me, Tate," I mumble, looking down at her as we stop outside, Brody on my heels.

I feel desperate, not knowing what could have happened in the short time she's been here. It might have been less than forty-five minutes … but that's more than enough time for a monster to claim his next victim.

I should have followed her out the door. But I was pissed, and I was being stubborn. All she's ever done is try to be independent. She doesn't realize that the world is dark and fucked up. Protecting her has always been an instinct, and I don't know how to turn it off.

"Oliver," she barely whispers, her lips trembling. "Please, just take me home." Her eyes glance around nervously before she burrows herself even closer against my body.

"You're safe, Tate. I promise," I murmur against her forehead, pressing my lips to her head. "Brody is going to take you to the truck. I'll be right there."

Clinging to my shirt, she shakes her head quickly. "No! Don't leave. Just take me home, Link. I'm fine. Just … please, I can't be here."

When I look down at her, my chest heaves as I try to steady my breathing, but I fucking fail miserably.

"Brody, let's go to the truck." I jerk my chin, giving him a knowing look.

There's no way I'm leaving here without finding Oliver and beating him senseless. Not a chance in hell. But I also need Tate to feel safe. So, once I get her securely in the truck with Brody, I can come back in.

When Brody steps closer, his eyes are nearly black. "Let me take care of him, Sterns. You'll get your chance." He looks down at Tate for a second before shifting his gaze back to me. "She needs you tonight, brother. Take her to the truck, and I'll be out in a bit."

I know he's right, but it doesn't make it easier to walk away without finding Oliver. She needs me right now. Besides, I know Brody enough to know he'll take care of it. And that kind of scares me because there's a darkness inside of him that not many people see. And when he unleashes it, it's hard for him to lock it back up.

Bolting away from me, he stalks back into the house.

Heading for the truck, I open the back door and pile both of us inside, keeping her on my lap. Her body is like ice, so I yank my hoodie off and pull it down over her.

Running my hand down her hair, I look at her. "Tell me what happened."

Her eyes look away from mine, and I stroke her cheek with my thumb.

"It's okay. You can tell me anything."

My mind goes to the worst-case scenario. That she was hurt or raped. That she'll never be the same again because he took that from her. And that I'll spend my life in jail because once Brody's finished with Oliver … I'll kill him.

"You'll hurt him," she whispers. "And then you'll get in trouble."

"Probably." I kiss her forehead. "Just tell me, Tate. Please."

"He wanted to go outside. He said there was a bonfire out there," her voice croaks. "But when we got outside … there was no one else. He said I wanted him. That I … was a tease." She finally looks at me. "He acted like this was all my fault. Like I'd asked for it."

The veins in my neck bulge, feeling like they could blow right out of my skin at any second. In my ears, I hear the whooshing sound of my own blood.

I wasn't there for her. She had to get away herself.

"How did you get away?" I whisper, seeing the tears in her eyes in the darkness of the truck.

"I punched him. And kneed him in the balls." She sniffles. "I never thought he'd do that. I'm so stupid. I'm such a fucking idiot. And a horrible judge of character."

"No, you aren't. I didn't think he would either. If I had, I never would have let you work with him." I shake my head. "Some people just hide their true selves better than others."

"All you do is save me, Link. And all I do is hurt you."

"I didn't save you tonight, Tate. You saved yourself."

I look at her. So beautiful and broken. She's always been like a lost soul that has never found its true place. She's wandered, but never really been found.

"You've never needed me to rescue you. And I guess, in some ways … I've always resented that. Because all I've ever wanted to do was be the person you relied on most. And you've never needed me." My thumb continues to graze her cheek. "Stop thinking of yourself as this frail creature. You're a fucking force."

I know why she did it. Why she left when things got complicated between us. When you grow up emotionally abused and neglected by your dad and watch the person who is supposed to be the most important male figure in your life treat his wife like crap … it affects you. I get it.

But there were still those moments when I needed her the most and she wasn't there.

The truth is, I'd been obsessed with her since the moment she had landed in Appleton. As we got older, I needed to see her before starting my day. I had to make sure she made it to school safely. Before a game, I had to get one of her hugs. And on my birthday, she was always there when I blew out that candle. And every year, I wished for the same thing.

I could have had any girl I wanted, but from the time I was twelve years old, I only belonged to her.

The door flies open, and Brody hops in. I don't miss his busted-up knuckles or the blood on his white T-shirt. Wasting no time turning the key in the ignition, he backs out of the driveway and tears toward our house.

Minutes later, when we get home and head inside, Tate pulls away from me to look at Brody's hands. "What did you do? What if you get kicked off the team?" There's no mistaking the panic in her voice.

Smirking, Brody walks to the sink and washes his hands. "There isn't any chance of that, Tater Tot. Trust me. Something in my gut tells me you aren't the first girl he's done that shit to. But if he learned his lesson tonight the way I think he did … you'll be the last."

After he dries his hands, Tate throws her arms around him. "Thank you, Brody."

"Hey, it's just another Saturday night for me." He shrugs as she releases him. "Just glad you're okay."

Her eyes shift to mine. Her smudged makeup and swollen lip prove just how fucked up this night was.

She gives me a small, sad smile. "I'm going to go shower and lie down. Thanks again."

I nod even though every part of me doesn't want her to be alone. I know she might not want to be around anyone right now, and I need to respect that.

"If you need anything, come get me," I tell her. "I mean it."

She doesn't say anything, just bobs her head up and down before walking upstairs. She's always been someone who deals with her shit alone. Never wanting to burden anyone else.

I want the burden. Even if it's so heavy that it breaks me. I'd gladly carry it if it meant I could save her from having to.

TATE

I toss and turn in bed. My mind reeling from the past few hours, never turning off long enough for me to rest. I took the longest and hottest shower, burning off any remains of Oliver. I got so lucky tonight. I guess the kickboxing and self-defense classes I've taken paid off because I'm certain if I hadn't learned those few moves, I probably wouldn't have gotten away.

I cringe, imagining his lips on mine. How he tasted like beer and cigarettes. A taste I can't seem to get out of my mouth, even after brushing my teeth three times and doubling down on mouthwash.

As I lie here, scared, I think about how pathetic I am. There are women who actually get raped. I got away. I'm fine.

So, why am I afraid to sleep?

After twenty more minutes, I throw my covers off and head into the hallway. And when my hand touches Link's doorknob, I can't stop myself from pushing the door open.

"Tate?" his deep voice drawls in the darkness.

"I can't sleep," I whisper, pushing my back to the door, closing it.

Sitting up, he pulls the covers down next to him. "Come on."

Wasting no time, I rush to the bed and climb in, snuggling next to him.

"I'm sorry if I woke you up."

"You didn't," he answers quickly, wrapping his arms around me protectively. "Get some rest, Tate."

And even though it makes no sense, with my body tucked against his, my eyes grow heavy.

And I do what he said. Not because I have to, but because being in the safety of his bed … my body leaves me no other choice. Because for the first time in as long as I can remember … I feel like I'm home.

The sound of feet on the stairs wakes me, and as I stir, my eyes flutter open. For a moment … I have no freaking clue where I am. That is, until I look around and remember coming into Link's room last night.

"Morning," Link says next to me. "You still grind your teeth when you're sleeping, by the way."

Turning toward him, I flick his shoulder. "I'm aware. It's when I'm stressed or tired. Though I can't imagine why I would be feeling like that, can you?" Yawning, I stretch my arms over my head. "You must have practice today?"

Setting his phone on the nightstand, he nods. "Yeah. Not till the afternoon though." He pauses. "We could, uh … get some breakfast?"

"I'd love that." I smile. "Thank you for being there for me. This feels like old times."

He puts his arm under me, his eyes looking pained. But still, he grins. "You know, there's no reason why it shouldn't be like old times. Maybe we fucked it up for a while. We complicated things with sex, and that was dumb. But you're here. So, let's just make the best of it."

My cheeks heat. "And what about the other times?" I swallow. "The classroom at the benefit dinner? Or … the shower yesterday?"

He shrugs. "I guess we fucked up a few more times, right?"

I know in my heart that it was much more than that. We did what we did because neither of us can keep our hands off of each other. The universe pulls us together with so much force that it's like we never even had a chance. But that doesn't change that he's going to be in the NHL soon. Or that I have big dreams with a career of my own. A career that wouldn't work with his schedule. I refuse to do long-distance even if he wasn't going to be a hotshot professional athlete.

Sitting up, he turns his body and looks down at me. "So, Tate Tracy … friends?"

Even though it shreds my heart into pieces when I hear it out loud, I fake a smile and swallow back the lump lodged in my throat. "Friends." I poke a finger into his chest. "So, does that mean you're going to attend the wedding from hell with me? As *friends*? Or …"

He cocks his head. "No, Tate."

My heart sinks. "Yeah, no. I—I don't blame you. I don't even want to go by myself, and he's my dad—" I start to say, but he puts a finger to my lips, silencing me.

"For whatever reason, your old man and his bitchy fiancée like to put you down. We're going to that wedding. But we aren't going as friends." He stops. "At least not as far as they're concerned."

"Really?" My eyes widen. "And what about after the wedding? Then, what?"

"Then, we'll have a really well performed breakup." He sighs. "I want to stay mad at you, Tate. I want to, but you know I can't. So, let's just have a little fun until it ends, yeah?"

"Yeah." I nod. "But what about—"

"But nothing. Just go with this." Slapping my leg, he slides out of bed. "Now, get your ass ready, and let's go get some food. Time's a ticking."

A part of me is so thankful to have my friend back. The other knows that he's given up on the idea of us. But that's what I wanted, right? That's why I pushed him away?

So, why does it feel like I'm having a heart attack right now? And why does he seem perfectly fine?

10

LINK

"**S**terns, what in the hell are you doing out there? Are you a ballerina or a hockey player, for Christ's sake?"

I snap back to practice, feeling all of my teammates' eyes on me. "Sorry, Coach."

"Dude, you good?" Cam skates next to me. "Because you suck ass right now. Not just ass, but like … donkey ass. Or, no … hippo ass."

"Fuck off." I shrug him off, moving away. "I'm fine."

"If you say so." He glances at Brody. "What in the hell did y'all do last night? He's useless."

I might be playing like crap, but Brody is better than ever. Not that I'm surprised. Not much affects him. He has this weird ability to separate hockey from everything else. And normally, I can too. But not today.

"It was a rough night, Hardy," Brody says, keeping his voice low. "Cut him some slack today. Remember how big of a pansy ass you were when Addy dumped you?"

"So, Link got dumped?" Cam grins. "By the hot roommate?"

Before I can answer, Brody frowns. "No. Nothing like that. Worse. She ran into some trouble last night, and we had to take care of it." Brody taps his stick against mine. "Took a toll on all of us—that's all. But everything's good now. Right, Sterns?"

"Oh, it's fucking peachy."

"Better be," Cam warns. "Now, move your ass. Coach has smoke comin' out of his ears because you're so awful."

As he skates away, I try to get my shit together for the remainder of practice. If this sport is the one main reason I can't have Tate … I'd better at least be fucking good at it.

I leave practice in my own truck. Before going home, I have a stop to make. Tate promised she was going to stay home with the door locked until I got back. I don't think Oliver would be dumb enough to fuck with her again … but you never know.

This morning, I told Tate we could be friends, like old times. I pretended like that was what I wanted, and it sucked ass to make it seem like I was actually okay with it. The last thing I want to do is be her friend. I want to strip her naked and taste every inch of her body. I want to thrust inside of her while she moans my name, scraping her nails into my skin. I want to bury my face between her thighs, letting her ride my tongue like a mechanical bull. I want to fuck the emptiness right from her eyes, making her feel everything all at once.

And I want to take her to breakfast, hand in hand. Kissing her across the booth.

But that would just complicate things worse than they already are. I've worked so hard to be known as one of the top college hockey players in the nation. If I lose focus now, it'll all be for nothing. But I can't just dispose of her the same way she did me. She means too much to me, and it was too fucking hard to treat her like shit before. So, if we have to be friends to make it through the remainder of the year together, I guess that's a price I'm willing to pay if it keeps her close and keeps her safe. I'll even pretend to be her boyfriend for her dad's outrageous wedding because I know, somehow, I'm helping her.

And maybe now that I know what it's like to lose her altogether, it will be easier for me to not cross the line. Maybe.

Pulling into the frat house, I jump out, slamming the door behind me. Brody might have taken care of Oliver last night, but it's my turn now.

Instead of knocking, I push the door open and walk inside. A few dudes look up from the television, but don't seem all that surprised. But then one I've seen around campus walks around the corner, heading toward me.

"Can I help you?" He throws his arms out to the sides. "I see you let yourself in."

"Where's Oliver?" I growl, stepping toward him.

"Your boy already proved his point, Sterns. Get out of here." His eyes narrow. "But pass this message along: Next time one of you comes into this house, to one of our parties, and attacks one of our guys? You'll have more to worry about than Oliver fucking your girl."

Reaching back, I nail him with a punch right in the jaw, gripping his shirt. "Is that what that fucking creep told you? You fucking heard wrong. He attacked her and tried to force himself on her." I tighten my grip, pulling him toward me. "So, fuckface, where is he?"

When he grabs me back, one of the dudes on the couch walks toward us. "Rayce, let him go." His face grows somber as he looks at me. "I saw the whole fucking thing."

Slowly, Rayce lets go of my shirt, never looking away from me. "Saw what, Benson? What the hell are you talking about?"

"I was on the roof, smoking a blunt." He cringes, his eyes traveling somewhere far away. "I heard yelling, so I looked down."

Finally, Rayce looks at his frat brother, his brow creasing.

"By the time I got downstairs, she had gotten away from him, and Brody O'Brien was out back, beating Oliver senseless."

Before Rayce can answer him, Benson nods toward me. "I'll take you to his room. Do what you wish. I have two sisters. I don't tolerate that fucking shit."

As he turns to head upstairs, I'm right on his heels. There's no erasing the memory of the way Tate's body shook against mine when I caught her running inside. Or the look of sheer panic in her wide eyes.

Oliver needs to pay.

Pushing the door open, he walks inside. "Fuck."

"What?" I walk in behind him and gaze around. "Motherfucker."

"He's gone," he whispers, more to himself than me.

Empty drawers are pulled from the dresser. There are no posters, pictures, or any remembrance to prove that this was a monster's room.

"If he comes back, I want to know," I mutter.

Turning toward me, he nods. "I meant what I said. I don't tolerate that. But I'll tell you, I saw his face after O'Brien was finished with him. He's hurting today. I promise."

"Not enough," I mumble and walk out.

It will never be enough for hurting my Tate. And he'll regret the day he ever put his fingers on her.

Tate

I sit on the couch while the guys are at practice. The show *Catfish* is playing, but I'm not really watching it.

Because my mother worries the way that she does and my dad would probably somehow spin it around on me, making me think it was my fault, I choose to keep last night's horror to myself. If I tell Meyer, she'll just freak out, so I decide to not tell her either. The thought of the attention being on me while I explain it all over again … I just can't do it.

I can't say that I haven't looked over my shoulder a thousand times today. And when Holly called me this morning, I ignored it. I'm supposed to work tomorrow night, but seeing as my boss is a complete creep, I think I'll sit that one out.

I feel like such a brat for ignoring Link's and Brody's warnings about the party. Maybe, in some way, I was being defiant. Since we were kids, Link basically tried to keep me in bubble wrap. The only good thing about being in Boston and away from him was that I could do as I pleased without having to listen to him constantly telling me to be careful. I always thought it was just because I was his best friend. It wasn't until graduation night that I realized it was because he loved me.

I had no idea why Link always thought of worst-case scenarios. Or why he was so scared to let me out of his sight. But I guess, last night, I can see why he is the way he is.

My head is filled with so many swirling thoughts, all pulling me one way or another. Some are crazy, telling me I need to go after what I want—Link. The others remind me of the real reasons why it would never work.

I want kids one day. I would never want their life as publicized as mine used to be. Now that I'm on my own, it's a lot better. Luckily, without my dad beside me, nobody really knows who I am. But I remember, as a kid, going to a movie or dinner and having the fans flock to him. I hated it. And I'd hate it even more if it was Link.

Besides, with celebrity comes a whole new world. Other famous people around you, glitz and glamour, and so much temptation. Link has no idea what's to come. But I do.

My phone buzzes, and I smile when I see it's Link. He texted me when he got to practice, asking if I was all right. He did again right after, making sure once again that I was okay and then telling me he had a quick stop to make and then he'd be home. And now, here he is again.

> *Link: You good?*

> *Me: Define good.*

Me: I'm just kidding. I'm watching Catfish and making a hat.

Link: You mean, you are knitting a hat.

I laugh when he sends the grandma emoji after it, but I send back a middle finger emoji.

Link: Be home in five.

Me: 10-4.

Link: Over and out.

I can't stop the stupid grin as I read his cheesy reply.

Seeing how much he worries and how much he cares about my general well-being has shown me something … Link really isn't like my father. But just because he is wired like an actual human being who can show empathy, does that really mean that fame and fortune wouldn't come between us if we ever did get together?

I just don't know.

LINK

I walk into the house, finding Tate on the living room couch, right where I left her. Her hair is pulled into a half ponytail, and she's wearing a baggy sweatshirt and sweatpants. Her fingers work vigorously with the light-gray yarn until she spots me.

"Hey," I say, tipping my chin up.

"Oh, hello." She grins, setting her project down before she squints her eyes at me. "What's behind your back, *friend?*"

"One hand has something in it that I feel like you might want." I cock my head. "So, pick a hand."

"I always love when we play this game." She strums her fingers on her chin, leaning forward. "Left. No … right. No … left. Definitely left. That's the one." Then, she glares playfully. "Although we both know you could switch it to the other one so that I don't get my treat."

"True." Revealing my left hand, I show her the huge-ass package of Reese's. "But I guess you lucked out."

Her eyes widen. "A king size? No way."

Tossing it to the seat next to her, I pull my other hand from behind my back and hand her a can of Diet Coke. She's always preferred fountain soda, but she says cans are the next best thing.

She looks up at me. "Link, thank you." Her hand slowly takes the soda from me, and she smiles, her eyes glossing over. "I'm so happy to have you back. I missed this."

"You missed treats, you mean?" I tease her.

Swatting at me as I take a seat next to her, she rests her head back and looks at me. "No, I missed having my person. I missed *you*. This you." She bites her lip nervously. "I get why you weren't the same to me when I came back."

She looks down, ashamed. "I'm so sorry. I'm sorry for how I left. But I'm mostly sorry that I wasn't there for you when you needed me the most." Her eyes find mine again. "I loved your mom so much. And it haunts me to this day that I wasn't there for her service." She places her hand over mine. "I messed up, Link. But I'll make it right. Or I'll do my best, trying to."

My heart must stop beating in my chest. I think, in life, we all have that one person we talk to about the deep, dark stuff. Those talks that would make you want to crawl under a rock if it were anyone else you were talking to. But when it's your one person—your soul mate, or whatever you'd call it—it somehow seems more tolerable.

"It's okay. I know you felt like you didn't have a choice." I swallow.

"There's always a choice," she whispers. "I'm sorry I made the wrong one."

I don't answer because, truthfully, I don't know what to say. The choice was so clear that night before she left. I was choosing her. And whether she went to Boston or came to Georgia, I wanted to make it work. It had taken me far too long to admit it out loud, but I was finally taking what I wanted.

But after all that has happened, it just doesn't seem that cut and dry anymore. And I no longer know what the fuck we were doing. But I know I want her around. And I know pretending to just be friends is a whole hell of a lot better than being mad at her all the time. Or worse, losing her altogether.

"How bad has it been?" she asks softly, taking my hand. "Everything with you, your dad … losing your mom."

"I've been fine," I say, trying to brush it off.

But when her eyes catch mine and she tilts her head, I know she knows I'm lying. It's wild that, yesterday, I still had a little hatred and anger in my heart toward her. But I guess a situation like last night can quickly snap us back to reality, and maybe, sometimes, we don't need to hang on to our anger and shit forever.

"I, uh … I guess I just never imagined I'd be this young without my mom. You know? I think back to the times I mouthed off as a teenager or when I did stupid shit that kept her awake, worrying, and it makes me want to go back and shake that kid. To tell my younger self to smarten the fuck up."

Tate doesn't talk. She just listens. Continuing to hold my hand, letting me know she's here.

"For so much time at the end, I had to travel back and forth from here to home." I close my eyes for a second. "I should have been around so much more, T. But just like you've always known … hockey comes first. I had to train, even in the offseason. And I had to keep my grades up just to stay on the team." I lean forward, looking away from her. "Dad resents me for it. I know he does. I should have done so much more, and I didn't."

"Link," she whispers, "she wouldn't have wanted you to give up your future. You did what you could. I know you. I know your heart. I know what kind of person you are." She wraps her arms around me. "You're a good man. A great human being. And so much of that was instilled in you from her. You're the person she raised you to be." She kisses my cheek. "She's proud of you—I know she is."

"This is the second person my love for hockey has hurt, Tate." My eyes shift to hers. "If I could go back, I would do more. I'd be there for her more." My throat feels raw. "Nobody tells you how many regrets you'll have once someone dies. How much you wish you had done things differently—better."

"I know." She strokes my hair, her fingers numbing the stabbing pain in my body. "But I promise, everyone feels this way. You did what you could."

"Do you remember when your father was out of town and your mom's cat got hit by a car? Your brothers were either too upset or too freaked out to dig a hole and bury it." She smiles at me sadly. "But you did. You even found a little stone."

"*We* dug a hole," I say, correcting her. "My mother loved that fucking cat. The thing was a dick to everyone else. But he sure loved Mom." I laugh. "The douchebag would claw me in my sleep."

"What about when you spent all of your money on Elton John tickets for her and your aunt freshman year? It was her favorite birthday present, hands down."

I think back to Tate and me staying up half the night, just waiting for the tickets to go on sale. I had saved up money from mowing lawns. Dad could have easily bought them for her, but I wanted to do it myself. So, I snuck over to Tate's, and we watched movies while we waited. Every good memory I have from the time she showed up in Appleton to the day she left revolves around her.

"Yeah, she came home hammered from that concert." I chuckle. "Said she had the best time. She loves that dude's crappy music."

"Crappy? How dare you! He's a freaking legend." She stares at me in disbelief. "Have you heard his new song with Britney Spears?"

"Wait, she's free? How fucking old is she now?" I scratch my head before my eyes widen. "Wait, how old is *he*? He's alive?"

She hits me on the arm. "Do you live under a rock? Yes, she's free! Finally!" Her mouth hangs open. "And of course he's alive! How would he sing a song if he was dead?"

Grabbing her phone, she hits the screen a few times, and some remix of "Tiny Dancer" starts to play.

"Terrible," I say, shaking my head. "Absolutely terrible."

"Give it a few times, and you'll be singing right along. Or humming it randomly. I promise." She turns the music off and flops back on the couch. "Here's what I say. I've never lost a parent, so I could never tell you how to feel. But I think however you feel is okay, Link. Just please, don't beat yourself up. Your mom wouldn't want that. You did so much while she was here. She knew you loved her."

"Yeah, yeah." I roll my eyes, smirking. "Enough feelings for today, deal?"

She laughs, throwing a pillow at me. "You know how much I avoid feelings. But sometimes, it's okay to lay it all out there. But, yeah, I agree. Enough for today." She holds up the remote. "*Catfish*?"

"That shit is fake," I tell her, like I probably have twenty times in the past.

I relax back, knowing I'll get sucked into what might be the most staged show I've ever watched. Aching to touch her, to pull her against me, but knowing I can't. Still, I feel lighter somehow. Just talking to her does that.

Since my mom died, I haven't talked about it with anyone. My father doesn't want to hear it. My brothers and I, well, we don't want to disrespect him by bringing her up, even to each other. And my friends … well, they might be like brothers on and off the ice, but they aren't my person. So, I keep it bottled up. I know that probably isn't the healthiest thing to do, but it's all I know. My mom was the one who would talk to us when we had a bad day. My dad is a good man, but he was brought up in a household where you just didn't talk about things like feelings. And unfortunately, he's carried that with him, even into parenthood.

It isn't going to be easy, letting Tate go again. But I guess I'll cross that bridge when I get to it.

11

TATE

The arena is cold, making Sloane and her friends complain. But not me because I get to wear my newest creation.

"You seriously made that?" Henley points to my head. "I'm insanely jealous right now. My nana tried to teach me to knit once. I just could *not* do it to save my life."

Like Ally and Sloane, Henley also dates a football player. Luckily, tonight, their men had an away game, so I guilted Sloane into all of them coming to the hockey game with me.

Sloane's head bobs up and down. "I want to learn. You have to teach me."

I laugh. "I will. Then, you can join my grandma club."

"I'll be honest," Ally says, chomping on her Skittles. "I have no interest in learning how to do it. I know I'd suck at it and fuck the entire thing up. But if you wanted to make me one with Brooks colors for football games, I would love you forever."

"Done." I grin.

"How's your living situation going anyway?" Ally mumbles, turning toward me. "Things better? And by better, I mean ... have you given him that earth-shattering blow job yet and made him forgive you already?"

I blush, thinking back to the shower. "Uh, it's going good. We've sort of called a truce. We're forgetting the few times we crossed the line, and we've decided to just be friends again."

Every one of their heads whips toward me, and their eyes narrow.

"Girl, that shit does not work," Henley says, her lips forming a straight line. "Take it from me—you can't do it."

"I agree. Once his penis enters your vajayjay, you can't come back from that." Ally gives me a sympathetic smile. "Why are you so hell-bent on being friends anyway? If he's your best friend yet you've hooked up before … it sounds like you might care about him more than on just a friend level."

"Not necessarily true," Henley corrects. "Sometimes, maybe you think you want something, and then you do it, and then once it's done, you're sitting there, probably crying, and you're like … *Wow, what did I do? Why would I have sex with my best friend's brother when I'm in love with my best friend?!*" She talks about a million words a minute. "And then everyone is mad, and you hurt your friend's feelings. And, yeah, it's a mess."

We all stare at her for a moment before Ally breaks the silence.

"We weren't talking about you and your Wade brother drama, good God." She turns back toward me. "Ignore her. She's a whole mess."

"I can hear you!" Henley growls.

"Don't mind them," Sloane finally says sweetly, widening her eyes as she looks at me and tilts her head back to her friends. "They are a bit nutty. So, what made this truce happen, if you don't mind me asking?" Her smile dies, and she looks worried. "We've all heard some things around campus. Things about last weekend." She whispers the words, not wanting to be too loud. "I just want to make sure you're okay, Tate."

"Well, I'm not sure what you've heard, but it could be true."

Sloane whispers in my ear basically the same thing that happened, even the part where Brody showed up and beat the crap out of Oliver. I tense up, watching out on the ice just as the Wolves come out into the arena.

"It's true, unfortunately," I mutter. "What a slimeball, huh?"

"What about work, Tate?" Sloane whispers. "You can't work there with him, obviously. I can see if we need anyone else in the library."

"Actually, he kind of vanished." I keep my voice low. "He gave the Astronomy Center notice that he was stepping down immediately. And he disappeared from the frat house and classes."

"Wow," Sloane utters. "Good."

"Yep." I pull a deep breath into my lungs and let it out, hoping like hell he's really gone for good. "So, yeah, it's been a week, and I'm really glad y'all agreed to come to the game with me."

I am so thankful they came tonight. Even though Oliver is gone, I still don't know where exactly he is. Or if he is coming back. I've told Brody and

Link countless times that I am fine and that I'm not worried. But truthfully, I am.

Oliver was a manager at the Astronomy Center, but he was only a student manager. So, a few days after it happened, before my next shift, I called the actual manager. The one who only seems to work from home and does the bare minimum for the public showings. I explained the situation, told her that there was no way I could work with Oliver again, and that I was quitting. She informed me he had already reached out via email. She planned to stand in as Oliver's replacement until they had time to interview new candidates. Which means I get to keep my job.

I told Holly what happened and warned her to stay as far away from Oliver as possible, if he ever did return. She felt awful for leaving me, but none of it was her fault.

"That sure doesn't look like a friend to me," Henley says, watching as Link looks up at me, tipping his chin up as he waves.

I give him a cheesy thumbs-up and smile. Even as he skates off, my eyes don't leave him.

When he's on the ice, a peace comes over him that I've never seen him have anywhere else. He should be the most on edge out there. Yet it's somehow his safe haven.

And that's why he's right. Hockey will always come first for him. And it should because I know all of his dreams are going to come true. I just wonder how much longer I have with him as ordinary Link before he can't even walk down the street without people freaking out.

I'm not ready for that yet.

LINK

"This is a real barn burner, huh?" Cam says, skating to me after Connecticut scores again.

"Yeah, too close for comfort." I squint up at the clock. "Especially this close to the end. We've gotta hold them down."

We are only leading by one goal. And with two minutes left on the clock, I don't like that. Not at all. If they score now, tying us up, we risk staying tied and going into overtime—or worse … them scoring again and winning.

"We need one more, Sterns." Cam's hand grips my shoulder. "We need a blue Wolf twenty-two."

My head swings to his. "You sure? Could be risky."

Skating backward away from me, he grins. "Guess we'll find out, won't we?"

So far this season, this has been the most intense game yet. We've met our match. For every strength our guys have, Connecticut has one similar or just as impressive. I'm dog-tired. This game has had no downtime and has been one of those where I find myself constantly doing damage control. We aren't trying to show off tonight. We're just trying to get out of here, undefeated.

I watch him head toward Brody, letting him and the others in on the play. No one will suspect this one—at least, that's the idea.

Moments later, the game is back on. Cam skates down the side, subtly passing the puck over to Brody, who calmly moves to the center of the blue line. The forward charges him, thinking he's going to pass it to Cam, Cade, or me. But what he isn't expecting is for him to take the shot himself. And just as planned, he comes at him from the front and not the side, leaving Brody a beautiful opening to slap shot the puck right into the goal.

And he does, sending it in with a whoosh of the net.

The other team tries to come up with something fast, but it's useless. And a minute later, when that horn blares, we leap into each other. Because there's no greater feeling than winning, especially in times like this, when we had to work hard for it.

As if needing her to make this win real, I gaze up. And seeing her smile ear to ear as she jumps up and down, I finally feel the gravity of it.

We won. And Tate's smile shows how proud she is of me. And as corny as it sounds, there's no trophy or award that could top that.

One day, I could find someone else. I could get married, maybe even have kids. But it'll never be like this. I'll never love anyone this fiercely.

And that really fucking sucks.

TATE

I watch the most adorable curly-haired girl run to Cam Hardy, leaping into his arms. Her mom walks up to them, and he kisses her, still holding the little girl protectively.

"You were so great," the girl gushes, keeping her stuffed wolf safely tucked in her arm. "Mommy was worried you were going to lose. I knew you wouldn't."

His eyes move to his girlfriend, who I know is Addison LaConte. I haven't formally met her, but they have to be the world's sweetest hockey couple.

"Is that right?" He lifts an eyebrow. "Doubting me, are you?"

"Me? Nope. Never," she answers before kissing him again.

I watch in what I guess is envy. She seems so confident, so sure in their relationship. Cam is also going to be heading to the pros soon. Yet here they are, living happily ever after.

Why can't I just be wired like everyone else?

I hate that I have this devil sitting on my shoulder, reminding me that I can't have that. Maybe I could. Perhaps it would be different than what I knew, growing up.

"There you are," Link says behind me, his hand touching my waist. "I know; I know. Hold the applause."

"Well, I'll applaud you. But I was waiting for this guy." I nod toward Brody walking out of the locker room. "Nice little stunt you pulled."

"Oh, yeah, that's right." Brody winks. "Please, please. No autographs, Tater Tot. I'm far too tired."

Link's mouth hangs open. "Hey! I scored two more goals than he did!"

"Eh, well, what can I say? That *working against the clock* thing did it for me," I tease him before putting my hand on his shoulder. "I'm joking. You were a beast, as always."

As Brody walks away, Link drops his duffel and wraps his arms around me, pulling me upward until my feet are off the ground. "That's what I thought."

Once he sets me down, I pull my lips to the side and sigh. "Hey, Link. Uh … does your dad ever come to your games?"

Grabbing his bag, he hikes it up on his shoulder and takes my hand as we start to walk toward the exit. "Nah, it's all good though."

"Link—"

"It's fine, T. I promise, I don't care. You hungry? Because I'm starving. There's a pretty kick-ass Italian restaurant. What do you say?"

"Garlic knots?" I raise an eyebrow.

"Obviously," he deadpans, still holding my hand in his. "But I think they have Pepsi products."

I stop walking, pulling my hand from his and crossing my arms across my chest. "Come again?"

"I would, but we agreed that shit's inappropriate for friends to do," he jokes until I punch him in the arm. "I'm kidding. Jesus."

Continuing to walk again, I tug him along with me. "Good. Let's go. Never speak of such things again."

"The coming or the Pepsi?" he drawls arrogantly. "Just to clarify, you know."

"The Pepsi—well, no, I mean … both!" Putting my hand to his mouth, I glare. "Now, shut your mouth, Mr. Inappropriate. Let's go eat."

My heart grows inside my chest as we walk out to his truck, just like we did after his high school games. This really does feel like old times.

Except for the part that, now, we've had sex, among other things. But that doesn't change anything, right?

Yeah … right.

12

TATE

"So, yeah … I'm not going to Dad's wedding," my sister says nonchalantly, chomping on some chips. "Sorry."

I pick my phone up, getting the screen closer to my face. "Bullshit you aren't."

She sighs. "No, I'm really not, T. When he called last night, we got into it. He was being a douche. And look, I've been trying to get better at setting boundaries for myself. Every single time I talk to the man, he manages to make me feel like I'm a failure in a matter of minutes." She shakes her head. "I hate to leave you hanging, but for my own mental well-being, I'm skipping out on this."

I slouch back in my bed. "Damn. How can I be mad when you put it like that?" I pinch the bridge of my nose.

Meyer has always been better at drawing a line and sticking to it. Me? I've always been afraid of hurting someone's feelings. Even if it is our dad—and he has been the definition of an asshole to me.

I draw in a deep breath. "If it makes you feel better, I won't be attending alone." I cringe. "Link is going with me. As my … well, fake boyfriend."

Her eyes widen, and she gets her face about an inch from the camera. "What?! Oh my gawd! Are you serious? Last I knew, he was pretending to hate you. Now, he's volunteered himself to go to the shit show that will be this wedding?" She squeals. "I need *all* the details."

Before I can respond, her forehead crinkles. "Wait, why would you need a fake boyfriend? I'm so confused."

"Honestly, I have no idea how or why it happened. At the benefit, I was talking to Dad and Margo. As always, they were being—"

"Fuckheads?" Meyer deadpans, interrupting me.

"Well, yeah. Dad did that thing where he basically calls me a failure. Margo was chipping in, making my job out to be a joke. Short story, Link appeared out of nowhere and was all, 'I'm her boyfriend. Of course I'll be at the wedding.' And Margo's face—" I laugh, throwing my head back. "She was *so* annoyed."

"Why wouldn't she be? She's signing herself up for old balls for life, and you're going to roll into her special day with a goddamn snack for everyone to look at." She snorts, giggling harder. "This is great."

"It's really crazy though. He went from hating me, to hating me but being sexy about it, to offering to be my fake date, to rescuing me, to now being my best friend again. It hasn't been a whirlwind. It's been a whole dang tornado."

"I bet. Wait, why did you say he rescued you?"

I swallow. *Dammit.* I didn't mean to let that slip. But then again, she'd want to know.

"Well, you know how I started that job at the Astronomy Center?"

She nods.

"So, my boss, Oliver, was having a party. I went to it, and … well, let's just say, he ended up being a creep." When I see her eyes look panicked, I quickly add, "And don't worry. I used my kickboxing and self-defense skills to get out of there before anything happened. And Link and Brody showed up right after and brought me home. But either way, it scared me." I scrunch my nose up. "And opened my eyes to knowing I need to be more careful."

"Why didn't you tell me?" She looks hurt.

I shrug my shoulders. "I was embarrassed. I didn't want to make it into a big deal."

"T, it *is* a big deal," she says boldly.

"I know." I smile sadly. "You know how I am sometimes."

Meyer knows that I have this thing where I stuff issues way down deep to avoid the discomfort of actually dealing with them.

"I'm just so glad Link was there for you, Tate. Thank God."

"Yeah," I mutter. "Now, enough with the shitty talk. Tell me something fun."

And then I listen to her tell me what's been going on in her life. From dating to hookups and everything in between. I'd be lying if I said I wasn't bummed she wouldn't be with me at the wedding. But I'm thankful Link will be.

A part of me knows the wedding weekend will be filled with backhanded comments and cringe-worthy moments, and I'll probably want to strangle my father a few times. But attending this wedding is just who I am. For my emotional well-being, it would be easier if I could just skip it and not think twice. Unfortunately, I know me, and I can't do that. So, I'll be there. And somehow, I know my fake date will make it all easier.

I just need to remember he's my fake boyfriend and not my real one.

LINK

I lace my skates up for practice, my head nodding to the music blaring from my AirPods, likely too loud.

A hand on my shoulder startles me, and when I pull the earbud out and crane my neck to look up, I find Cam and Brody. Both grinning like morons.

"Sunday, we're going on a guys' fishin' trip," Cam drawls, raising his eyebrows. "Your ass had better be there."

"Manly man's day," Brody boasts. "Beer and fishing. All. Day. Long."

I clear my throat and finish lacing my skates. "Yeah, I can't. Got plans for Sunday. Y'all have fun though."

Cam's hand comes down on my shoulder again. "Dude. Besides hockey, we ain't hung out in a long damn time. Sunday, we have the whole day to fuck off. And Monday, we don't have to be at practice till the afternoon. So, this is the perfect chance. You know, get a little buzz on, pretend we know shit about fishing, and chill."

I stand, holding my arms out at my sides. "I'm sorry. It sounds fun, but I'm going to Florida. I have to go to a wedding."

Brody narrows his eyes. "Wait a second. Tater Tot is going to her daddy's wedding this weekend." His face lights up. "You're going with her? Aren't you, you romantic fuck?" He wiggles his eyebrows. "I've noticed you two have been putting off the good vibes and shit."

"Is that true?" Cam leans on his hockey stick. "If so, you get a pass. Only because Brody says she's nice and I'd love for you to stop being a dick to this poor chick. And this, well, this would sure be a start." He cringes. "Annnd … I feel guilty that I potentially fucked up you guys getting together sooner by telling the poor girl you were banging someone else and then not telling you."

"Yeah, that was a dickhead move," I point out. "And we're friends," I say, trying to appear uninterested. "Her old man is a prick. And his soon-to-be bride's no better. Tate's taken a lot of shit from him over the years. I'm only going to make sure the entire event doesn't consist of her being a punching bag."

Brody and Cam share a look, both seeming amused, before Brody slaps me on the back. "Attaboy. I knew you'd come around."

"Glad to see I won't be the only whipped one on the team from here on out." Cam nods in agreement, smirking. "Hey, maybe we could double date."

"We're fucking friends, you clowns!" I groan before heading toward the door. "Are we practicing? Or y'all wanna play matchmaker all damn day? And for the record, you both suck at it. Tate's my best friend, nothing else. Not anymore anyway. We tried that; it doesn't work. So, shut up, and let's go work."

Cam continues to grin, strutting by me. "Yes, sir. If you say so."

Brody mopes behind him. "I thought I was your best friend, dick." He pouts.

Clasping my arm around his shoulders, I laugh. "Oh, you are too, O'Brien. You are too."

And I mean it. He and Tate are both my best friends. Cam too.

But the thing that separates Tate from my other best friends is ... the dirty thoughts constantly running through my brain, involving her.

132

13

TATE

"All ready?" Link says, poking his head into my room.

When his eyes drink me in, only in my tank top and cheeky panties, he swallows. "Sorry … I'll, uh … I'll come back."

Snatching my jeans, I shimmy into them. "Oh, shut up. Nothing you haven't seen before, right?" Grabbing my Brooks long-sleeved crew-neck shirt, I pull it over my head. "And I'm as ready as I'll ever be."

His hand grips my duffel bag, and he hoists it up. "Is this all set? I'll go put it in the truck. I even got us a sweet playlist to listen to on the drive."

"Ooh, should we get snacks? Like Nerds Rope, Starburst, and chips? You know, all the good stuff?"

His eyes twinkle as he grins proudly. "Already on it. I stopped at the store on the way back from morning practice." He starts toward the hallway but turns. "I'll be in the truck. Go to the bathroom. We aren't stopping every half hour for potty breaks."

"Who does that? Not me." I shrug.

"Yeah … right," he grunts and heads downstairs, knowing I am that person who feels the need to go to any restroom I pass. Even if I don't really need to pee that bad, I get it in my head that I do.

It seems exactly like old times, before things shifted and then were awful. It's strange that we can suddenly be so close again. I don't deserve this from him, but this just goes to show how good of a person Link is. And even though it's only two nights and we have to attend something I'd rather not … I'm actually excited for this time with him.

The trouble is, I'm mostly excited to pretend he's my boyfriend. Because for a few hours … that means I'll get to feel like he's mine.

LINK

I plaster on a fake smile, pretending it's all good. Fronting that I'm having fun. But deep down, I'm fucking hurting.

I don't know why I thought we could be friends. Why I volunteered myself as tribute to fake being her man when that's all I actually want in reality. At least, it won't be hard to play along. I just won't want to stop acting. Even once we're back at Brooks.

"Bailey Zimmerman is my favorite!" She smiles. "His songs are sad. I like that."

I knew he was one of her favorites when I added the songs to this playlist. She plays music in her room constantly—never too loud though. She's never liked her music so loud that it gives her a headache. But it's always been clear that she has music for every mood.

"So, T, what's on the agenda tonight?" I glance over at her. "Anything fun?"

"Rehearsal dinner." She sighs. "I can't believe I have to stand there with Margo without Meyer."

Tate told me Meyer wasn't coming. I can't really say I blame the girl. Meyer has always been wired more like I am. She has no problem cutting someone off if she wants to. Tate has never been able to set a boundary with her father. That's why it seemed so out of character when she took off to Boston, leaving me behind. She'd always done her best not to hurt anyone. Yet there she was, tearing me to pieces from across the country.

"We could put some eye drops in her drink, make her shit herself in front of everyone." I cringe. "Although I'd never be able to look at a white dress the same."

"That's tempting," she says, chewing on a piece of Nerds Rope. "If she wasn't pregnant, I'd be sold on that."

I can feel the pain in her voice. Her dad is finally getting the son he's always wanted, and I'm sure, Tate being his daughter, that has to sting a little. Just because he is having a boy, it doesn't mean the child is promised to be some big-shot hockey player. But I don't think anyone could tell her father that.

Changing the subject, she pops her feet up onto the dashboard and looks at me. "They're going to be able to tell—you know that, right?"

"Tell what?" I ask, confused.

"That we aren't actually a couple." She leans her seat back. "Margo will sniff us out within an hour. Guaranteed."

I look straight ahead at the road for a moment, thinking. She might not be wrong. Ever since the shower that day, we haven't done anything stepping over the line of friendship. Even though it's killed me not to. I don't want to scare her away.

Suddenly, I get an idea.

"So … we need to practice then." I swing my eyes to her. "Once we get there, we'll only have an hour or so before the rehearsal dinner. So, I guess we'd better get started right now." I grin. "You know, *if* we want to really sell it."

Her eyes widen as she swallows nervously.

"Okay," she mumbles. "Let's practice."

TATE

"Look, a Starbucks full of people," Link muses, pulling the truck into the parking lot. "Lesson one: public affection. Let's get to work."

I eagerly unbuckle my seat belt and climb out of the truck. Maybe I'm excited to learn, to make sure we really sell this *we are a couple* thing. Or maybe I just want the treatment of being Link's girlfriend without actually having to commit to it.

As we walk toward the door, he looks my way. "Damn, T. You're already failing."

I think for a second before quickly grabbing his hand. His fingers lace with mine, instantly making the butterflies that were asleep in my stomach wake up.

"Better," he says, pulling the door open with his free hand and letting me in first.

We head to the line, and he positions my body in front of his. Placing his hands on my waist, he holds me there. But I do him one better by taking half a step back, pressing my ass into his body.

"That's it," he mumbles, his chin on my shoulder and his mouth close to my ear.

I crane my neck to look at him, and all I want to do is connect my lips to his. I know I can't. This is simply practice for tonight. But when he's so close and he smells this good … damn, it's hard not to.

Instead, I press my forehead to his.

That is, until the barista yells, "Next."

In the midst of everything, I forgot to look at the menu.

"Oh Lord." I nervously gaze at the long list of items before looking at him again. "I don't even know, Link."

"Me neither. This shit is fancier than Dunkin' Donuts." His eyes land on something, and he steps around me, keeping his arm around my waist. "We'll take two of those cookie crumble things."

"Size?" the barista with blue hair and bright green glasses mumbles, looking unimpressed.

"Uh … large, I guess?" Link shrugs.

"Venti," she corrects him.

"Maybe?" He tilts his head.

She looks annoyed but presses the screen a few times. "Is that all?"

His eyes scan the cooler, and he jerks his chin upward. "Nah, she'll take a birthday cake pop." Pulling me to him, he kisses my forehead. "Is that all, babe?"

Knowing damn well I don't need a cake pop after the amount of candy I just ingested and Lord knows how much sugar is in that drink he ordered us, I smile up at him anyway. "Sounds perfect to me. You're the best." Pressing my lips to his as quickly as I can, I turn back toward the counter before my eyes catch his.

I didn't need to kiss him to sell it to this random person that we're a couple. I just did it because I couldn't help myself.

We both know we're walking a dangerous line, acting this way. But I don't think either of us has the ability to stop.

Besides, everyone knows that Link Sterns as a fake boyfriend still beats the hell out of anyone else as a real boyfriend any day of the week.

Once we gather our order, we head toward the door, hand in hand.

"Excuse me, miss. Are you Harvey Tracy's daughter?" a man says, coming alongside us. "Is … is he here too?"

I stare at him for a few seconds before appearing confused. "Harvey? No. My father's name is Donald."

His eyes widen, and he steps back, murmuring, "Oh, whoops. Sorry," before walking away.

I don't need to look at Link to know he's grinning at me. He's seen me do that countless times. Sometimes, I pretend like I don't speak English. Sometimes, I say I don't have a father and fake cry. And some days, I just make up a fake name for my dad. Because the truth is, I don't have any interest in entertaining his fans. Maybe that makes me a bitch, but I guess I'm okay with it.

14

LINK

I stare out the window, watching the waves crash onto the sandy white beach before rolling back, only to crash again.

When we arrived, I quickly showered and changed into a button-up shirt. Tate has been in the bathroom, getting ready for the rehearsal dinner. I can tell she's nervous about this whole event, yet she's trying her best to remain optimistic.

"All right," she says softly from behind me, "let's go get step one of the shit show over with, shall we?"

Turning slowly, I pull a deep breath into my chest from the sight of her. She's wearing a strapless baby-blue dress, her hair pulled up in a bun, leaving her back and neck bare. Her brown eyes look like a deer in headlights, and I know it's because she's uncomfortable with how this night is about to go. Not because of me, but because her father always seems to put her on edge. He enjoys it too, almost treating it like a job.

"You look, uh, good." I swallow, stuffing my hands in my pockets to stop myself from reaching for her. "Really good."

No other woman could ever put me at ease one minute while making me squirm the next the way Tate does. She's my greatest comfort while also making me insane.

"Thanks." She smiles nervously, and suddenly, it feels like we're headed to the fucking prom or some shit. "Should we go?"

"Yeah, yeah. Let's head over." I nod, pulling my hands from my pockets and opening the door. "It's just up the beach, right?"

"Yep. So, if we need to escape, at least we know we won't be far," she jokes, but I know there's actually some truth to her words.

As we head onto the beach, her hand finds mine.

"Never know when they could be watching, right?" she says softly when I look at her.

"Right," I answer.

Trudging along, I wonder if she's only holding my hand because it's an act, or does she want to? And if she wants to, is it saving her the way she's always saved me?

"Link," she whispers, "thank you for being here. For doing this. But mostly, just for letting me in again." She pauses, suddenly looking sad. "I know if that awful night hadn't happened, we wouldn't be here together. So, I guess something good came out of it. Right?"

I stop, turning toward her. "No matter what, we would have found our way back. There's no way we wouldn't have." My chest rises as I drag in a breath. "I'm real sorry for what happened when you showed up at my dorm. I wish … I wish I had known you were there."

She smiles sadly, attempting to chuckle. "Why? Would you have stopped what you were doing?" I hear the pain, and I know that must have hurt her when it happened.

"Yes," I say bluntly. "In a fucking heartbeat."

Just as my hand reaches for her cheek, I hear Margo's grating voice in the distance.

I cup Tate's face. "Don't freeze up, T. Just go along with it this weekend. After that, we can go back to normal."

TATE

Normal.

My heart feels like a sharp pain is running through it. I don't even know what our normal is.

Taking a breath, I nod slowly. And when his lips touch mine, my eyes flutter shut, and I turn my brain off, savoring every second of him kissing me. My mind knows that this kiss doesn't mean anything, yet every single cell in my body feels it. And somehow, it feels anything but meaningless. Or fake.

It feels right. And even though I made the rule to not date athletes to keep myself safe … I want more.

He tastes like mint and feels like heaven. And when he pulls back, I find myself inching forward, wishing for it to go on forever.

"I think we sold it, T," he utters, though he isn't smiling.

As he starts walking again, his hand finds mine, and I trail behind him silently. My brain has so many thoughts that I barely hear Margo's voice calling to us again. And even when it registers, I continue looking down, lost in a world where Link kisses me deeply and it never has to end.

"Babe," Link says, giving my hand a slight squeeze, "Margo here is talking to you."

I move my gaze from the sand to the lady in front of me. In her flowy white sundress and her deep red hair in waves down her back, she looks like Princess Ariel. Only her soul is ugly.

"Sorry, what?" I say, still frazzled.

"I asked if you've seen your father. He said something about going to get ice earlier and never came back." She doesn't hide the eye roll. "I figured he came to visit you or something. You know, to see if he could do anything for his *Princess*."

Just like she didn't hide her eye roll, I don't hold back the laugh that comes from my mouth. "Um, no. No, he didn't." Suddenly, I frown. "In fact, when has he ever seen if he could do anything for me?"

"Oh, like paying for your college, you mean? Or your car?"

"You have no idea what you're talking about," I growl in a tone of voice that I have never used on Margo or my father.

"Oh, but I do. All so that you can be a bitch to us," she hisses.

I step toward her. It's clear she's stressed today, and the last thing I want to do is upset a pregnant girl more. But she's out of line, and she's about to find that out.

"Student loans, Margo. I have a lot of them. Why, might you ask? Because I refuse to take a dime from that man. As for my car? I bought that relic with the money I'd saved in high school from waitressing." My nose almost touches hers, the steam rolling from my body. "And if by being a bitch, you mean, taking both of your shit with a smile and always feeling like a complete failure … then I guess I am!"

"What in the world is going on here?" Dad appears, coming to Margo's side. "Tate, I know you aren't causing trouble on our big day, are you?"

"No," I say smugly. "Your big day is tomorrow, right?"

"It was nothing, Harvey. I was simply trying to calm her down. She's just … so unstable today." She mutters the last part, and even though I've never hit another person in my life—aside from Oliver—I would right now, if only she wasn't pregnant.

"Tate, if you're going to cause trouble, you can go," my dad says, pulling her against him. "I know this is hard for you. I know you've probably had your mother in your ear for days. But please, this day is important to us."

"I'm not going to cause trouble, Dad." I fight the urge to cry because, frankly, the shell of a man in front of me who I call Dad doesn't deserve my tears.

"And if you had been here a minute or two sooner, you'd have seen your bride here treating your daughter—your own blood—like garbage," Link says, glaring at my father.

"I don't know what type of shit you've been feeding Margo here, but we both know you don't do shit for either of your daughters. Hence why one of them isn't here." Link holds my hand protectively, stepping a little closer to my dad. "But Tate's here. She's here because she loves you and because it's who she is. So, make it easier on her and try to act like a goddamn parent." He shrugs. "Or we can head on back to Brooks. Choice is yours."

I feel the heat radiate from Link.

"Also, I'm not afraid to ruin your big day if you do anything to upset my girl, I promise."

"You're out of line, son. Just because you're a hotshot *college* hockey player doesn't mean you can act big and bad. You aren't shit," Dad growls, eyeing Link over. Eventually, his eyes move to mine, and he gives me the smallest nod. "I appreciate you being here. Maybe, for both your and Margo's sake, you ought to just watch the ceremony. You know, instead of being in it."

Both relief and hurt wash over me. But the relief outweighs the hurt, and I nod once. "Maybe that's for the best."

"Oh, that's sad," Margo says, pretending to care. "But I suppose that means you're free tonight. Since this dinner is for the wedding party only."

"Margo, I think we can make an excep—"

"No, it's okay," I cut my father off, giving Margo a sickly-sweet smile. "She's right. Enjoy! We'll see you tomorrow. For the *big* day."

Before another word can be said, I turn, pulling Link with me before my father changes Margo's mind and I'm stuck with the she-devil all damn night.

"Well, that was … interesting," Link drawls, pulling my body closer to his. "Now what?"

"Now, we hit this all-inclusive resort's bar. Courtesy of the future Mr. and Mrs. Tracy." I look at him and raise an eyebrow. "What do you say?"

"I say, hell fucking yes."

I look down at our hands and sigh. "Guess we don't need to pretend. You know, since we won't be around them."

His hand drops mine quickly before he smirks. "Yeah, but you never know where they have eyes." And then he scoops me up, carrying me across the sand. "Still gotta sell it. Besides, don't actors say it's easier to stay in character?"

"That's what I hear," I say, looking up at him.

"I'm sorry your dad sucks, T." He looks straight ahead, walking us across the sand effortlessly. "You're a good person for coming down here, you know? Had it been my dad, I would have been Meyer in this situation and skipped out."

"You say that, but look at you right now. Here with me, even after everything I've done." I lick my lips. "We aren't that different, you and I."

"That's just how I am with you, Tate," his voice almost rasps. "Nobody else gets this side, I promise."

And then we're both quiet. Because we're aware that if we say much else, we'll both know that when it comes to pretending we're just friends … it's bullshit.

LINK

The sun begins to set as Tate slides another shot glass my way and laughs, tipping her own back.

I watch her throat bob as the liquid goes down, and even though she's had quite a few by now … she still scrunches her nose up and slaps her palm against the wooden bar.

Her dad might be a douche, but he booked us—well, her—a private villa at the same all-inclusive resort his wedding is at. And judging by the amount Tate has laughed tonight, she's having a hell of a time. Even in spite of the run-in with Margo, the meanest bride to ever grace this beautiful beach.

Maybe this time, the ball will be in my court. I'll get a call from the NHL anytime now. And when I do, I'll be the one leaving. Only I won't leave without a good-bye.

"Remember that time when you tried to teach me how to drive a stick shift?" She snorts, putting her head against my shoulder as she laughs. "That was terrible."

"No, *you* were terrible," I remind her. "I taught my younger brothers how to drive a stick, and they did just fine. I think, in your case, it was the student who failed and not the teacher."

She picks her head up and pouts. "So mean, Link. So. Mean." She takes her finger and touches my nose. "Always trying to hurt my feelings."

I take a sip from my beer and throw my head back. "I could have been a lot meaner."

She bites her lip as her eyes float down my face. "Maybe."

She gazes at my lips for a moment before, finally, she blinks a few times. Standing up, she grabs my hands and pulls me. "Dance with me, big guy. And make it good. Remember … you never know where there could be eyes watching us."

Just as she leads us to the dance floor, "Thinkin' Bout Me" by Morgan Wallen comes on, making it a slower beat.

My hands find her waist as she moves in my grasp, tossing her head back. Her body looks so hot as she gazes up at me. Her slender arms wrap around my neck, and I move my hands to her back, sliding them down lower and lower until I palm her ass. Not giving a fuck if we're selling this boyfriend-girlfriend thing or not. The only thing I'm thinking about right now is how bad I want her.

I dip my head down, hovering my lips not even an inch from hers, but never making contact. My heart clenches in my chest because I don't know how I'm supposed to walk away this time.

It took me a while last time to feel semi-normal. And even then, I wasn't great. This time, there've been too many lines crossed. I'm never coming back from this. And to be honest, I don't really care. Because a night like this? It'll make it worth it.

Even while we're dancing, not saying a word, it's like her soul travels into mine. I've never felt so close to another human being in my entire life, and I doubt I ever will.

We dance through a few more songs, now with her ass to me, making my cock ache with need. Both a sweaty mess and tipsy from the shots. And that's when my phone starts to vibrate in my pocket. Pulling one hand away from her, I take it from my pocket, frowning when I see a weird number.

I consider ignoring it, but with three brothers, a father, and a shit ton of friends, I just never know when something could be an emergency.

Turning her toward me, I put my mouth to her ear. "I'll be right back. I gotta take this. I'll stay right there," I say, pointing to a spot just outside the bar, where I'll be able to see her. "I'll watch and make sure everything's okay."

Giving me a cheesy thumbs-up, she swipes the back of her hand against her forehead, brushing the loose strands from her skin.

Once I get far enough away from the speakers to where I can hear, but close enough to see Tate, I swipe my thumb across the screen.

"Hello?"

"Hello, Link Sterns?" a deep voice answers from the other end.

"Uh, yep. That's me."

"Oh good. I hope this isn't a bad time." He chuckles. "It's a little loud on your end."

"No, it's a fine time. Who is this?"

"Well, this is Rob Blake. I'm the general manager of the—"

"Los Angeles Kings," I say, finishing his sentence.

"Yes, sir. Do you have any idea why I'm calling you?"

"Uh, well … I've got an idea." I continue to watch Tate, making sure nobody goes around her. And so far, they don't.

"We've been watching you for quite some time now. Especially this season, you really have unlocked a whole new level of potential. The sky's the limit, kid. And if you say yes, we'd love to have you join the team. We want you to be a King, Link."

"Holy shit, really?" I rest my head on a beam post.

I've been working my entire life for this—to get drafted into the NHL. Even though I hoped this day was coming, it's still beyond what I ever imagined. It was the goal, but I never knew for certain that I'd make it here. It's surreal.

"Really." He laughs. "We'd need you here right after the school year ends to start training. So, what do you say?"

Tate's eyes find me, and she continues to dance, almost like she's putting on a show just for me. My heart sinks, and I swallow.

"When do you need an answer by?"

"Ideally, right now," he tosses back. "But I'll tell you what. You've probably got family, and I know you have to talk about this with Coach LaConte. So, I'll give you a few weeks. Does that work?"

"Yes." I nod. "That's perfect. Thanks."

"Talk to you soon, Mr. Sterns. Have yourself a good night."

And when he ends the call, I stare down at my phone. Months ago, before she came back, I wouldn't have needed a few weeks. I would have said yes, absolutely. But now, she's here. And even though I would never choose anyone over hockey, I just wish I could have both.

But Tate has a rule. And she isn't going to change it now.

By the time I gather myself up and walk back to Tate, she's getting another drink at the bar. She's giggling, her cheeks a deep red from a combination of alcohol and dancing.

Downing her shot, she throws her arms around my neck. "I missed you!" she squeals. "Who were you talking to?"

I shouldn't pile on to her weekend. It's already fucked up enough. But if I don't tell her now, when would be the better time? I've got to eventually, so why wait?

"The general manager of the Los Angeles Kings." I swallow, watching her shrink into herself. "They offered me a position on their team."

Slowly, her fingers unhook from my neck, and she slides onto the stool next to me. "When?"

"After this school year is over, I'd have to go out there."

Her eyes gloss over for a split second before she blinks it away and plasters on that same smile she gives everyone. Even when it hurts. Hugging me again, she buries her face into my neck. "That's great, Link. I'm so proud of you. Your whole life has led up to this moment. All your dreams are coming true." And when she kisses my cheek before letting me go, I swear I see a tear roll down her face. "I always knew you'd make it."

Before that phone call, it did seem like all of my dreams were coming true. I was holding her close. She was laughing. Now, I'm not sure.

I've been grinding my way up this mountain, the NHL being the finish line. But I don't want to stand at the top alone. I want Tate next to me, and I can't have her.

Her eyes lock with mine. "You're leaving anyway," she yells over the music.

"What?"

"You're leaving anyway," she says again, moving toward me and stepping between my legs. "Can we just stay here, in this bubble, until Monday? Just pretending like I'm yours and you're mine." Her lips connect with mine, and she kisses me hard before pulling back. "We both know that once you go to LA, you aren't going to have any time for me. If all I'm going to have is now … I want it to be enough to last me the rest of my life."

I want to give in to her so fucking badly. I want to throw her over my shoulder and take her back to our villa. Keep her up all night, devouring every inch of her body and memorizing it to have forever.

But when she sobers up in the morning, she could bolt again. And I'd take the rest of the school year as her friend, just to keep her close by.

"Tate, we can't." I push her back softly, shaking my head. "We just got back to being good. Last time we had a night like this … it ruined everything."

She looks hurt, her eyes shining with tears.

"Yeah. What was I thinking?" She tries to shrug it off. "I'm going to go back to the villa. You should stay and celebrate."

And then she leaves the bar, walking back onto the beach. And as I squint my eyes through the window, I watch as she takes off just as fast as her legs will take her down the beach.

Before I can stop myself, I'm running after her. I had no idea it was raining, but I feel it now as it pelts against my face, stinging my skin.

"Tate," I yell, putting my arms around her waist and stopping her, pulling her ass against me. "Why are you running away?"

"Link, stop!" She tries to push my hands away, but I anchor her down.

I spin her around, cupping her cheeks. "Talk to me."

"The lines are blurred. Everything seems better, but it's so fucked up," she cries, her face dripping with raindrops. "I'm so happy that you made it. The NHL is what you've wanted for as long as I've known you. But I'm going to lose you—again. So, why can't we give it all we've got this weekend? Why can't we pretend to ourselves that everything is okay and that you aren't leaving? And that I'm staying?"

Her pouty lips pull in a breath. "We'll never be able to be friends, Link. Maybe it's been easy for you these past few weeks, but they've been hell for me. Just like before."

"You think it's been easy for me?" I growl, stepping closer so that our bodies are touching. "Do you think it's easy for me, knowing you've been across the hall and I can't come in there and fucking touch you? Or when you're eating breakfast in the morning and all I want is to throw you on the countertop and eat you for breakfast?" My hand slides down her cheek, and I brush my thumb against her lips. "I can't kiss you good-bye in the morning, and I can't hold you in my arms while I drift off to sleep." I dip my head lower. "Pretending we're just friends isn't hell for me, Tate. It's worse."

Pulling my hands from her face, I slide them down her back and under her ass. When I hoist her into the air, her legs wrap around my waist, and I kiss her. I kiss her so hard that when I finally pull back, her lips are swollen and red.

"Take me to bed, Link," she whimpers, grinding herself against me. "I need you right now. And we'll deal with the consequences tomorrow. Together."

I walk us toward our villa, her lips on mine, her tongue teasing me of what's to come.

Walking the few stairs to the front door, I slide it open and step inside.

Tossing her on the bed, I look down at her soaking dress, which is now completely transparent. Her full breasts are visible through the fabric, her perfect nipples poking through, making all the blood rush to my cock.

Leaning forward, I pull it over her head, tossing it to the side of the bed in a pile. Sliding my hand down between her breasts, I stop at the wet fabric of her thong before tearing it off.

"You're the most beautiful thing in the world," I say, looking down at her. "An angel."

"Link," she whispers, "please."

Unbuttoning my shirt, I throw it before dropping to my knees and inching forward toward the bed. Hooking my hands behind her thighs, I pull her toward me.

"I've wanted to taste you for so long, T." I gaze up at her. "So perfect. And so ready for me, aren't you?"

She nods slowly but looks nervous. "No one's ever … done this." She swallows. "You've had all my firsts, Link. And you always will."

Something swells inside my chest because I know that no man will ever be able to claim that. She's given me all of her firsts, and that's the best gift she could have given me.

But I don't just want her firsts. I want her lasts too.

My tongue dips inside of her, and I continue to grip her thighs, spreading her wider.

Leaning forward to get a better look, she grips my hair.

She's so much sweeter than I ever imagined she'd be. The truth is, this is a first for me too. I've never wanted to do anything this personal with anyone else. And knowing no other man has been here on Tate means something to me.

I put her feet on my shoulders, diving in deeper before slipping a finger inside.

"Link," she moans as my tongue draws circles on her sensitive spot. "Oh … my … God."

Her grip on my hair tightens, and her hips move greedily. "Wait, Link. I'm—"

I gaze up at her, never backing down or slowing my movements as her moans turn to cries and her hips buck faster. I feel her pulsating as she continues to yank my hair.

Coming down slowly, she tosses her head back on the bed and drags in a few shaky breaths. "Wow," she says, breathless. "Wow. Wow. Wow."

Climbing over her, I smirk. "Good, huh?"

"Something like that," she says before looking me up and down. "Why are you still in shorts and I'm naked?"

"Tate, if you don't want to have—"

"I want everything," she answers, sitting up and unbuttoning my shorts. "Don't stop loving me tonight."

Tugging my shorts off, Tate moves her hand to my cock and strokes a few times, making me hiss.

Lying down, she opens her legs bravely. "Give me all of you." Her voice sounds gritty and so not her usual self. "I don't want anything between us."

When I stare at her, she bites her lip. "I'm on birth control. You're the only person I've been with."

"What?" I whisper. "You weren't … in Boston?"

She shakes her head shyly. "I hated anyone else's hands on my body. It made me feel sick." Her voice is barely a whisper. "It's always been you. And tonight, I just want to be as close to you as I can. So, as long as you're clean—"

"I am," I say quickly. "I promise."

Knowing I'm about to feel her has me sucking in a breath. Like, really *feel* her. Nothing between us, just me and Tate.

I stare down at her, palming myself for a moment as I take in the most beautiful angel I've ever laid eyes on.

Gently, I lower myself onto her. As I nudge inside of her, my hands grip hers, pressing hers to the bed.

She winces as I move deeper inside of her.

"I'll take it slow," I whisper, kissing her quickly. "If it hurts, tell me."

She might not be a virgin, but she's only had sex one time. The last thing I want to do is hurt her and make this not good for her.

"Link," she whispers as tears gather in her eyes, "I love you. I'm sorry I am the way I am."

"Shh." I kiss her again. "It's okay, Tate. Don't apologize for anything."

Pushing in further, I freeze when she whimpers.

"Don't stop." Her grip on my hand tightens. "Don't you dare stop."

Moving again, I kiss her neck to help her relax. Dragging my tongue down her chest, I pull her nipple into my mouth and feel her dripping on my cock.

"You all right?" I ask, pulling back and looking at her.

"Never better," she whispers. "It's okay. You won't hurt me."

"Oh, I could. But I won't." I pick up the pace, moving in and out of her faster and deeper with each thrust. "Is this okay?"

"Yes." She grits her teeth before releasing my hands and moving them to my back.

Her nails dig into my flesh as she hooks her feet behind my back. And when her tongue drags up my neck, my balls start to tingle just as I feel her begin to squeeze me back.

"Link, I'm going to—"

"Me too, baby. I'm right there with you," I grunt, thrusting faster just as her hand reaches down and cups my balls, making me come even harder.

I'm spinning. And falling. And frozen in time as everything goes black and I pour myself inside of her, claiming her with my seed.

And when I can finally see again, I kiss her forehead and grin.

"Damn." I laugh.

"Yeah … damn." She smiles. And unlike the last time we did this, she doesn't look sad or spooked.

She looks happy. And I just want to keep that smile on her face. If she'll let me.

15

TATE

I watch my father and Margo stare at each other while the pastor reads the vows. I knew they wouldn't write their own. My father just doesn't run that deep. In fact, he's about as shallow as a puddle on a paved driveway in a rainstorm. And Margo … well, she's not the sharpest tool either. I'm not one to question someone's intelligence, but the way she spoke to her fiancé's daughter yesterday is proof that she's a few sandwiches short of a picnic. Or she's just really, really mean.

Link's hand splays across my thigh, and when I peer over at him, he winks. Despite the fact that my father's reaction hurt my feelings, I'm more than grateful to *not* be standing up there next to my soon-to-be stepmother.

Meyer was flying home to be with our mom today. She was going to surprise her, knowing our mother needed her. A part of me feels like an ass because I'm here and not there, but I'm trying to remind myself that I can only do so much. My mom knows I love her, and I guess that's what matters most.

"I now pronounce you husband and wife. You may kiss the bride," the pastor says proudly.

I watch my dad's lips attack Margo's. I swear I even see some tongue.

"It's like watching the beginning of a really weird porno," Link mumbles in my ear. "I feel like this kiss shouldn't last this long."

We continue watching them basically dry-hump each other, and Link groans.

"Yeah … wrap it up," he mutters under his breath. "Wrap. It. Up."

When they finally pull apart, I snort while trying to cover up my laugh. "We should show them up, shouldn't we?"

"Don't tempt me, T." He squeezes my thigh. "Trust me, I don't plan to stick around this reception long." His finger drags up my thigh slightly. "How could I when you look this good? And when there're so many other ways I plan to take you before we leave tomorrow."

A shiver runs down my spine, wrapping around to my belly. "If you fake an emergency at the reception, I'll owe you something."

As my dad and Margo hold their joint hands up, everyone stands.

"All right, you've piqued my interest. What kind of something?" His eyes darken.

Gazing around, I make sure no one is looking before I move in front of Link and lift his hand up. Taking one of his fingers deep into my mouth, I run my tongue down the length of it before releasing it and standing on my tiptoes, kissing him on the cheek. "Use your imagination."

Groaning, he looks upward as I move back to my own spot.

"One fake emergency, coming right up," he utters. "Fuck, now, I'm so hard that I can hardly stand myself."

It doesn't feel like we're faking anything. Nor does it seem like we're waiting for something to end. It's like we're finally getting what we've both wanted for so long. And that feels pretty damn good.

Like the good daughter that I am, I play along with all the shameless wedding shenanigans. I even agree to share a dance with my father when it comes time. So, here I am, swaying around with a man who feels like a stranger.

"I'm sorry for yesterday, Tate." He actually looks ashamed. "And for all the other times."

I shrug, suddenly feeling uncomfortable. "It's all right."

He shakes his head once. "It's not. I heard what you said to Margo, about not taking anything from me. I'm sorry I led her to believe otherwise. I guess I just didn't want her to think that I completely failed as a father. I know I suck at every other aspect of it, but I thought … if I at least pretend to financially be there, I'm not a monster."

I sigh. "To be fair, you have tried to be there financially. I just didn't want it."

"I know you didn't. And I find that admirable." He looks pained. "I know I messed up with you and Meyer." He cringes. "And your mother … I did so much wrong." He jerks his head toward where Margo stands, dancing with her friends as they all ogle my fake boyfriend. "This is my fresh start. My chance to do better. With Margo and our son. I'm going to be the best man I can for them."

A lump forms in my throat, burning as I try to swallow it down. I've always been too timid to say how I feel to my father. I guess, in some way, it makes me feel ungrateful. If it wasn't for him, I wouldn't have the life I have today. But after having a few drinks today and feeling the confidence of being here with Link, I stop moving and look at my dad.

"A fresh start with them," I say softly. "Not with me or Meyer. But with them." I hold no judgment in my voice, just understanding.

He breathes out the smallest laugh and shrugs. "You and Meyer are grown now. And you have your mother. And each other. And I guess … it seems like it's too late for us now. It's just hard to make time for everyone."

My heart breaks. "No, Dad. It's that you don't want to make room for me and Meyer in your new life." I take a step back. "Thank you."

"For what?" He looks confused.

"For finally giving me the clarity I needed. It's not me. It's you." A tear runs down my cheek. "There's nothing wrong with me, Dad. It's you, Not me. Not Meyer. You." I shrug. "I'm done trying. I'll never be enough for you, but I'm more than enough for others." I swing my gaze to Link, who watches us curiously from the bar. "Bye, Dad. Congratulations and best of luck."

And as I start toward Link, I'm aware my father is calling out to me. I just don't care.

LINK

"Let's go," she says, grabbing my hand.

But before I follow her, she notices Margo's friends desperately trying to get my attention. Standing in front of me, she smirks over at them before pushing onto her tiptoes and kissing me—hard. And when she releases me, she winks at them before pulling my hand to follow her.

"Wait, what about the emergency?"

"Don't need one," she says flatly, pulling her shoes off and strutting away from the venue.

Once we're out of sight of the reception and around the corner on a private, completely secluded beach, she lets go of my hand and starts running toward the water. Letting her hair down, she strips her dress off and drops it on the sand.

"Swim with me?" she says seductively, walking into the water.

I look around, not seeing a soul, but still knowing someone could easily walk out here. But when I watch her unclasp her bra and head into the water … I don't really give a fuck who might see us.

Stripping behind her, I head into the ocean in just my boxer briefs.

Once we're out deep enough, she hooks her legs around my waist and tips her head back in the water.

"You plan on telling me what this is about?" I hold her asscheeks, pushing her body against my already-aching cock. "Don't get me wrong. I have no complaints right now. But I need to know you're okay."

When she sits back up, her now-slicked-back hair drips droplets down her face and onto her lips.

"I'm good," she tries to assure me before fastening her thighs tighter and attacking my lips with her own. "Make me feel better, Link. Take the pain out of me."

I've also never seen her so vulnerable. It's clear she's hurting. I watched her entire dance and conversation with her father, and she was in pain.

Moving my hand to her nape, I grip her neck, running my lips over it, tasting the salt from the water on my tongue. Parting her legs wider, I push her panties to the side and nudge the tip of my cock inside.

"I was never going to be enough," she barely whispers. "I don't even know why I'm here."

Staring at her, I kiss her before pulling back. "I'm not him, Tate. I'm never going to be either."

She cries as I push further inside of her, inch by inch.

"I'll love you from afar, if that's what you need me to do. But that isn't what I want, T." I tangle my lips with hers, swallowing her moans. "I want you. I want you next to me through it all. My dreams coming true. The bad times. All of it. And I want to be there for you too."

I bend my head down, running my tongue across each nipple. Gliding my hands to her hips, I move her up and down on my length harder, rougher. The water splashes between us, and her eyes haze over as she stares at me.

I feel her body start to tense up, and she squeezes my cock as she bites her lip. We don't speak. We don't need to as my entire body shudders and I come inside of her and she continues to greedily squeeze me, getting every ounce of pleasure from her orgasm.

"I can't fix you, Tate. And I don't want to. But I can love you just the way you are. If you'll let me?"

She collapses against me, crying harder. "I wish I had been there for you when you needed me. I don't deserve you." She pulls back, looking up into my eyes. "I'm sorry you lost your mom, Link. If I could take back that entire day ... I would."

"Yeah. Me too."

I know she didn't give me an answer if she'd let me love her, but that's okay. For now anyway.

TATE

We walk into our villa, both covered in sand and a complete mess from our little swim in the ocean.

"I need a shower," he says, peeling his clothes back off. "I smell like salty ass." Looking at me, he tilts his head to the side. "So do you. Only worse."

I swat at him. "Do not." I smell my arm. "Okay, fine. Yes. Yes, I do."

"You still owe me, you know." His eyes twinkle. "Don't think I forgot."

Putting a hand on my hip, I narrow my eyes. "Uh, no. The deal was, I would owe you if you faked an emergency. Only you didn't have to do that." Strutting toward him, I place my hands on his bare abdomen. "But I'll tell you what. I'll meet you in the shower, and if you're a good boy ... you might get rewarded anyway."

He rolls his eyes, sliding my hand down a little further. "Psht. Yeah, right. More like, *if* you're a good girl, I'll let you suck my dick."

His crudeness sends a shiver through my whole body. And even though we just had wild ocean sex, an ache resides between my legs.

Moving backward, he pulls his briefs down and heads to the bathroom. But not without a cocky smirk first. "See you soon, babe."

As much as I want to run for the bathroom and redo the last shower we took together, I haven't checked my phone in hours. And I know I need to in case anyone has tried to call.

When I pick my phone up, my mouth falls open. "Holy shit."

Meyer called me twenty-seven times and sent me countless texts. Without reading them, I quickly dial her number.

"There you are! I've been trying to call you for over an hour!" I can tell right away that she's crying. "It's Mom, Tate," she sobs. "She's in the hospital. I'm here with her now."

"What are you talking about?" I blurt out, pushing my hair nervously away from my face. "Wh-what happened!"

"I flew home to surprise her." She sniffles. "But when I got to the house, it was quiet—too quiet." Her voice lowers to almost a whisper. "I found her in the bathtub. She had taken a bottle of pills."

In the past, it wasn't unusual for our mother to take antidepressants during hard times. The times when her marriage was put under a microscope. Or when Dad messed up. She'd go through dark times, sure. But she never tried to intentionally hurt herself.

Guilt strikes me in the gut. I know my coming to the wedding probably didn't help. Pulling my wet dress off, I yank my suitcase open and pull on a pair of shorts and a T-shirt. I know I'm dirty, but no part of me cares.

"I'll be there as soon as I can," I say quickly. "Are you at Western Light?"

"Yes," she says, confirming she's at the hospital closest to our house. "Tate?"

"Yeah?"

"Don't blame yourself, please," she squeaks. "None of this was our fault."

"Yeah," is all I say again. "Talk to you soon."

I end the call and throw my stuff together before charging into the bathroom and getting Link. This day went from bad, to okay, to worse. And somehow, I don't think it's going to get better anytime soon.

LINK

I run my fingers through Tate's hair as she sleeps restlessly, twitching every few minutes. We got to the hospital last night, and here it is, five in the morning on Monday, and there's no change in her mother.

Even in her sleep, still dirty from the beach and the salt water, she's breathtaking. Brown and blonde pieces hang over her face, and I push them away.

Even though Tate and Meyer have always downplayed it, their mother has struggled with depression for a long time. She'd have high highs and low lows. I never imagined she'd go as far as she did this time though. To put a burden like this on her daughters is unimaginable to me. And even though I know it shouldn't, it pisses me off to think she gave her kids yet another unbearably heavy thing to carry on their shoulders.

I'll be there for Tate as long as she'll let me. I remember the day I needed her the most, and even though she didn't even know me back then, she was there.

"That must be the people moving into the Hudsons' old house," Travis said, sitting next to me. "Anyone will be better than them. They were stuck-up assholes."

"Yeah," was all I said back.

We'd just found out the worst news of our lives. Our mother had breast cancer and was going to be starting treatments, along with undergoing surgeries. I didn't give a fuck about who was moving in across the street. I didn't care at all.

The door on the driver's side opened, and a man about my father's age hopped out. And when the passenger side opened, I knew right then that I did care who was moving into that house.

She was scrawny. Her legs were long and bony, and her arms were gangly and awkward. She wore a pair of overalls with flowers or some shit on them. Her Converse looked worn out despite the truck she rode in, and the SUV behind it had probably cost as much as most people's houses did.

Her brown hair looked like it had gotten some sun from the summer, lightening it at the ends. And even though she was the cutest girl I'd ever seen, that wasn't what had me standing up and walking across the road. No, it was the way her shoulders slumped as she walked behind her dad. Her dad, who I quickly realized was Harvey Tracy. One of the NHL's most talented players. Still, I couldn't pull my eyes from her. Analyzing the nothingness in her eyes when she caught sight of me. Yet her lips turned up the smallest bit, and she smiled.

Her dad continued to talk on the phone, and I watched her mother and sister climb out of the SUV and run inside. But she didn't follow. Instead, she waited for me to reach her.

"Hi," I said.

"Hi," she muttered back, shifting around on her feet uncomfortably.

"I'm Link."

"I'm Tate." She inhaled. "I guess I'm your new neighbor."

Her eyes studied me for a moment before her brows pulled together. "Are you okay? You look like … well, you look like maybe you're sad."

"My mom has cancer." I blurted out the words to a girl I'd only known for a matter of thirty seconds. "She just told us. Me and my brothers."

Within a split second, her hand reached for mine. "I'm so sorry, Link. I hope she's going to be okay."

I swallowed. "Yeah. Me too."

Our hands dropped, breaking apart as we stood there in her driveway.

Her face lit up before she reached in her pocket and pulled out the tiniest plastic bag I'd ever seen.

"Before we left our old house this morning, I found this." She looked down at it. "I hoped it would bring me good luck. You see, I wasn't all that excited about moving to a new home."

Holding her hand out, she placed the tiny bag in my hand. "Maybe it will help you. Maybe it could help your mom."

When she pulled her hand away, I looked down at my hand. In it lay a tiny four-leaf clover that had some sort of shiny coating over it.

"I preserved it," she added, seeming to clarify the question I had been asking myself, wondering how it looked that … perfect. "That way, I could keep it forever."

Her mother called her name from the front porch, and she started to back away from me.

"It was nice to meet you, Link." She frowned. "I'm really sorry that your mom is sick."

"Wait," I said, holding my hand up. "What about your good luck? Don't you need this?"

Giving me the smallest smile, she shrugged. "I think I might have just found mine."

And then she turned, her brown hair swishing on her shoulders as she ran up the stairs to where her mother stood.

And I thought that the hardest day had just gotten a lot better. And I knew right then, she was mine.

My four-leaf clover.

TATE

We wait. And wait. And wait some more. Meyer and I take turns pacing the hallway. It's been over twenty-four hours since I got here, and there's still no change in my mom's status.

Link got excused from practice tonight, but I know he needs to be there for tomorrow afternoon's practice. He can't just not go.

"T, wanna walk to the nurses' station and see if the doctors have any new information from her most recent blood work?" Meyer says, pressing her back to the wall in our mother's small room.

"Wouldn't hurt to check, I suppose."

I gaze at Mom, unsure if I should leave her or not. I hate to think that she could wake up and not have us here. But then again, two sets of ears are better than one. And while Meyer isn't the one to ask questions, she does remember most details.

"I'll sit here with her," Link says from the doorway. "Y'all go, and if there's any change, I'll let you know."

Taking one last look at my mom, I head to where he stands and press a kiss to his cheek. I nod at Meyer, and we head to the nurses' station.

"So, are you still pretending to date for my benefit?" She grins, elbowing me. "Because that shit looks awfullllly real."

"No. Yes. I don't know." I blow out a breath. "Everything is a mess right now. Mom. Me. Dad. She-devil Margo. It's all a damn disaster."

"You didn't mention Link's name in that," she says curiously.

"I know," I mutter. "That's because in a world full of disaster ... he's the one good thing. And I know that makes no sense. And I'm aware ... I'm sort of breaking our rule."

She laughs softly. "T, we both know that rule has never applied to Link." She links her arm with mine. "He's one man who isn't and will never be our dad." Her voice drops to a whisper. "Guys don't love girls *that* much in real life. Link Sterns looks at you like you're the damn sun and he's been in the dark his whole life." She puts her head to mine as we take the last few steps. "I say, go for it. Because if you don't, I promise, you'll never find that again "

Link's face flashes in my mind, smiling at me, making it all better.

"Yeah, I know."

LINK

I offered to stay here, but, hell, I'll be nervous as hell if she starts to wake up and isn't okay when I'm the only one here. The doctor said that she had those pills in her stomach for too long before someone found her. I watched Tate break before me as she heard the words, no doubt blaming herself.

I wish her mom had thought about that before she did it. I wish so badly she could have just stopped and thought about these two girls and how they'd been through enough. But she didn't, and even as she lies here, hooked to machines ... I'm livid.

I have her and Tate's father to thank for completely fucking Tate up to the point of no return. She won't ever believe that she's enough. But more than that, I know she's afraid of the lifestyle that comes with being a professional athlete's wife.

I think back to Starbucks. That dude asked if she was Harvey Tracy's daughter. She smiled and shook her head. It was so well acted out that if I hadn't known her, I'd have believed it. I'd seen her do that countless times before, and every time, it seemed so natural. That's how good she's gotten at staying out of the limelight. And I know that if I want to play for the Kings, which I do, it'll put her in a situation she doesn't want to be in.

But we can make it work. I know we can.

"Link." Meg's voice breaks me from my thoughts, and I stand as soon as I hear her.

"Meg, you're awake." I rush to her side, pulling my phone out. "Let me call the girls. I told them I would."

Slowly, her hand reaches out, splaying her fingers over my phone.

"Wait," she says, her voice hoarse. "Please, just wait."

Unsure, I stare at her for a moment before I drop my phone down at my side. "Do you need something? Water?"

Gradually, her head moves up and down. "Water would be great, thanks."

Walking to the counter, I pour a small amount into a paper cup and hand it to her.

"I know you're mad at me," she utters, never looking directly at me. "And I'm sorry."

Taken aback, I rear my head back. "Why would I be mad?"

"Because I hurt her," she says flatly. So not like the woman I grew up knowing.

She seems almost put out that she woke up. Or that I'm here.

Meg has always been warm, kind, a light in a dark room.

Just like Tate is.

Yet right now, she isn't that woman. She seems … frustrated or annoyed.

"I really should call them. I promised I would."

"I wasn't always like this, you know," she whispers sadly. "I'm *not* always like this either." She looks out the window, wiping her eyes. "People can be cruel. And if you don't have a strong foundation under you … it's easy to crack. When I married a man who was so loved by the world, seen as such a larger-than-life figure, I should have known it wasn't going to be easy." She pauses, taking a few breaths. "Sure, the cheating was rough. And when it was publicized? Awful. But do you know what the worst part of being married to that man was, Link?"

"What?"

She turns toward me, and for the first time since knowing her, I see her age before my eyes. The wrinkles around her eyes are more prominent. And the bags under them are much deeper than I remember.

"Having to deal with people who didn't even know me having an opinion about me. If I was out with friends, having a few glasses of wine, I was a drunk who needed my kids to be taken from me. If I went out on a girls' weekend, I was a whore who didn't take care of my babies." She looks down at her hands. "If I gained ten pounds, I was called a pig in the tabloids. But when I worked out and lost some weight, I was anorexic because, you know, I just *had* to be depressed about the affairs."

She grabs a tissue from the nightstand and wipes her nose. "Meyer's vocal about what bothers her most. That's why I don't worry about her. If she's in trouble, she'll tell me or her sister. But Tate?" Her eyebrows pull together. "She bottles it up. And she's sensitive and thoughtful. She overthinks things and almost never puts herself first. When she was a kid, before you came along, she was afraid to go in public without some sort of disguise."

I take in her words, knowing what she's saying. And even though I don't want to hear it, I get it. And I guess a part of me already knew it too.

"We moved to Appleton to get away from the city. And, yes, Harvey was gone most of the time, but that was for the better. We needed to live our lives without the constant pressure of being watched or judged." Her hands wring together.

"Harvey didn't ruin me, Link. The public did. And it will ruin her too. She's got her own dreams to follow. Just like you have yours. Just take a hard look at me. Is this really what you want for her?" Pulling her hands apart, she wipes her eyes again. "Just like me, she isn't strong enough for the pressure of the harsh, cruel world. And I love her way too much to let anyone destroy her."

She tips her head back. "You've always been so good to my girl, Link. But the two of you … I just worry it's a recipe for disaster. She isn't what you're going to need, and your lifestyle will cause her so much stress. She is brilliant. And the thought of her losing her spark"—she sniffles—"it kills me. Much more than myself going through it."

I stand there, dumbfounded. Before finally straightening myself out.

"You're wrong. Tate is the strongest person I know." I look at the door to make sure the girls aren't walking in. "But if you and her dad continue this way, you will break her and Meyer both. So, if you really love them—and I know you do—you'll get the help you need, and you'll get better. They deserve it."

"I will do whatever I need to do to never be in this bed again," she croaks. "But you're going to let my daughter go. I know you love her, but it's not fair to drag her along when you know once you're in the NHL, you won't have the time for her that she deserves. I want the best for her, Link. I want her to stand on her own two feet and not depend on someone else to hold her up."

"You're asking me to leave her?" My nostrils flare.

"I'm protecting my daughter," she says softly. "I love you. You're a good man. I've known that since the day I met you. And you might even be her man. But with you comes a whole darkness that she won't be able to escape."

She pats the bed with both hands. "This is what the darkness looks like when it closes in."

My body stiffens to stone just as I hear Meyer squeal and see Tate run to her mom's side.

"You woke up!" Her eyes fly to me. "When?! You didn't call—"

"It just happened," I say, trying my best to look pleasant. "I wanted to make sure she was okay before I called you—that's all."

I watch them hug their mother, all three of them bawling their eyes out. As they should.

"I'll let y'all catch up," I say, nodding my head toward the door and walking outside.

"Link, wait." Tate follows me out the door and throws her arms around my neck. "You should head back to Brooks. You have classes and practice tomorrow."

All I want to do is pull her against me and not let go. But with her mother's words in the back of my mind, I kiss her forehead before stepping back. "You sure you'll be all right?"

"I'm sure." She smiles. "Thank you. For … everything."

I nod, putting my hand on her waist. "No problem. Call me if you need anything."

And before I can turn to leave, her lips crash against mine.

"We'll figure it out, right?" she whispers, her eyes dancing between mine. "All of it?"

Swallowing hard, I suck in a breath. "Yeah. Definitely."

I can't tell her the truth. Not here. Not now.

I'll just be another human being who makes her feel like she's less than she is. When the reality is, she's everything. And she's all I've ever wanted. And yet here the universe is, throwing another mountain in our way to break us apart.

As I release her and walk away, I wonder if that's the last time I'll ever kiss her again. And if it is … well, that fucking sucks.

This world continues to push us together, only to pull us apart. And at some point, I just have to let her go.

And I think this is that point.

16

TATE

"I feel like the worst human being on the planet," I tell my sister once my mother leaves and goes to her appointment. "I can't leave today."

Two weeks ago to the day was when I received that awful phone call. Two weeks ago, I wasn't sure if I'd even have a mother the next day. But now, she's acting like herself again. Herself during the highs, that is. She started going to therapy, and that seems to be going surprisingly well. Still, the thought of being a few hours away from her terrifies me.

The good part of being here these past few weeks is, I finally got to see Mrs. Fenton now that she's back home. She's doing much better, but it's not hard to tell that being so sick took a lot out of her. It breaks my heart to see how much she's aged since before going into the hospital.

"Don't. I'll be here for another few weeks. I've already cleared it with my professors to do my assignments online," she assures me. "She knows she needs help to feel better, and she's getting that help now. I know you feel bad, Tate. I know how your mind works. But now, it's time for you to go." She looks at me, giving me the same sympathetic smile my mother always does when she doesn't want me to feel bad. "You can't always carry the weight of everyone else's shit. So, at least for the next few weeks, let me do it."

"Yeah," I whisper. "I just … feel bad. She's taken care of us our whole lives, and now, I'm just leaving her alone. I wish Brooks were closer to home. I'm taking off to study crap that probably doesn't matter and ditching my mom when she needs me."

"Stuff that doesn't matter?" She tilts her head to the side. "You were one of the few accepted into Brooks's rocket-building program." She flips her hair. "My, my. I have a badass sister."

"A nerdy sister is more like it." I laugh. "Thanks for making me feel better. And thank you for staying back. I know the last place you want to be is here in Appleton."

She shrugs. "It's not so bad. I've just always wanted to be anywhere but home, you know?" Sighing, she picks up a rag and wipes the counter off. "It will be good for me and Mom to have a few weeks alone. Maybe now, I'll get to be the favorite." She sticks her tongue out.

"Uh, I hate to tell you, but I think you already are."

"Oh, bullshit!" She attempts to snap me with the rag, but luckily fails. "You always do the right thing. *Even* if it hurts you. Me? I just avoid it all."

"Trust me, I wish I could avoid it. It would be a lot better for my whole mental health if I could." I lean against the counter. "Man, we're a couple of screwed up girls, huh?" I giggle, fighting the sadness.

"The most screwed up." She winks. "But I think we're doing okay. Especially you these days. Aren't you happy to be headed back to your sexy roommate?"

"Well, which one?" I raise an eyebrow. "Because there's Link. Who is … yum. And then there's Brody. Who is a bit of a caveman and walks around with his shirt off, showing off his insane abdomen and tattoos."

She fans herself with her hand before stopping. "We both know you only have eyes for Link. So, tell me, on a scale of one to ten, how much are you going to jump his bones when you walk through that door?"

"I guess we'll see." I try to keep my voice cheerful, but it's hard. "I said my good-byes to Mom before she left for her appointment." Holding my arms out to Meyer, I pull her against me. "If you get in over your head with her or if you need to head back to school early, call me. I can be here in a few hours."

Hugging me back, she sniffles and nods. "I will. Now, go get your man. Go get Link."

When I step back, my heart sinks. "I will. Bye."

"Bye, sis." She blows a kiss.

As I head toward the door, a worry churns in my gut. Truthfully, he's been weird ever since he went back to Brooks. His messages are extremely short, if he answers at all. And the times I've tried to call him, he doesn't answer. Instead, he'll text me that he's right in the middle of something.

Maybe he really did just use me so that he could leave. The same way I'd left.

I'm not letting him get away that easily. I might be scared of a future with an NHL player, but I'm more scared of a future without Link.

"There's my favorite Tater Tot!" Brody beams, strutting toward the door. "Do you have anything else you need lugged in?"

"No, just this." I hike my bag up on my shoulder. "Thanks though."

Taking it from me, he kisses the top of my head. "I'm sorry for all the crappy shit you've had going on."

"Thanks, Brody. And thank you for bringing my car down earlier this week. Sorry I missed you when you did."

"It's no big deal. Link and I were due for a little road trip anyway. Would have loved to see you, but Sterns said you were busy."

"Did he now?" I answer, tight-lipped.

His words cause my heart to stop beating for a split second. Link said he couldn't bring my car to me, so he supposedly asked Brody and Hunter. The entire time, it was actually him? And he didn't even try to come in and see me.

The sight of someone behind him catches my eye, and I see the most beautiful, towheaded girl waving at me.

"Hey, Tate!" She walks over, holding her hand out. "I'm Bria."

My eyes move from Brody back to this goddess girl, Bria, and I smile. "Nice to meet you, Bria."

Brody winks, giving me a knowing smirk before he turns and jogs up the stairs with my bag. Moments later, he returns, and I look around.

"Is Link not home? His truck's here. So …"

Brody scratches the back of his head. A tell that he's nervous or uncomfortable, I've come to realize. "Uh, yeah … he's—"

"He's in his room," Bria interrupts him, glaring at Brody. "He should be down here, helping her bring in her things instead of being a damn baby up there."

I look at her, confused, before heading toward the stairs. "It was nice to meet you. I'm going to … I guess go deal with him."

"Good luck. Call if you need reinforcements!" she calls behind me.

Pushing the door open, I find Link, freshly showered with nothing but a towel around his waist. His hair is still wet as I close it behind me.

"Did it mean nothing?" I whisper. "Did *I* mean nothing?"

"What?" he answers lazily, like I'm fucking bothering him or some shit.

Marching to him, I get in his space. "What was that weekend? Huh? Was that you trying to get me right where you wanted me so you could hurt me like I'd hurt you?"

When he ignores me, pulling a shirt over his head, something in me snaps.

Grabbing a fistful of it, I pull until I hear the fabric tear. "Was that all it was, Link?! Was it?!"

"Yeah," he mutters mindlessly, backing out of my hold. "Pretty much."

I stare in disbelief. Even though it began with us acting for my father, it felt real. There was no part of it that wasn't.

"Are you serious right now?"

"What's the difference, Tate? I fucked you, and you left for Boston the next day. Why is it any different if the roles are reversed? So, what, you can do what you please, and I can't?"

"That isn't fair, and you know it." I try to grab for him again, but he pushes my hands away. "You don't mean this! We said we were going to figure it out! All of it!"

"Tate, stop." He steps back. "I'm leaving for Los Angeles in a few months. It was never going to work anyway. You had to know that."

"Why couldn't it work?" I sniffle. "Maybe it can. Those days in Florida at the beach were the best of my life."

"It just can't." His face grows solemn. "And even if it could, I don't want it to."

"You son of a bitch," I hiss, my vision growing cloudy from the tears forming in my eyes. "Fuck you, Link. Fuck. You."

"I'm sorry." He looks down. "Just … go."

Without thinking, I tear my own shirt over my head and throw it onto the floor. "You love me. I know you do."

Picking it up off the floor, he presses it to my chest. "Put your shirt back on, for fuck's sake."

Unclasping my bra, I let it fall before pulling my jeans down. "Or what, Link?" I sniffle, letting more tears gather in my eyes before blinking to clear my vision. "What are you going to do? Hmm?" I shove his chest. "Are you going to pretend to hate me? Or maybe just ignore me? What?" I shove him again, yelling, "What are you going to do!"

"I can't do this." He looks away from me, running his hand down the back of his neck. "I can't fucking do this. Leave."

"No," I cry. Dropping to my knees, I gaze up at him. "I won't leave."

Reaching up, I pull the towel off, and his hard length springs free.

"You want me," I croak. "I know you do."

"I can't have you," he utters. "I was stupid to ever think I could."

"So, this is really it then?" The words burn my throat like a straight shot of whiskey coming out.

"Yes," he states with no hesitation.

"At least give me one last time then. If I'm losing your friendship and you, all in one day … help me get through it."

"That won't help, Tate. Haven't you learned anything?" he growls.

Inching forward, I open my mouth the smallest bit before licking my lips. "Let me," I whimper. "Let this be what you remember if you ever have another woman on her knees. Because I promise you, I'll never want another man's hands or mouth on my body after you, Link."

He squeezes his eyes shut for a moment, as if willing himself to just stay strong. So, I make it harder for him to do that by reaching out and stroking his length.

"Link," I whisper, "please. What would one last time hurt?"

"It'll break me—that's what. Every time with you leaves me wanting more, Tate. It will never be just one last time. But it has to be. This time, it has to be over," his deep voice rasps before his hand grips the back of my head and he pushes himself into my mouth.

Little by little, I open my throat and move my head back and forth. Letting the length of him slide out before plunging back in. Cupping the bottom of him with my tongue over and over before sucking harder.

All at once, he pulls me off of my knees and lifts me up. Pushing me against the wall, he drives himself inside of me. We're nose to nose, our eyes burning into each other like stars colliding in the dark sky.

"Kiss me, Link." My voice sounds so desperate that I barely recognize myself. "I'm sorry. If I could go back and never get in that car to drive to Massachusetts … I would. I'd do it all differently."

He kisses me, anchoring one hand under my ass as the other snakes around, gripping my arm and pressing the back of my hand to the drywall.

He pounds into me, and my spine digging against the hard wall makes me wince, but not enough to stop him.

His thrusts slow just as my entire body begins to tingle. His face drives into my neck as his chest heaves against mine. As he pours himself inside of me, his fingertips dig into the flesh of my ass.

I cry out, throwing my head back as we come together for what I refuse to believe could really be the last time. It can't be.

Setting me down slowly, he takes my hands in his and dips his head down. "It wasn't a plan. I'd never do anything to intentionally hurt you, Tate. Even if I still resented you, I wouldn't do that." His eyes gloss over, and his hands drop. "It's just not going to work. You were right to leave that first time." Backing away, he reaches for his clothes.

Quickly, I grab my own clothes and throw them on myself, knowing I'm a complete mess but still desperate to get him to listen to me.

"You aren't even giving it a chance! I know what I said. I know my rule, but I changed my mind, Link! Just let me try!" I back him into a corner, my hands flying to my chest as my heart feels like it's being cut out from my body. "Please. Please, don't do this. I'm begging you."

Cupping my cheeks, he kisses me long and deep before pulling back. His face looks pained as he flinches before the next words even leave his lips.

"You're my best friend, Tate. I love you. And I know you love me too. But we both know being friends doesn't work for us anymore." He swallows, his Adam's apple bobbing. "If you want to give me what I need, you'll leave me alone. I'm going to move into the other hockey house so that you don't have to see me." His voice turns hoarse. "It's over, Tate. Time to let it go."

I stand there, frozen. Every second that passes, he somehow feels further away even though he's right in front of me. I lost him because I let my daddy issues shape my entire life. Nobody is to blame but me.

"If you mean that, tell me you never want to be with me. Ever," I sob, wiping my nose with my sleeve. "Say it."

When he stares at me, I hit his chest.

"Say it, dammit! Fucking say it! If you really do mean this, you'd better be sure, Link." I suck in a breath. "Because I can't … I can't go through this again."

"I don't want to be with you, Tate. Not now. Not ever."

Reaching in his duffel bag on the floor, he grabs something before handing it to me. And when I look at my hand and see the four-leaf clover, I feel the familiar sensation of spinning, followed by nausea, and I know I have to get out of this room before I faint or throw up. Damn this stupid condition I've had for most of my life. I've become good at trying to avoid triggers, but situations like this are beyond my control.

It's all too much, and my body physically can't take it. But I know Link, and he'll still want to care for me and make sure I'm all right. Fuck that, is what I have to say. If he doesn't want me around him anymore, he doesn't need to save me.

Backing up slowly, I turn toward the door, steadying myself by gripping his dresser.

"Tate, are you all right?" I hear Link's voice from behind me.

I take a few steps out of his room … and then it all goes dark.

Link

"Are you sure she's okay?" Bria kneels down. "I don't like this. Not one fucking bit."

"She faints sometimes," Brody answers her, repeating the words I told him the first night he saw her do it. "Gets worse when she's overstressed." He stretches the last word out, and I feel his eyes burning into the side of my head.

I knew when she started to turn that something wasn't right. And when all the color drained from her face and she had to grab hold of my dresser, I could see what was coming next even though she tried to get out of my room before it happened.

Brody and Bria were in his room and heard her come down hard in the hallway. And now, we sit, her between my legs, her head draped over my shoulder as we wait for her to wake up.

She normally comes to within a few seconds. This time, it's been at least thirty seconds, but slowly, she starts to stir.

"Damn, girl, you scared me," Bria says, crouching down and pushing Tate's hair from her face. "You good?"

As if realizing she's on me, she scoots away from me, putting her back to the other side of the hallway. "I'm fine."

When I move toward her, her eyes go wide, and she puts a hand up. "No, don't touch me."

"Tate—" I open my mouth to calm her down, but her eyes fill with tears.

"Stop trying to save me. You aren't my hero, Link." She looks down, lacing her hands together. "You're the villain." Her eyes shift to mine, darker than I've ever seen them. "Stop pretending like you aren't."

Slowly pushing herself up, she brushes past me and walks into her room, slamming the door behind her.

"Well … that went well," Brody says, rubbing the back of his neck. "We'll be in my room. Try not to make Tater Tot faint again, would you?"

Brody tugs Bria along, and they head back toward his room. But before they get there, Bria stops at Tate's door.

"I'll be over in a minute, okay?" she whispers to Brody. "Let me just talk to her. Girl to girl."

Nodding, he walks into his room.

And I watch someone else be there for her. For once, it isn't me.

And I wish so fucking bad it were.

TATE

"Tate, it's me, Bria."

I lie in my bed, staring up at the ceiling. My throat hurts, my nose is stuffy from crying, and my eyes burn.

Slowly pushing the door open, she walks inside and sits on the edge of my bed.

"Are you okay? Did you hit your head?"

I shake my head once. "No. My body just hates me and likes to do embarrassing shit."

"I'm not the best at the whole girl-talk thing, but I'm here, if you need me." She pats my hand. "I've heard Brody and Link talk enough to know you've had a rough couple of weeks. And now, with Link doing whatever weird shit he's doing, that can't be helping."

"I need to find a new apartment," I say flatly, knowing I can't let Link move out when this was his place to begin with. "I should just move home to help my mom, but she told me she wants me to stay at Brooks." I close my eyes, my head pounding. "Can anything just be simple? Like … for one day?"

"In my opinion, no. When it comes to parent issues, I'm your girl. If you ever want to talk or, hell, even compare notes"—she laughs—"I'm game. We can see which one of us is more screwed up."

I crack my eyes open and look at her. "I traveled hours to attend my father's wedding, and he basically told me he wanted to start over with his new wife and unborn child and that he didn't have room for me in his life."

"Ouch. My dad once sold my bicycle to buy drugs." She shrugs nonchalantly. "Damn thing was a birthday present too. Was a freaking Schwinn."

"Wow, that's awful." I scrunch my nose up. "Is it normal for us to bond over trauma?"

Patting my leg, she nods slowly, smiling. "Hell yeah, it is. Whatever we have to do to get through it is normal." She pauses, looking like she's thinking before her face lights up. "Hey, I have an idea. I have this adorable two-bedroom apartment with no roommate." She tilts her head to the side. "What do you say? Wanna move in with me? I know we just met, but this trauma shit sort of bonds us for life, don't you think?"

Looking at her for a moment, finally, I sit up. "I say, hell yes."

"Yay!" She claps. "I'll warn you, I don't know how to cook, I'm sort of messy, and I'm known to leave candles burning from time to time."

"I'm annoyingly particular and organized. I love to cook and stress-eat often. Oh, and as you just saw, I faint when I'm hungry, anxious, or sometimes just because."

I hold my hand out, and she takes it and smiles.

"Sounds like a perfect match."

I nod. "I agree."

This day might suck, but at least it's suddenly looking a little brighter.

LINK

"You realize you wanted her to move out, right?" Brody says to me as I all but pull my hair out, watching Tate's car pull out of our driveway. "You ended whatever weird fucking shit you had going on. Your love-hate crap."

"No, I said *I* would move next door to the other hockey house. That way, I could still keep an eye on her," I growl, annoyed. "We don't know where Oliver went, O'Brien. How the fuck will I know if she's safe when she's on the other side of campus?"

"I spend some time over there with Bria, dude. We'll just have to keep an eye on the situation—that's all." He leans against the wall. "I don't think he's coming back, Sterns. Like … I really don't."

"But you don't know that for sure, and now, she's in a different fucking house!" I bark, pounding my hand against the wall. "Fuck!"

"And whose fault is that, big man?" He walks toward me. "She loves you, and you pushed her away. You've got yourself to blame and no one else."

"You don't know what you're talking about," I say, glaring at him. "So, don't start with me, O'Brien. Trust me, you don't want to fuck with me right now."

I know it's not Brody's fault that she's leaving. It's nobody's fault but her mother's. And mine, for being so damn selfish when it comes to hockey. If I were just an ordinary guy—going to college to be an accountant, doctor, or some shit—we'd be together. Hell, she never would have left years ago. But hockey is all I know. And without it, I'm afraid of the monster I'd be.

About like the monster I am without her, I suppose.

"You're mad. You're hurting. So, for that, I'm going to let you have your little tantrum, just like Hardy did when he went through this same shit. But not for long, Link. I won't let it go forever." He points at me. "So, figure your shit out—and fast. And if it affects your game, sit your ass on the bench."

"Fuck you," I grumble.

"I already did when I was in the shower." He smirks before strutting away.

Walking away from the window, I head upstairs. Deciding to torture myself further, I walk into her room and look around. Even with all of her things gone, it still smells like her in here. Fruity, but not overwhelming.

I gaze around, seeing she didn't leave anything behind. She won't have to stop by in hopes of running into me. She made sure of that.

I crane my neck to her bed, and that's when I see it. The tiny pouch on her nightstand. Beside it lies a short note.

For when you need a little luck.

Thanks for always being mine.

—T

And I pick it up. The last thing I have of her.
The four-leaf clover.
Our four-leaf clover.

TATE

The thing about falling in love with your best friend is, when it goes south, not only are you heartbroken, but you also no longer have your best friend to make you feel better.

The years in Boston without him were downright awful. But then I entertained the idea of giving us a go. A real chance. Only for that to get shot down, sending it into flames. And now, we share a campus, never running into each other, yet I'm painfully aware he's always nearby. At least for now, he is. Until he leaves for LA and forgets all about me.

Leaving the clover, our one symbolic thing from our friendship, was my Hail Mary. My last attempt to make him think about me when I was gone. But I moved out three weeks ago, and I haven't heard a peep from him. Brody stops in—a lot. And even though I know it's probably just my imagination, I swear I hear the same rumble of Link's car driving by late at night. And even though I know it's wishful thinking, when Brody shows up with some of my favorite treats for Bria and me, I wonder if Link told him to bring them.

That's how pathetic I am these days. Every single thing that happens, I look for some sign that it isn't over. Because truthfully, I can't imagine never laughing with Link again. I can't stand the thought that he'll never wrap me up in one of his bear hugs. And what I really don't like to picture is going through life's milestones without our friendship.

I think somewhere deep down, subconsciously, I knew that if I came back to Georgia, we'd reconnect. Maybe something inside me knew we weren't done yet. Like we had one more chapter to write.

But I guess in the story of Tate and Link, it isn't ending with that happily ever after we all hope for when we open a book to begin with.

On a brighter note, my mother is doing so good. And that makes things a whole lot easier. And when I went back to work at the Astronomy Center, the manager asked if I would fill Oliver's shoes. It's much more paperwork than I had before, but I only work at the building a few days a week, and the rest I can do from home. Which is perfect since I've been traveling home once a week to check in on Mom.

She apologized for putting Meyer and me through what she did. And her doctor said that the medications she was on for depression and anxiety seemed to have more of a negative effect on her than a positive. So, after switching them around, she's much more stable.

I guess that even something as awful as her attempted suicide had a silver lining because she got the help she needed. Maybe in the game of life, the worst things all hit you at the same time for a reason. I'm just not sure what that reason is yet.

"I'm in need of carbs and ice cream," Bria says, coming out of her room. "Pizza first, and then we can hit up the store for some Breyers?"

"Breyers? Oh, hell no." I stand, shaking my head. "Ben & Jerry's, lady. There's no other brand."

She laughs. "All righty then, Ben & Jerry's it is."

I follow her to the door, thankful that she gave me the opportunity to move in with her. She's the easiest person to get along with, and though she's a little messy, she offsets my constant need for perfection. Turns out, she's sort of the yin to my yang.

"Thanks for hanging out with me," I say, sliding my sandals on. "Brody is probably missing you tonight."

"Eh, I don't know about that." She frowns, her body language turning rigid. "Let's just say, we both need a time-out. For now anyway."

I give her a knowing look. "Let me guess. Being 'friends' became too complicated."

Her mouth forms a line, and she shrugs. "Something like that, yeah."

Pulling the door open, I hold my fist out to her. "Hos over bros?"

Bumping hers to mine, she laughs. "Hos over broooos."

LINK

"Brody's in a bad mood. Link's *always* in a bad mood. And Hunter won't put his phone down long enough to shoot the shit with me." Cam pouts, sitting at the bar of a pizza place just off campus. "You all suck. I'm going home to Addy and Isla. They'll talk to me."

Hunter looks up and shrugs. "Sorry, Cap. You know how it is."

"Go play unicorns and butterflies," I tease him, elbowing his side.

"Better than being with a bunch of Debbie Downers," he tosses back. "I'm out."

Lifting my beer to my lips, I roll my eyes. "Pansy."

"Better than being a Grumpy Gus," he says, patting my shoulder before leaving.

He's not wrong. Brody has had a hair across his ass all day. And when I asked him why he was in a bad mood, he got pissed and walked off. So, now, here we all sit. Grumpy and silent.

I should be celebrating, seeing's last week, I gave my verbal answer to the GM of the Los Angeles Kings, telling him I wanted to come on board and be a part of the team. Something about that phone call didn't feel right though. Truthfully, I felt slimy in some way. Like I was finally selling my soul just to cash in on claiming I'd made it to the pros.

"We meet again, Mr. Sterns," a semi-familiar voice says next to me.

I watch as Kaylee takes Cam's seat, quickly ordering some sort of a mixed drink.

"Another dare?" I try to joke, but it comes off emotionless.

"Nah, not tonight." She takes a sip from her drink and smiles at me. "How have you been? How's your … history?"

Relaxing in my stool, I sigh. "In the past for good now, I guess."

Resting her head closer to my shoulder, she doesn't come off as flirtatious as much as someone just trying to get to know me better.

"And how do you feel about that? Because I have to tell you, Link, I've come here a few times the past week, and every single time, you've been sitting on this stool, staring straight ahead."

"Stalker," I mutter. "And maybe I just like this stool. Ever thought of that?"

We continue to talk about basically nothing, both ordering drinks as Brody and Hunter sit silently beside me. Eventually, Hunter leaves, but Brody stays in the same spot, ordering beer after beer. And I realize, it's the first time I've seen him drink in weeks.

After enough beers, I tell Kaylee more about Tate and how much the entire situation sucks ass. A few times, I even laugh. For the first time in weeks, that stabbing pain dulls the smallest bit.

That is, until I hear *her* voice coming from the other side of the room. And when I turn my head to follow the sound, my breath hitches when I take in the sight of her.

She looks tired and maybe even a little thinner than she did a few weeks ago. But, goddamn, she's perfect. Like an angel in a dark room, she lights the entire place up. She smiles at Bria as they wait to be seated, but that smile quickly dies when she spots me and her eyes shift to Kaylee's hand on my forearm.

Even across the room, I watch her flinch, like she's been slapped. And when she whispers to Bria and Bria takes in what I'm sure looks like me on a date, they quickly turn and leave the restaurant like the place is on fire.

I shouldn't run after her. I should stay here and continue talking to this nice girl, who probably doesn't have a fucking wheelbarrow full of baggage, like Tate does, or a mother who basically forbids me to see her. I should. Fuck, I know I should.

"I'll be right back," I tell her before standing up.

"Okey dokey," she says sweetly, and it's so clear she's a nice girl. But she isn't my girl.

Pushing through the crowd of people waiting for a table, I spot her approaching Bria's car.

"Tate," I shout, walking toward her. "Wait."

"No," she quips back, flinging the door open. "Here's an idea: go fuck yourself."

"It's not what it looks like," I say quickly, pushing the door shut before she can get in.

"I don't care what it looks like. Get away from me," she snarls, suddenly looking like an angry wolf. "Go back inside, Link."

"T, stop. I can tell you're mad—"

"Do *not* call me T. My friends and family call me T. And people who are assholes don't need to talk to me, so they call me nothing."

She glares, crossing her arms over her chest, and fucking hell if my cock doesn't twitch at the sight.

"You dumped me, if we can even call it that since we weren't actually ever together. So, guess what. I'll hook up with who I want, and you hook up with who you want, like you clearly already are. Stop trying to have control over me. Got it?"

"What do you mean, you'll hook up with whoever you want?" My nostrils flare. "You're seeing someone already? Is that what you're fucking saying?"

"You lost your right to ask me that," she says, tilting her head. "So, unless you want to be with me—like *really* be with me—walk away right now. Stop fucking with my head."

"Tate, I can't—"

"Yeah, that's what I thought. Just want to toy around with me some more. No thanks."

"Sterns, what's going on?" Brody calls from behind us. "You guys all right?"

"We're fine, Brody," Tate answers softly. "Y'all have a good night."

Ducking under my arm, she yanks open the door and climbs in. Letting Bria drive her away without so much as a second glance.

"I fucked up," I whisper, sinking down as their taillights disappear. "I really, *really* fucked up."

Standing next to me, Brody rests his hand on my shoulder. "Yeah. Me too."

They say timing is everything. I guess they're right because when I was ready to commit, it spooked her. Now, she's ready, and I can't do it because of her mother.

I say, fuck timing. And fuck falling in love with friends.

LINK

I might be struggling in everyday life, but I'm sure as hell not about to bring that on the ice. We're nearing halfway through the season, and if we keep playing the way we are, we might just secure our spot in the Frozen Four if we're lucky.

Aside from practice, homework, and driving by Tate's apartment at random hours of the night to make sure nothing seems amiss, I have nothing to do besides work out and train. The temptation to continue hanging out at the bar still gets me some nights when the house is really quiet, but for the most part, I'm trying to just focus on the game. After all, I'm all in on it.

We defeated my brother Logan's team last weekend, and that was bittersweet. I know he was both bummed out to lose and happy to see my team continue to make our way through an undefeated season. I wish he had come to Brooks too. With him on our team, we would have been even more of a threat.

In the second half of the last period, our opponents seem to be getting fatigued. Coach LaConte might be a hard-ass, but his program has made sure that getting tired isn't something that happens easily for us. We're all in the best shape I think any of us have ever been in, and that's because of him. I might curse him some days for it, but not in games like this one. Against a team that comes out so strong, keeping us on our toes, only to eventually get sloppy and worn out. That doesn't mean we'll let up though. Hell no.

Sometimes, on the ice, I swear Cam and I know each other just as well as we know ourselves. I know his next move before he makes it even if we have to scramble and it isn't part of the original plan. And I'd be lying if I said I wasn't disappointed that this will be our last season working together. Everything the dude does in the arena is with grace. Almost seeming effortless even though I know that's not the case. He's just that good.

Tonight's no different as we go goal for goal, working together seamlessly till that final buzzer sounds.

And just like I always do, I look for her. Even the years she was in Boston, I'd do a quick sweep of the crowd. Knowing she wasn't there to watch me, but wishing she were.

Maybe the four-leaf clover I always bring everywhere with me doesn't help on nights like this. And, yeah, it's probably all a coincidence when we win and I happen to have it. But she gave it to me. So, I'll carry it always, just like I have since I was twelve.

Everyone in the locker room showers and dresses at the speed of light. Rushing around quickly, trying their best to get the hell out of here. Me? I didn't want the game to end. When the clock runs out of time and I'm forced to leave the ice, it's just me and my thoughts of Tate.

Besides, so many of them hurry out to their families who came to watch them. My brothers have their own shit going on with sports. And I know my dad sure as hell isn't making the trip down.

Guilt strikes me because I haven't talked to him since I was home for the benefit dinner for Mrs. Fenton. But now that she's home and doing better, I know I need to drive home and visit her and Clyde.

And my old man.

But I always feel like I'm in the way when I go home. If I stay here, I'm not bothering anyone.

As I slowly pull my shirt over my head, Hunter comes next to me.

"You all right, ol' boy?" he says, eyeing me over. "You've seemed off lately. Which is weird for a man who's a goddamn LA King these days."

"I'm fine." I pull my sneakers on and grin up at him. "No therapy today, please."

"You fuckers always need my therapy," he deadpans. "Hell, I should be getting paid for this shit."

"He's not wrong," Cam says, duffel bag in hand. "But then there was that one time your ass tried to steal my girl, so I think we're even. Especially since I didn't beat the fuck out of you."

Hunter holds his hands up. "It was *one* dinner date—"

"Wasn't a date!" Cam interrupts him. "It was like … an awkward meal. Shared between two complete strangers. While one was thinking about me the entire time." He fists-bumps Brody.

"I was. You got me." Hunter shrugs.

Cam rolls his eyes. "I meant Addy, you dick."

Last year, Cam and Addison had some sort of secret relationship, and when they were on the outs, Hunter asked her to dinner. Cam didn't like it and essentially crashed their date in true Cam Hardy fashion. It all worked out because Hunter was only doing it to make his then ex-girlfriend jealous anyway. And now, we're all back to being best friends.

I look up at Brody. "You look all spiffed up. Where are you headed?"

"His old lady is at Club 83. He's gotta roll in there and protect what's his," Cam chimes in, smirking like an idiot. "Ain't that right, O'Brien?"

Brody looks annoyed and dips his head closer to Cam, whose eyes widen.

"Fuck, sorry," Cam mutters, his eyes finding me.

Standing, I stalk toward Brody. "Let me guess. *She's* there."

"I have it covered, Sterns. I'm headed there now. I'll keep an eye out from a distance." He pats my shoulder. "I'm not going to let anything happen to her."

Backing away from him, I quickly grab my bag and head toward the door.

Oliver could be at the club too, watching from the shadows. Waiting for the perfect time to attack her again.

I have to be there to make sure that doesn't happen.

TATE

"Girl, this is what we needed," Bria cheers, taking a long sip from her drink.

I look around Club 83 and try not to let the thought of something bad happening creep in. Oliver is gone—at least, I hope he is. And I can't let one incident shape the rest of my college career. Besides, since it happened, I've brushed up on my self-defense, and I even bought a small Taser and pepper spray to stow away in my tiny crossbody purse. If someone wants to mess with me, they'll be in for a rude awakening.

"Brody's going to be mad you weren't at the game tonight, you know," I yell over the music. "He's sensitive about that type of stuff."

Though they seem to still be in a weird place with their friendship, they are talking again, which makes me happy. Brody is stubborn, and underneath the shirtless, tattooed beefcake of a man … he's damaged. And a strong woman like Bria would be the best thing that's ever happened to him. *If* he could just figure his shit out enough to let her in, that is.

"He'll deal. Besides, they won, so he won't care who was there," she tosses back. "He knows I was bringing you out for some fun tonight." Bumping her shoulder to mine, she smiles. "And you having fun was much more important to him than me being at the game. His words, not mine."

"He's a good one," I tell her, knowing she already knows. "Most people don't know just how good he is. I'm glad you do."

Her expression grows somber for a second before she brushes it off. "Let's dance!" she yells, raising an eyebrow. "What do you say, *Tater Tot?*"

Taking a long draw from my beer, finishing it off, I stand. "I say, hell yes!"

Beelining it for the dance floor, I think we both try to forget our boy troubles and just shake our asses and act like the college girls we are. And the one good thing about Bria and Brody not figuring their crap out and being a couple? She can be my wingwoman when it comes to dancing with cute boys.

I carry my purse on me at all times, just in case. And I make sure we stay in a well-lit spot on the dance floor with lots of other people.

With Bria in front of me, we dance to "Flowers" by Miley Cyrus. Both singing the lyrics and laughing hysterically at how awful we sound. I'm sweaty, and I'm probably starting to stink. But I'm actually having fun. Something I never thought would happen again.

The song switches to "10:35" by Tate McRae, and a few of the guys we've hung out with most of the night make their way back behind us. I dance in a guy's arms, completely letting loose and not caring about a damn thing.

My brain plays tricks on me again, making me feel like Link's eyes are on me. And even though I know I'm imagining it … it makes me want to dance sexier. And like a completely crazy person, I pretend the dude behind me is him. I squeeze my eyes shut, imagining it's Link's hands on my waist, not this random person's. And I will myself to recall Link's scent, breathing it in.

When "Last Night" by Morgan Wallen comes on, I open my eyes and notice Brody has found Bria. And even though he's trying to play it cool that she's dancing with another man, it's clear he's irked.

"I'm going to run to the restroom," I yell to them, and they both nod.

Making my way through the crowd, I push the door open and take in the sight of two drunk girls giggling as they look at the mirror. At the sight of me, they frown in true mean-girl form and brush past me, going back out to the club.

I grab a paper towel and wet it, dabbing it on my face and chest to cool myself down. My eyes are slightly bloodshot, and my hair is a damn mess from dancing.

The door flies open, but I don't bother looking to see who it is. That is, until a pair of arms traps me against the sink and a pair of familiar blue eyes stares back at me in the mirror.

"Link," I whisper, staring at his reflection.

"How do you do it?" he rasps.

"How do I do what?"

"How do you dance with another man's hands all over your body when I can't even stand the thought of someone else touching me?" His eyes darken. "It's worse than getting stabbed in the chest, T, watching the shit I just had to see."

Turning quickly, I glare up at him with his arms still trapping me against the sink. "I have a solution for you. It's simple really." I grit my teeth. "Stop. Watching. Me."

His hand grips the back of my neck as his chest heaves and his nostrils flare. "I wish I could do that, Tate. It would make my life so much fucking easier."

Before I can object, his mouth is on mine, kissing me dizzy, making me forget everything that's wrong with this picture as I moan into his mouth.

Sliding a hand under my ass, he yanks me upward and walks us into the stall, closing the door behind him and pressing me against the door.

Unable to control myself, I kiss him back, the tip of my tongue slipping inside of his mouth. His jeans are down without me even realizing it, and he pulls my dress up, pushing my thong to the side and driving inside of me, all at once, making me yelp.

He pulls back, burying his face against my neck as he thrusts in and out, pushing me against the cool metal of the door over and over again. His hands hook around my thighs, digging into my flesh.

It's fast and furious. And neither of us says a word. And just when he pulls back to look at me is the second my body lets go. Giving in to a man who probably doesn't deserve this, but I need it. And apparently, he does, too, because I feel him twitch inside of me, coming undone just as the door opens and someone rushes in.

I fight back the urge to cry out as I reach the peak of my orgasm, and when the smallest moan escapes me, he places his hand over my mouth, somehow making the intensity grow.

Finally, whoever it is opens the door and walks out. Leaving us once again alone. Only this time, I'm not blinded by pure, desperate need. But hit with the cold, hard reality of what we just did. And the fact that it probably put me back weeks in my healing process. At least.

Stepping back, he lets my feet slide to the floor. I quickly slide my dress down and step around him.

My hand's on the door when I catch sight of him in the mirror. He doesn't look proud or satisfied.

He looks broken. He looks like that same boy who just found out his mother had cancer, the one I so desperately wanted to save.

But just like Link found out with me, you can't save someone who won't let you. And even though it kills me to do it, I open the door ... and I walk away from my best friend.

And this time, I never look back.

20

LINK

The calendar reads December 25. *Christmas Day*. But like every other year since Mom's been gone, it just feels like another day. Only more depressing.

There's just a darkness that settles over my brothers and me on the holidays. Dad too. For Thanksgiving, I was lucky enough to not come home. But Trav thought that we needed to be here for Christmas, and even though it's pretty apparent our father doesn't want us here, we're here nonetheless.

Nobody has been at Tate's mom's since I got here last night. I have no idea what they are doing for the holiday, but it's clear they aren't celebrating it at home. I've kept tabs on Tate's mom through Brody. And even though I'd be lying if I said I didn't hate that woman now, I'm happy for Tate to hear her mom's doing well and finally got her shit figured out. When it comes down to it, Tate needs her mom more than she'll ever need me. So, even though it killed me to do it, my decision to walk away was easy.

We finish eating our Christmas dinner. And by dinner, I mean, the pizza, wings, and breadsticks Logan and I went out and got. There was no tree, so Carter found a tiny one in the attic and brought it downstairs.

Dad doesn't give out any gifts. He hasn't in years. I guess he probably never had to do it before because Mom always did the shopping. And now, well, I guess he just doesn't want to deal with it,

My brothers and I buy each other something every year. And every year, we join up to give our father something too.

He always awkwardly opens it, muttering, "Thank you," before he gets up and cleans up the mess he thinks we've made.

This year is no different.

He opens the new shop vac we got him for work, along with some new tools and work pants, and utters, "Thank you," and now, he's nowhere to be seen.

Looking out the window, I squint when I see Clyde using a leaf blower to clean his driveway off. Jumping up from the couch, I pull my sneakers on and run across the road.

"Hey, let me do that for you, Clyde." I hold my hand out, and he grins at me.

"Merry Christmas, Link," he says cheerfully. "Why in the hell would you want to clean an old bastard's driveway on Christmas?"

"Trust me, it beats what I was doing—" I stop before saying anything else. "I've got nothin' else going on. Besides, you said you were old. How are you going to know you aren't missing piles of dirt with your old-ass eyes?"

He laughs, passing me the blower. "I suppose you do have a point there, my boy. And then Caroline will be bitchin' at me for not doing a good enough job." Turning toward the house, he points. "You come in and see us when you're done, you hear?"

I nod. "Well, of course. I wouldn't just take off without coming to see y'all—you know better."

"Good man," he says before walking inside, and I cringe, knowing I'm really not all that good.

TATE

The sound of the boat cutting through the water and the sun beaming down on my skin have me stretching my arms over my head with a yawn. I close my book and glance over at Meyer, who I can tell is bouncing out of her seat to go do something fun. And Mom, who keeps her eyes closed but I know she isn't sleeping.

This year, we decided to do something different for the holiday. My mom didn't want to be at the house because she said it held too many memories. Meyer didn't want to have Christmas there because, honestly, I think she was still traumatized from finding our mother in the bathtub a month ago. And me? I didn't want to risk running into Link. So, when Meyer proposed a cruise to the Bahamas, it was a no-brainer.

We've had a few people come up to us, asking if we are Harvey Tracy's family. We played dumb, pretending we didn't know who he was. Another time, we even pretended we didn't speak English, and that got rid of them fast.

It's been good for all three of us to spend this time together, and I'm sad it'll end in a few days.

"All right," Meyer says, standing, "that's it. I'm going to find us an activity to do later. Be back in twenty."

As she walks off, my mom's eyes open, and she giggles. "That kid, I tell you. We've been relaxing for forty-five minutes, and she already can't stand it."

I smile. And even though I'm happy to be here, that pain is still very much there in my chest. The pain that started the day I went to Boston but then went away the night Link made me that damn grilled cheese. Only to return weeks later when he decided to break my heart.

Every particle of what makes me who I am misses him. I wake up, exhausted, and that's how I go through my days. They say time heals all broken hearts. God, I hope that's true.

"Talk to me, Tate girl," my mom says, flipping onto her side to face me. "We're on a boat, floating in the ocean. The food is to die for. The staff is superb." She looks sad. "So, what's wrong? Where do you go when you check out mentally sometimes?"

"Is it that noticeable?" I mutter. "Sorry, I hope I haven't been a Debbie Downer."

Reaching for my hand, she shakes her head. "No, no, baby. You haven't. But you haven't been yourself in quite some time. Actually, I don't really remember when the last time was. I get a glimpse of you, but then you're … different. Is it school? Is it your dad?"

Sitting up, I brush my hair away from my face and swallow back the emotions rising up. "No, it's Link."

She shoots up in her seat, her eyes widening a fraction. "Link?"

Slowly, I nod. "I miss him every hour of every day. I wish I hadn't been so stupid years ago. I let my fear of ending up like—" I pause, panicked that I almost just blamed my issues on my mother with her sitting next to me.

"Me?" her voice squeaks. "You were worried about ending up like me?"

I sigh, giving her a long look before deciding to be honest. "Yeah, I was. And now, I realize I let fear stop me from living my life. I love him, Mom. And at the end of the day, he isn't my dad."

"But the reporters? The paparazzi? He's going to be dealing with all of that," she blurts out. "Do you remember how much you hated that when your father was at his peak?" Her eyes grow glossy. "I thought … I thought they'd ruin you. You were so unhappy."

"I'd take a thousand reporters, following me around every day, if it just meant he'd be coming home to me every night." I let the tears fall. "Some people are just worth going through the uncomfortable stuff for. And Link, he's that someone for me." I wipe my face with the back of my hand. "But I ruined it. And now, he'll never be mine."

Grabbing my hands, she looks at me with a sheer look of panic on her face.

"I messed up," she whispers. "I really, really messed up."

LINK

Leaf blowing Clyde and Caroline's driveway quickly turned into me cleaning their entire yard, ridding it of all the sticks and debris from the last windstorm and trimming a few branches that were starting to be overgrown.

Brushing my hands together, I put everything back in the shed before heading toward the house.

I know I don't have to knock. If I did, Caroline would scold me that I didn't have to do that. So, just like I always have, I slowly push the door open and walk in.

The smell of gingerbread hits my nose right away. As long as I've known her, Caroline has always had something baking. Heck, I think she fed my family for months after Mom died.

"There's my boy," she says from the love seat as I walk into the living room. "I gave Clyde holy hell for putting you to work on Christmas Day."

Clyde holds his hands up. "He insisted." He peers out the window. "I guess you did all right."

"He did great," she scolds him before she looks at me again. "Merry Christmas, Link. I'm awfully glad you stopped by. It just isn't the same on this street now that the kiddos are all grown up."

I take a seat in the empty recliner. "Merry Christmas. How was y'all's day?"

"Same as every day, I suppose," Clyde drawls slowly. "How's your dad?"

Sitting back, I rest my arms on the sides of the chair. "Same as every day, I suppose." I mimic his words. "He's … managing, I guess."

"Yeah, well, that's all we can do, right?" She frowns. "You should have taken him on one of those vacations, like Tate and Meyer took their mother on for Christmas. Now, *that's* the way to spend a holiday."

"What kind of trip is that?" I try not to seem too surprised, playing it off like it's nothing to me. "Where'd they go?"

"Oh, Tate didn't tell you?" Caroline sounds stunned. "They went on a Christmas cruise. Huge ship that goes to the Bahamas." She shakes her head again, confused. "I still can't believe you didn't know this already. Why, I didn't think Tate did anything without you knowing about it."

I look down, gripping my hands together as I try to think of something, anything, to change the subject, but Caroline doesn't give up.

"Link, what's going on with you and Tate?" When I don't respond, she points toward me. "Don't make me come over there and beat it out of you, child. Tell me what happened."

Taking a breath, I push it out. "We aren't really friends right now. Actually, we aren't even talking."

"And why the hell not?" Clyde gripes. "What'd you do?"

I throw my hand up. "Why do you just assume it was me? Jeez."

"Boy, I know it was," he says back quickly. "Now, the question is, what are you gonna do to fix it?"

"Clyde," Caroline hisses in warning, "cool it."

I sit back again, resting my head on the plush back of the chair. "Not a damn thing."

"You ain't got a brain in there, kid," Clyde grumbles. "That's a shame. Never seen two kids take to each other quite like the pair of you did. From day one, you were a moth to a flame."

"It's complicated, all right? I'm no good for her. I'm not what she needs." I drag my hand over my face. "Hell, even her mama thinks so. I'm telling you, if there was something I could do, I'd do it. But I can't."

Slowly, Caroline stands. "I'm going to let you men talk." She takes a few steps before stopping in front of me and reaching for my hand. "Best make sure you let Tate decide what's good for her." Giving my hand a squeeze, she lets it go and pats my cheek. "Merry Christmas, Link," she whispers sweetly and goes into the kitchen.

"You're telling me, her mom, Meg, doesn't want you with Tate?" He looks around thoughtfully. "And why on earth would that be?"

"Because, Clyde, after this school year, I'm headed to California." I swallow. "I'm going to be an LA King."

His head snaps back, and his eyes widen. "You're saying you made it to the NHL?"

"Well, yeah. I accepted verbally, but before signing anything, I told them I wanted to fly out there and meet everyone and talk about the details."

"And remind me why this affects you and Tate?" he scoffs. "Heck, you two ought to be celebrating."

"Her old man. He's made it so she'll never see a future with me."

"Let me tell you, kid. You sure as hell ain't her shithead daddy." His nose scrunches up. "Now, that's a man who needs a good ass-kickin'."

"It's not just that." Leaning forward, I rest my arms on my legs and clap my hands together. "I'm going to be in the media. The news. The internet." My face twists. "Everything she can't handle. And she shouldn't have to either. Not after what her father put his family through."

"I see," he says thoughtfully. "And Tate told you this? That she couldn't handle it?"

"Well, no."

"Then, where the heck did you come up with it? Your big, old brain?"

I look at him nervously. "I can't say."

"Bullshit," he says quickly. "You can, and you will."

When I don't answer, he guesses, "Meg. She told you to stay away, and Tate has no idea."

"Pretty much," I sigh. "It was more complicated than that. But I'll say, she didn't leave me a choice. And I don't fault her for it either. She's scared. She's terrified of losing her daughter."

"I don't like the sound of this, not one bit," he grumbles, looking over his glasses at me. "But let me ask you this, Link. How much does that girl mean to you?"

"It doesn't matter, Clyde—"

"Dammit, for being a smart kid, you sure are dumb sometimes," he hollers, slapping his hand down on the armrest. "Now, answer the question."

"She means everything to me. Not a thing matters now that she's gone," I say genuinely. "And it won't matter, not even when I'm playing on that ice as a King in a packed arena." I look him in the eyes. "I could be surrounded by a sea of people, all chanting my name, and I'd still look for her." My heart aches. "Every. Single. Time."

"Well then, I reckon you know what you have to do, don't you?"

Raking my hand over the top of my head, I shrug. "Not really. What about Meg?"

"Meg is a scared mother, trying to protect her daughter from getting hurt the way she has been," he answers bluntly. "But she's hurting her instead of helping her right now. So, I say, she'll have to deal with it, won't she?"

"I said some things." I cringe. "I don't know if she even wants me anymore."

"If you plan on being together forever, you're gonna say a helluva lot more things that'll piss her off." He chuckles. "I promise you that. But it doesn't matter what tears you apart in those moments of anger and frustration. It matters that you go back and fix it." Standing up, he clasps his hand on my shoulder. "Make it right, Link. Be a damn shame to lose a girl like Tate who looks at a knucklehead like you the way that she does."

My chest suddenly feels lighter, and breathing becomes easier as I look at him and laugh. For the first time in weeks, I believe that maybe, just maybe, everything will be okay.

TATE

Once we've moved from the public ship deck to our stateroom, my mom sits down on the edge of the bed and pats the spot next to her, wanting me to do the same.

"You're blaming yourself for how things ended with Link?" she asks, keeping her voice calm.

"Well, yeah," I say, looking at the carpet. "For the entire time I've known him, I have voiced over and over how I'd never be able to be with someone who was a professional athlete. I fixated on it." I bite my lip as I suck in a breath. "It's no wonder when he got that call from the Kings that he assumed I'd never want to go with him. Or why he thought being in the public eye would get to me."

"And would it?" She clears her throat. "Would it get to you, in a negative way, being back in the public eye?" Her hand touches my shoulder as she brushes my hair back. "Honestly."

"It wouldn't be easy—I know that much." I turn toward her, tears in my eyes. "But it wouldn't be nearly as difficult as not having him around." I sniffle. "This is hell, Mom. Literal hell. Day in and day out. And I can't sleep. I can barely eat." I swallow or attempt to. "He's my best friend, yeah. But he's also the man I love. I've been in love with him since we were kids." I shrug. "I know they say it's normal to not get over your first love, but this isn't like that. It's so much more."

Her hand rakes down my head before she cups my cheek with her palm. "I'm so sorry, Tate."

A tiny, sad, pathetic laugh bubbles from me. "For what? It's not like you did anything."

"No, I did," she says, staring at me nervously. "Please promise me you'll forgive me for what I'm about to tell you. I can't lose you, baby girl."

"What—what are you talking about?" My head rears back from her touch. "What did you do?"

"I thought it was for the best," she whispers. "I was scared that if you continued down that road, chasing Link's dreams instead of your own, that you'd lose yourself. I didn't want *them*, the judgmental pricks in this world, to ruin you the way they ruined me."

"So, what?" I feel dizzy. "You sent him away?"

"Yes. At the hospital that day. I was just waking up, and I saw him there. Even though I hadn't been in my right mind when I took those pills, I'd still known what taking them meant. The very thought that, one day, that could be you?" Her voice breaks. "I just didn't want them to get to you too. You've been doing so good now that you're older and you have separated yourself more from your dad and his fans."

I stand quickly, putting some space between us.

I pace back and forth, unable to fully grasp what she's saying.

Pushing herself up, she follows me. "If I had known then what I know now, I never would have done it! But I was bitter. I woke up, embarrassed and ashamed. And I just knew the way he was carrying himself, how light he was, that you and he were together. And I looked around at my reality, and I panicked." Stopping me, she holds my face, putting her forehead against mine. "Everything I did was out of love then. Just like it is right now too."

"I can't believe you'd do that behind my back," my voice croaks. "I trusted you. You, Link, and Meyer are the only three people I trust. And now, I know you and Link kept this from me."

"Don't blame him, sweetheart," she says quickly. "I'm not proud to admit this, but I didn't really leave him a choice. And doing this? It broke him."

Sitting on the edge of the bed again, I drop my head down. "So, now what? What the hell am I supposed to do with this information, Mom?"

Coming to my side, she sighs. "Well, when we get off this ship in a few days, I guess you'll make your choice. But I don't think it'll be hard for you, will it?"

When I don't answer, she pats my arm. "You can be angry with me as long as you need to be. I understand. I really, really messed up. I'm so sorry, Tate. Like your dad, I let you down."

I hear her words, but I don't respond. Because frankly, I am pissed. And I need time to process this all and cool off.

It might have taken me some time to fully understand it. But the truth is, choosing Link will never be a hard decision. I'll choose him every time. But now, the question is … will he still choose me?

God, I hope so.

LINK

The past three days have been a whirlwind of a shit show, to put it lightly.

Christmas Day, I realized I had walked away too easily. I hadn't fought for what I wanted, and talking to an old fuck like Clyde, I knew I had taken the coward's way out. I couldn't just call Tate and tell her the truth. She needed something more.

Besides, I called her phone countless times, and it went to voice mail. So, after some investigating, I found out exactly what port the ship was coming back to and what time. So, after traveling back to Brooks for practice, I hit the road.

Now, here I am. Standing at the port terminal with a bouquet of Tate's favorite flowers—lilies—and a four-leaf clover in my pocket because after the way I acted, I can use all the help I can get.

Tate has never made me nervous. We've always been too close for that. But right here, in this moment ... I'm fucking terrified.

A large crowd of people slowly enters the port terminal building, making their way to the other side of it before walking outside. Pulling suitcases and pushing strollers, people brush past me as I stand in the dead center of the building, looking for her face.

Coming through the open double doors, she moves slowly between Meyer and Meg. She takes each stride with caution, not wanting to push anyone out of the way or step on anyone's toes. And when she looks in my direction, I lose my breath just at the sight of her.

Her skin glows from being in the sun all week, and her hair is back to plain brown. She's wearing cutoff shorts and a fitted white top, making my palms sweat with the need to touch her.

Her eyes squint as she looks directly at me before her entire face lights up and she smiles.

Taking off in a jog, I push through the crowd until I'm right in front of her.

"Hi," I say, looking down at her as I tuck her hair behind her ear.

"Um … hi." She looks up at me, eyes wide. "What are—how are you here right now? Did my mom call you?"

"I would have if my damn phone had worked," Meg says next to us. "But, no, I didn't. We're going to be out in the waiting area." She pats my arm, but my eyes never break away from her daughter's. "Take your time."

Setting the flowers down on top of her suitcase, I open my mouth to explain everything. But before I can, Tate's voice, small but clear, beats me to it.

"She told me the truth," she whispers. "I really can't believe she did that. I'm so mad that she came between us."

Even though I'm still pissed at Meg for what she did, I know she did it out of love. Deep down, I'm sure Tate does too.

"I'm mad too, T. She was just afraid," I say, cupping her face. "But she doesn't have to be. Neither do you."

Her eyes fill with tears, and she bites her lip. "I know. I … I shouldn't have ever put you in the same category as my father. You're not him."

"No, I'm not. And I never will be either," I answer sharply. "But I understand why you were scared."

I brush my thumb across her cheek, wiping a tear away. "Tate, I've only had two loves in my life. Hockey and you. But I'd walk away from the game right now if it meant you were mine forever." I swallow. "I wouldn't think twice about it."

"You won't have to," she says faintly, her hands resting on my waist. "Hockey is what you were made for. And now that I've had time to reflect on everything, I know the passion you have to be the best you can be at it is another thing I love about you. I'm ready to be there, beside you, on this next step. Like I should have been this entire time."

"I wasn't made to play hockey, Tate. I was made to love you. And I'm going to do that from here on out. Above everything else. *Even* hockey." Finally leaning down, I kiss her. "I promise you, I'll never put you in a situation where you could get hurt. And I swear, however hectic this life gets, we'll have something your mom didn't. We'll have each other."

She sniffles, pulling in a breath through her nose. "I believe you. And I trust you with my whole heart." She smiles, nodding slowly. "I promise that when you leave for California, we will figure out a way to make it work. Even while I finish school."

"We won't need to," I say casually. "Not yet anyway."

"What—what do you mean?" Her eyes show panic. "What did you do?"

"I called the general manager yesterday. I told him I wanted to be a King for sure. Just not yet. Because I'm going to be staying another year at Brooks and graduating—with you. Well, at least while you get your bachelor's." I kiss her again. "I know that you'll still have another year of schooling after that, but we'll cross that bridge when we get to it. But for now, I'll get to stay and play another year as a Wolf. The only stipulation is, you're required to be at all of my home games, cheering me on." I wink. "Oh, and in my jersey, which I'll rip off of you each night after a game. So, what do you say, Tate Tracy? Do you take the deal?"

"Are you sure? Like, *really* sure?" Her eyes move between mine nervously. "I mean, you don't think you'll resent me?"

"Fuck no." I laugh. "It's never been about the fame or even the money for me. It's been about the feeling I get when I'm on the ice." I shrug. "I get that every time I play for Brooks, with my guys. And you know what always makes it even better?"

"What?" she whispers.

"When you're there. You're the only one who matters, T. Someday, thousands of people might know my name. But you're the only person I need cheering me on. As long as I have you, I'll be fine."

"I love you," she utters before launching herself into my arms. "I love you so much."

Lifting her up, I hold her thighs as her mouth attacks mine. We might be in a building full of people, but that isn't stopping us one bit.

"It only took us nine years for us to figure our shit out. But here we are," I mumble against her lips. "Nine years and a lot of fuckups."

"Better late than never," she says thoughtfully, pressing her forehead against mine. "Besides, it wasn't all bad. In fact, all but two of those nine years still had the best days of my life."

"Yeah, me too." I nod before kissing her again. "Especially that time in our old homeroom classroom."

Her cheeks turn red, and she squeezes her eyes shut. "I can't believe we did that."

Slowly setting her onto her feet, I curse the blood continuing to run to my cock, making it ache in a way it shouldn't in a public place.

"Let's go home. You ready?"

"I thought you'd never ask." She sighs. "I'm ready to start the next chapter in the *Chronicles of Tate and Link*."

"You and me both. But the new chapter has to still consist of blow jobs in the shower from time to time."

"Perhaps," she singsongs back.

Taking her suitcase from her, I throw my arm around her as we walk out of the terminal and outside. Like she said, to start whatever the hell this next chapter is. Shit, maybe it's even a whole new book.

It took us too long to get here, but I still wouldn't change any of it. Because even as a best friend, I had gotten to have Tate Tracy close to me for a long time. I've always belonged to her even if she didn't realize it.

TATE

There was no way we were making it back home before climbing each other like a tree. So, after saying good-bye to Meyer and my mother and getting inside the truck, we started kissing. Kissing turned to touching. Which somehow led to me naked in the backseat of his truck as he now kisses his way down my stomach, parting my legs with his hand.

"Christ, it's been too long since I've tasted you," his gruff voice murmurs against my flesh before he looks up at me. "So damn beautiful, T."

My fingers fist into his hair as I watch his head move between my legs, and he dips his tongue inside of me, making me whimper with deep-rooted desperation in its purest, most potent form.

"Fuck me sideways," he coos, pulling back. "Just as sweet as I remember." His tongue slips inside again. "Like a fucking cupcake."

One hand gripping his hair and the other on the edge of the seat, I moan as his tongue hits me just right, awakening every cell in my body. My spine stiffens, and goose bumps break out over my skin. As my thighs tighten around his neck greedily, I pull him in deeper.

"Link," I cry out.

He looks up at me, continuing to do whatever magical shit he's doing, making me shiver. Something about the visual of him deep between my thighs, completely ravaging me like I'm his prey … it's so much hotter than I could have anticipated.

Abruptly, I need him closer, and I yank him upward. "I need more. I need you right now."

He smirks. "Tell me what you need, sweet thing."

"You to fuck me. Hard." I swallow. "Now."

Pulling his jeans down just enough to expose his hard length, he crawls over me and takes my hands in one of his. Then, he parts my legs before slowly pushing himself inside.

"You're always so ready for me, aren't you?" he grumbles against my neck. "Did you think about me while you were gone?"

"Every damn second," I moan, my hips lifting up to meet his thrust, making him hit deeper, and I wince.

"Look at you, taking my cock so good." He pounds into me harder as my back presses against the leather seat.

"You're so perfect," he rasps, his hand releasing my own and cupping my neck. "This body was made for me to worship."

When my legs wrap around his waist, dragging him in closer with every thrust, I start to drift into a heavenly bliss as my body succumbs to him. Being without him and the intensity of this day have my body unable to fight this release. A loud moan escapes my lips, and when he bites my shoulder, I'm clawing his back.

Everything begins to tingle. As his moves become slower, I feel him twitch inside of me, telling me we're in this together.

"Fuck," he mutters. "That's right, squeeze me like a good girl." He bites down, this time on my neck. "So greedy for every inch as you drip on my cock."

"Yes," I cry out, letting my head fall back on the seat. "Oh, Link. Dear God—"

The sound of heavy breathing, along with our bodies colliding, is the only thing filling the cab of the truck. And as our movements slow, he kisses up my neck, around my jawline, to my cheek before stopping at my lips.

"Missed me, did you?" He smirks. "Who knew you were going to be so fucking filthy?"

Swatting him, I cover my face with my hand. "Shut up."

"I dig it, babe. And to be honest, it'll come in handy. Because I plan to fuck you in every position over the course of the next few days." Giving me a peck on the lips, he winks. "Gotta make up for lost time. Besides, years apart meant my imagination was working overtime." Putting a finger to his temple, he taps. "Lots of ideas up here."

Slowly, we sit up and pull our clothes back on. The entire time, we're grinning like fools because for once in the whole time we've known each other, it all feels like it's going to work out.

And I really hope that's true. Because I am finally getting exactly what I've always wanted.

Him.

TATE

"I don't want you to go." I pout, poking my bottom lip out as I watch my newly declared boyfriend get dressed to head out to his away game tonight. "Who will keep me warm?"

Bria and I were going to go, but we opted for a girls' night instead.

"Lady, the way you've been jumping my bones lately, there aren't enough protein shakes or steaks in the world to replenish the nutrients I'm losing, fucking you every way to Sunday."

I sigh. "Oh, so does that mean you don't want to take a shower with me when you get back?" I stand, pulling my lips to the side innocently. "I guess I'll just go take one now. With lots and lots of sudsy bubbles."

Quickly planting his hands on my waist, he throws me over his shoulder. "Don't you fucking dare. These tits are mine to suds up, you hear?"

He brings his hand down on my ass before tossing me on the bed. Walking over to his duffel bag, he pulls out a pack of Reese's and a can of Diet Coke and throws them to me softly.

"This should keep you busy for, like ... five minutes. But if you still get the urge to *shower*, maybe this will stop you." Throwing me a package of Ruffle's All Dressed chips, he cringes. "Those are the world's grossest chips, by the way. I felt like a sick motherfucker even buying them."

Leaning down, he kisses me. "I'll be back late tonight. I love you."

Holding up the package of candy, I tear it open. Biting into the chocolate peanut butter perfection, I moan. "I love you too, but only because you bring me treats."

"Yeah, yeah." He rolls his eyes. "If you're good, I'll have you spread those pretty legs while I eat one of those right off of you when I get back." Kissing me one last time, he smirks. "But I'll be honest, I like the way you taste better."

"Is that a promise?" I raise an eyebrow and slap his butt when he stands. "Good luck."

"Thanks, babe."

I watch him leave and pull a pillow over my face, smiling at absolutely no one like a complete moron.

Two weeks ago, all of my dreams finally came true. And even though I know there will be tough times ahead, my heart is bursting at the seams with happiness at this moment.

I only wish I had grown up sooner and seen what was in front of me. But I was scared. Either way, I guess we all get to where we're going in due time.

And maybe, just maybe, love is enough sometimes.

LINK

"Ain't you out there, looking like a hotshot?" Cam drawls, skating beside me. "What did you do before this, coke?"

"Oh, yeah. And crack," I deadpan. "No, just having a good night, I guess."

"That's what happens when you get you a lady." He winks. "Some good ol' lovin' nightly. It's wholesome for the soul."

"Can Coach read lips?" I nod toward Coach LaConte, who is glaring at Cam. "Because if looks could kill, you'd be fucking dead right now."

"Shit," Cam mutters. "That ain't good."

As he skates off, I chuckle, shaking my head before halftime ends and it's back to game time. Maybe it's knowing Tate is watching me from home that pushes me to go as hard as I have. Either way, I used to not want the game to end because I didn't want to be alone with my thoughts. Now, I can't wait for the buzzer to sound, so I get to go home.

Brody saunters by, and I jerk my chin up at him.

"Your ass going to be back in that penalty box this second half, O'Brien?"

He's always rough. And if I were on the other team, I'd shit my pants to see him coming at me. But each move he makes, every time he gets aggressive, it's all because he's protecting his teammates. We are brothers. And Brody and Cam have become my family.

Holding one arm out to his side, he grins. "Is a frog's ass watertight?"

"So, that's a no, I take it?"

"It'd be like me asking you, *Sterns, you gonna score again?*" He shrugs. "What would you say to that?"

"I'd say, does Dolly Parton sleep on her back?"

"Fucking right she does." He nods, smirking like an idiot before giving me a fist bump. "Let's get this shit done."

I skate behind him. "Let's go."

TATE

Once the game is over, I flip the TV off and yawn, stretching my arms above my head. "I'm tired. But I'm also starving. Pizza?"

"I'm hungry too," Bria says, sticking her bottom lip out in a pout. "I just remembered I do have to finish research for the paper I'm writing. It should only take me an hour, tops."

"Why don't I go pick up a pizza while you finish that?" I stand, twirling around. "And Ben & Jerry's. *And* Diet Coke."

"Fuck your aspartame." She scowls. "I want regular sugary Coke."

"Chicken bacon ranch?" I raise an eyebrow. "And breadsticks?"

"Tate Tracy, if I were into women, I'd wife you up right now." She sighs before reaching in her pocket and handing me some cash. "My mouth is watering, just thinking about food."

Grabbing my phone from the coffee table, I call and order the food.

Pulling my sneakers on, I yank my hair into a messy bun. "I'll leave now. I need to grab a few things at the store anyway. Any requests?"

"Get a bottle of ranch. They are stingy with that shit," she says, opening her laptop. "You da best."

"BRB!" I call cheerfully before rushing out to my car.

I'm so thankful for the relationship I have with Bria. We are so alike while also being completely different at the same time. She's quickly become one of my closest friends. Not like that would take much, seeing's my roster is pretty pathetic.

Once a week, we go on a hike because that's something she loves to do. And when I started a new kickboxing class, she volunteered to go with me.

And now, here we are, about to pig out on enough food to feed six people with absolutely no shame.

I drive to the store, listening to my playlist that consists of Morgan Wallen, Luke Combs, and Bailey Zimmerman. I sing along to all my favorites, knowing my voice is shit.

Turning into the parking lot, I park the car and step out.

Even though I look like a moron, I'm still smiling the smallest bit. Because, one, my boyfriend's team is so close to a guaranteed spot in the Frozen Four. And, two, life is good. Despite that I haven't spoken to my father since his wedding day. That's something I have to leave in the past. My mother is doing great, and Meyer is happy. And finally, Link and I have found our happily ever after.

It's funny how, not long ago, it seemed like it would be the end of the world to be married to a professional hockey player. Now, I find myself excited for our future. I know we'll have to figure out the logistics of me finishing my degree and him moving to LA, but I have no doubt we'll make a plan that is perfect for us. We might have a few hiccups or roadblocks along the way—because it's us and that's our norm. But together … we've got this.

As I walk into the store and head to the pizza counter, a voice stops me.

"Tate?" a man says.

I turn slowly to find Oliver taking a few steps toward me.

My eyes widen, and panic rises in my gut, but he quickly stops moving when he sees my reaction.

"I'm not going to hurt you." He cringes. "But I can see why you'd be scared." His eyebrows pull together. "I don't remember a whole lot from that night, but from what I do remember and the things I've been told … I was a monster." He swallows. "I'm sorry, Tate. I was drunk, and … well, I guess it's no secret now that I was attracted to you."

I stare at him, unable to form any words.

Finally, he sighs. "Look, I'm just back here to tie up a few loose ends. I'm not staying, so don't worry. But for what it's worth, which I'm sure isn't much, I'm so sorry for the way I acted. I don't expect you to forgive me. I just needed to tell you that."

Eventually, I nod. "All right," I whisper.

And then I walk away. Because life is pretty great and the last thing I want to do is dwell on the past.

24

TATE
FOUR MONTHS LATER

"Look, Tate! Look, I'm wearing the hat you made me," the cutest little voice says from behind me as I feel a tiny hand on my shoulder. "And Mommy is wearing hers too!"

Turning, I see Isla and her mom, Addison, standing behind her. Both wearing the blue-and-gray hats I made in Brooks colors. I had seen the two of them at team events and a few times when the guys hung out, but one day, Addison brought Isla into the Astronomy Center, and I got to know Isla more and adored her. So much that I had gone to the store that day and gotten new yarn and pom-poms for their hats.

"They look so good!" I beam at them. "I'm so glad they fit!"

"They fit perfectly. And that means you're a good knitter lady because my mommy says I have a big noggin and most kids hats are too tight."

I laugh, looking at Addison, who shrugs. "It's true. It must be that big brain of yours!"

"Me and Cam watched a show that said a bigger brain actually makes you stupider." Isla scowls. "And I'm smart for my age. So, that means my brain isn't ginormous."

"Lovely," Addison murmurs, squeezing her eyes shut, and I have to fight a chuckle.

"*Anyway*"—Addison shakes her head—"thanks again for the hats! Let's do lunch or coffee soon."

"That sounds gre—" I start to say.

"I can't have coffee. So, let's do lunch," Isla says, turning her head to the side and tapping her foot. "I'm not missing out on girl time."

"Well, obviously not!" I wink. "What would a girls' day be without Isla?"

She widens her eyes. "That's what I'm saying."

Once they find their seats, I turn my attention back to the ice just as the Wolves skate into the arena. The crowd goes wild, everyone standing and cheering loudly.

This is it. The game of their lives.

The Frozen Four.

Just as number twenty-two turns and finds me, lifting his head to the crowd, I hear a throat clear.

"Is this seat taken? Actually, this whole row? The boys should be here soon."

My eyes find Link's dad, and I can't help the smile that spreads across my face. "Reed. Hi! You made it."

He looks sort of like a fish out of water, looking around at the crowd around us, but eventually nods. "Oh, yes. I … I couldn't miss this."

He sits next to me, and I pat his arm.

"It will mean everything to him that you're here. Thank you."

He shifts nervously. That is, until his eyes look out at the ice, and suddenly, his face lights up as he holds his hand up.

When I swing my gaze to the arena, my heart cracks at the sight of Link. He waves to his dad, and even through his helmet, I know he's happy.

I think this is the first game his dad has ever come and watched. For so long, he was hurting from losing his wife. He lost sight of things, even his own kids. But he's here now. That's what matters.

Link deserves to have his family here, cheering him on. And when I hear his brothers all making their way toward us, likely turning every head in this place, I feel tears spring in my eyes. Because I know Link is looking up here, so content and feeling loved. And that's all I want for him.

LINK

I stare at the scoreboard, completely in shock.

It's over. One of the biggest games of my life, done. And we did it.

We fucking did it!

"Yeah, buddy!" Cam throws his arm around my neck, pulling me against him.

We're both sweaty, and we likely smell like ass, but neither of us cares.

"Aren't you glad you got hurt last year and couldn't leave us for the Bruins early?" I grin. "You would have missed this. Hell, this wouldn't have even been possible."

"Fucking right I am." He releases me, shoving me the slightest bit. "We had a hell of a season, Sterns. It's been an honor, skating with you."

Cam is leaving Brooks after this school year. We both feel the weight of the realization that this is it for all of us playing on one team. The entire team does. As lame as it sounds, Cam is the glue that holds the team together. It isn't going to be the same without him.

"Don't get emotional on me, Hardy," I tease him. "I'm already a wreck from this win. You don't want to see me crying and shit."

"Aw-shucks," Brody says, coming next to us. "If you get to crying, you know I'll snuggle you."

"Thanks, O'Brien. You always have my back."

"Damn right I do." He winks, pinching my nipple. "Go get your girls," he says to both of us. "They're waiting!"

Looking at the Plexiglas, I hold up a finger, telling Tate to give me a second, before quickly skating to the bench and grabbing something from under my seat.

Just like every game since we got together, Tate is waiting for me, and I know that this will always be my favorite part of each game. Win or lose, it's knowing she'll be there after.

She's like coming home. And I'm so excited to spend my life with her.

Skating to the exit, I make my way up the stairs. When I spot her, I cup my hands around my mouth and call her name until she sees me. Her face lights up, and within seconds, she's running through the bleachers, headed for me.

Lifting her up, I kiss her, squeezing her against me.

"You did it!" she cheers, looking so fucking beautiful in my jersey. "I'm so proud of you! Does it feel like a dream come true?"

"Almost," I say, setting her down.

Slowly, I sink to one knee, pulling the small velvet box from my waistband.

Her hands fly to her mouth, and her eyes widen. I knew that no matter the outcome of the game, I wanted to do this tonight. But knowing my dad and brothers are all here, watching this, it means so much more. It doesn't matter to me that there's a crowd because, in this moment, it feels like it's just her and me.

"I know you hate being the center of attention, so I'm sorry for doing this right now. But truthfully, I couldn't wait. So, just focus on me and no one else. Okay?" I hold her gaze as she nods.

"I didn't know if we would win tonight or not. But I knew whatever happened, you'd be here. You are my biggest supporter. In the times where I celebrate, you're who I want to open a beer and cheers with. And in the times when everything goes wrong, you're what I need to lift me from the darkness. You are home. My compass. My arrow. My four-leaf clover. Everything that I am is because of you. I'm better because I want to be the man you see when you look at me. I'm patient because I've learned it from you. I'm honest because I can't stand the thought of ever hurting you. I'm strong because I want to be strong for you."

I take her hand in mine. "Yes, I love you. Yes, I'm in love with you. But you and I are so much more than that, Tate. And maybe this seems fast, but to be honest, I feel like I've waited for this my entire life."

I swallow. "Marriage, I suppose, is just a piece of paper, but to me, it's a promise. And I promise, whatever comes our way, we'll face it together. No matter what. As husband and wife. If you want that, that is. So, Tate Tracy, do you want to be my wife? Will you marry me?"

She sobs, still covering her mouth with her free hand. "Yes. Yes. One million times, yes."

I slide the ring onto her finger just before she yanks me upward, throwing herself into my arms.

I kiss her, lifting her body to mine and pressing my forehead against hers. "Now, it feels like a dream come true."

She sniffles, nodding slowly. "It really does."

I hear the stadium erupt into applause and my brothers come behind me, cheering. And when I finally set Tate down, my dad comes next to me, throwing his arms around my shoulders.

"My boy," he says, his eyes filling with tears. "You did good. I'm so proud."

"Thanks for being here, Dad." I nod as he steps back. "Means … so much."

"I should have been here the whole time. At all the games," he yells over the noise before jerking his chin up toward Tate. "Your mom always knew she was the one for you. She said, no matter what happened to her with her cancer, she knew you'd have Tate." He smiles. "Guess she was right."

Looking down at Tate, I pull her into my side. "Yeah, she was."

My brothers all hug us. Most muttering, "About fucking time."

They've always known how I felt about this girl. There was no hiding it.

"Damn, brother. You sure know how to make the fact that my team didn't make it here tonight hurt less." Logan grins, rubbing the top of my head. "Hell, I even got a little fucking teary-eyed. Who knew my brother could be so damn romantic?"

Laughing, I shove him off of me. "Yeah, yeah. Whatever you say." Throwing one arm around him, I pull him against me. "Thanks for being here."

"Like I'd have missed it. Besides, next year, it'll be me here, and your ass will be sitting on the bleachers, watching."

"Whatever helps you sleep at night," I joke, releasing him.

"Mom's looking down, smiling so much that it probably hurts," he says softly.

I drag in a breath through my nose just as Tate's hand finds mine.

Looking at Tate, I squeeze her hand. "I love you. So fucking much."

"I love you more." She smiles. "Always."

I know that the journey leading up to this was far from perfect. But if you ask me, perfect isn't even a real thing. Maybe it's just an illusion we're all made to think we need. Whatever it is, I'll take our story over anyone else's. No matter how flawed it might be.

epilogue

TATE
THREE YEARS LATER

I look around at the hundreds of faces in front of me, attempting to explain the process of how long the journey would take to travel to Mars for research. The last few words leave my mouth just as another sharp pain shoots through my stomach.

Looking down at my belly, I sigh. If I can just get through the remaining five minutes of the presentation, the projector will come on, and I can go to the hospital to see if I'm in labor.

Just as I open my mouth to talk, I feel a pop and a small gush of fluid, trickling down my leg slowly. It's not a huge rush, like I've seen in the movies, but unfortunately, it's enough for all the eyes in this entire freaking room to dart to the floor while everyone gasps.

"She peed!" a girl shrieks. "She just peed her pants!"

"Ew, gross!" adds a teenage boy. "I want my money back!"

"You dumbass, her water broke," a guy calls back. "Can't you tell she's pregnant?"

Looking around, I feel my cheeks burning.

Inching my way away from the light, I swallow hard. "Well, I guess the actual show will begin now. Because apparently, my baby wants to come three weeks early." I shrug, taking a few steps back. "Y'all have a good day. Thanks for visiting Griffith Observatory." I point to the girl who yelled first. "And, no, I didn't pee my pants. It's part of the birthing process!"

The room erupts into cheers as I exit the stage as quickly as I can. With every step I take, more water rushes out, leaving an embarrassing trail behind me.

Taking my phone out, I hit Link's contact, breathing through yet another contraction. Panic sets in that I'm about to push an actual human being out of my vagina. Because I know it's going to hurt like an absolute bitch.

LINK

I turn the shower off and dry off before wrapping my towel around my waist. As I head to my locker, my teammate Jake Buck points to my locker.

"Dude, do you have a vibrator in there or something?" He smirks. "Something is buzzing like crazzzy."

"No, you dildo. It's probably my phone." My eyes widen as I run over. "Shit!"

Opening it, I grab my phone, seeing an incoming call from Tate, her picture on the screen.

"T? Are you all right?" I blurt into the phone.

Now that she's due this month, every five seconds, I've been ready for her to call and say she's in labor.

"I'm on my way to the hospital," she says, her voice sounding breathier than normal. "Rebecca is driving me. Can you meet me—ahhhh, fuck, that hurts," she growls. "Shit. Shit. Ow."

"Breathe, baby. Just breathe. Like the classes taught you—"

"Shut the fuck up! Your asshole and vagina aren't being ripped out of your own body right now!" she hisses. "That's what it feels like! Like my asshole is being suctioned out of me! So, shut up!"

"Well, to be fair, if I had a vagina, we probably wouldn't be in this predicament to begin with," I tease her, but that stops quickly when she growls my name in warning.

Pulling my jeans on, I keep my phone between my ear and my shoulder. "I'll be there as soon as I can! I love you. You're going to do so good."

"This is going to suck, Link," she whines, completely changing her tone from angry to sad, like a crazy person. "I'm a baby. You know I hate pain. And this baby is going to come out of my vagina." She sobs harder. "I'll probably shit all over the place. And tear to my asshole. You'll be disgusted by me."

"Tear to your asshole?" I grimace just as a few of my teammates nod their heads slowly, telling me it's a real fucking thing. "Can you give Rebecca the phone?"

I hear her shifting around for a few seconds.

"Hello?" Rebecca, her coworker, says politely, though I can tell she's nervous.

"I'm leaving the stadium. I'll be there soon. If you get there before I do, please make sure she reminds the nurses that she has a condition that makes her faint. Also, she's been going in and getting iron in—"

"Infusions," she cuts me off. "I know; I know. They'll have all of this in her chart. But just in case, I'll tell every doctor and nurse I come across. We'll see you soon."

I hear the line go dead, and I know she hung up.

Running into the parking lot, I see the ambulance with Freddy, the paramedic, who's always around during games, cleaning the rig.

"Freddy! I'm about to be a daddy! You know what would sure be helpful during afternoon traffic?"

He raises an eyebrow. "Let me guess. You want a lift?"

"Hell yes, I do." I nod, clasping his shoulder. "What do you say?"

"I could get in trouble," he deadpans.

"And maybe I'm having a heart attack." I shrug. "Are you going to let me die right now?"

Groaning, he jerks his chin toward the front. "Let's go, Sterns."

"You are the real motherfucking MVP, Freddy. Let's roll."

"You sore, T?" I say, pulling my eyes from our new baby boy. "Do you need anything?"

She's as pale as a ghost, and she looks like she's been hit by a truck. Still, she takes my breath away as she attempts to sit up further.

"I'm good, thanks." She smiles. "Well, it's not exactly the birth story I had in mind." She stares at Crew. "But when it came to that point, I was just ready to have him out of me." She scrunches her nose up. "Who knew twenty-eight hours of labor could be *that* intense?"

Leaning forward, I cradle Crew while planting a kiss on her lips. "You did so fucking good though. You're so strong." I widen my eyes. "And look on the bright side. You didn't shit, and you didn't rip to your asshole."

"This is all true." She giggles, but I can tell it causes her pain. "Lordy, those incisions are sore. Don't make me laugh."

"I'll do my best."

Crew Harris Sterns came into the world just like everything else seems to in our life. Completely not the way we had planned.

Even though Tate had this perfect birth plan in her mind—one that involved no pain medications, maybe a whirlpool bath, and watching Animal Planet and the Space Channel on TV—it turned into an emergency C-section, where Tate inevitably had one of her passing-out spells. Not that I could blame her. If I knew they were cutting me open, I'd pass the fuck out too. The nurse also thought it would be good to tell me how many layers of skin they were going through. And *that* led to me passing out too. So, there we were, Tate and I, in one big fainting party.

But when I got back up, just as they were taking him out, it was the scariest and most beautiful few minutes of my life. Because the second they lifted him up and Tate woke up and heard his cry … hell, I get teary-eyed, just thinking back to it. Even if it was only hours ago.

Harris was my mother's maiden name. We had talked about, if we had a girl, we should name her after my mom, but we quickly had to come up with plan B when we learned our baby was indeed a boy. Tate mentioned Harris, and I knew it was the one.

"Get some rest, babe. You know our family all got the first flight out this morning. They'll be here by tonight." I sit back in my seat, getting comfortable. "My brothers will be loud as fuck. So, sleep. I've got him."

"I love you," she whispers, giving me a sleepy smile. "Both of you."

"We love you right back."

Yawning, she pulls her blanket up to her chin, and within a few minutes, she's out like a light.

"You are the luckiest boy in the whole world," I whisper down at Crew even though he's asleep too. "Because you get to have her as your mama. She'll protect you; she'll love you, even when you mess up; and she'll always see the best in you. Just like she does me." I bend down, kissing his forehead. "We made you, little man. I can't believe you and your mom are mine." My voice grows hoarse with emotion. "I don't know what I ever did to deserve this."

Maybe my mother sent me this beautiful gift, wrapped in a blue blanket. Maybe she is the reason why Tate and I made our way back to each other. I know she's smiling down, wishing she were here. I wish she were here too. I guess having that four-leaf clover all this time really was something.

Because now, I have everything I've ever wanted, times a million.

THE END

Have you read Cam's story? If not, it's available now!

Already needing more Brody? Preorder *Filthy Boy* now!

OTHER BOOKS BY HANNAH GRAY

NE UNIVERSITY SERIES

Chasing Sunshine
Seeing Red
Losing Memphis

BROOKS UNIVERSITY SERIES

Love, Ally
Forget Me, Sloane
Hate You, Henley

FLORIDA EAST UNIVERSITY

Playing Dane
Stealing Bama
Catching Kye

THE PUCK BOYS OF BROOKS UNIVERSITY

Puck Boy
Broken Boy
Filthy Boy

acknowledgments

If you're reading this, thank you for taking another journey with me! I hope you loved Link and Tate's story as much as I did. Although it was a completely different experience writing it compared to Cam and Addison's story, I really adored this couple. Something about a love that travels back to childhood pulls at my heartstrings. And this was no exception.

Without my family, I doubt I'd even have the inspiration to write words. My husband reminds me daily by actions, not just words, that I am not only enough, but also that I'm more. My kids—though they drive me insane at times—are my heart beating outside of my body. For them, I'll always try my best to make them proud and remind them they can do anything.

My mama, who is the most selfless, boldest, kindest, stubbornest, funniest, and smartest human being. And who has the biggest heart I've ever had the chance to know—Thank you for making me who I am. You love unconditionally. It has no limits. No end. No boundaries. You're often easy to anger, but quicker to forgive. I love you so much. Thank you for believing in me, especially on those days I question myself.

My dad, who is undoubtedly the hardest worker I've ever known—Thank you. Thank you for teaching me to push the limits. To take the risks. To follow my heart on something even if it's scary. Watching you in all of your business endeavors has helped shape me into the person that I am. I love you.

My best friend, Kayla—I'm so proud of everything you've accomplished in your life. A mother of two, wife, and business owner … you're killing it. I'm glad to be right next to you on this crazy journey we call life. Thank you for inspiring me every day to put all of my heart into what I love to do.

Tatum Hanscom, who is not only one of my best friends, but also one of the few I trust to read my stories while they are still rough in places—When I get a bad review, you're the one pepping me up, reminding me of all the good reviews I've earned. You're one of my biggest cheerleaders and steady supporters. You also were a huge inspiration for Tate's character. Her love for knitting. Her unwavering need to have the backs of the ones she loves. How she can see the good, even in the darkness. And most importantly, what a good friend and sister she is. I love you!

My brother—We don't see each other nearly as often as I wish we did. That doesn't change the fact that we will always have each other's back, cheer each other on, and understand each other like most people don't. I love you. Thanks for being my brother.

My sister-in-law, Tara, who is also one of my very best friends—Gosh, I love you so freaking much! I love your long late-night text messages that you send after you finish reading my newest book. I love our inside jokes. And I love watching our babies grow up together. Thanks for being a part of the Gray family. We hit the jackpot, getting you as a bonus family member.

My mother-in-law and father-in-law—I love you guys! I can't believe I've legally been a part of your family for ten years now! Thank you for believing in all of my dreams. Even if those dreams involve writing dirty books!

My editor, the fabulous Jovana with Unforeseen Editing—I wonder if you're tired of reading these every few months since you've been stuck with me. I hope not because there will be many more to come! Truly, it's always a pleasure working with you. You are a human I look up to as not only a businesswoman, but also a successful business owner, who, like me, is also a mama. You are a badass boss lady, and I love you!

My Autumn—At this point, let's just keep adding more titles to your name in these acknowledgments. Agent. Publicist. Assistant. Mentor. Advice giver when my babies are sick. Tough-love disher-outer when I need it. I really, really love working with you. And I hope you know that, without you, I likely would have never published my first novel. Love you. #lifers

My beta readers, Jaimie Davidson and Candice Butchino—I appreciate you all so much for taking time from your busy lives to help me perfect my stories. You are amazing. Not only have you helped me so much by proofreading my words, but you are all some of my favorite people I have met on this writing journey.

Amy Queau with Q Designs—Thank you for creating such a gorgeous cover for me. It is exactly what I pictured. And thank you for always being so easy to work with.

Sarah Grim Sentz at Enchanting Romance Designs—You hit it out of the park with the alternative covers for this series! I am obsessed! Thank you for being such a sweet human being and for being so easy to work with.

Thank you to Michelle Lancaster, owner of lanefotograf—As always, you had the picture that fit the bill perfectly for my character. Your gift is truly a rare art, and I'm so thankful that I have been lucky enough to not only see these photos, but to also have them on my covers.

For my cover model, Chase Mattson—Anyone who knows me knows that you were my unicorn pick for who I wanted on a future cover. But I knew in order to do so, I first had to establish some success in this industry. The day that Michelle sent me your gallery and I locked in on the perfect one was a big deal. Thank you for sharing your beauty with the world. And also for helping me create the perfect cover for *Broken Boy*.

My readers—Gosh … I love you! As my group continues to grow, I meet new and amazing people constantly, and it really does feel like I've found my place in the world. And my place is among all of you who live somewhere between reality and our favorite novels. Getting lost in words and falling in love with characters, feeling like they are our family. Thank you all for being so incredible to me.

about the author

Hannah Gray spends her days in vacationland, living in a small, quaint town on the coast of Maine. She is an avid reader of contemporary romance and is always in competition with herself to read more books every year.

During the day, she loves on her three perfect-to-her daughters and tries to be the best mom she can be. But once she tucks them in at night—okay, scratch that. Once they fall asleep next to her in her bed—because their bedrooms apparently have monsters in them—she dives into her own fantasy world, staying awake well into the late-night hours, typing away stories about her characters. As much as she loves being a wife and mom—and she certainly does love it—reading and writing are her outlet, giving her a place to travel far away while still physically being with her family.

She married her better half in 2013, and he's been putting up with her craziness every day since. As her anchor, he's her one constant in this insane, forever-changing world.

Made in the USA
Las Vegas, NV
19 February 2025